CHRISTMAS
ON THE
Prairie

© 2004 *One Wintry Night* by Pamela Griffin
© 2004 *The Christmas Necklace* by Maryn Langer
© 2004 *Colder Than Ice* by Jill Stengl
© 2004 *Take Me Home* by Tracey V. Bateman

ISBN 1-59310-537-1

Scripture quotations are taken from the King James Version of the Bible.

Cover image © Photodisc

Illustrations by Mari Goering

This book is a work of fiction. Names, characters, places, and incidents are either products of the author's imagination or used fictitiously. Any similarity to actual people, organizations, and/or events is purely coincidental.

Published by Barbour Publishing, Inc., P.O. Box 719, Uhrichsville, Ohio 44683, www.barbourbooks.com

Our mission is to publish and distribute inspirational products offering exceptional value and biblical encouragement to the masses.

ecpa Member of the
Evangelical Christian
Publishers Association

Printed in the United States of America.
5 4 3 2 1

INTRODUCTION

One Wintry Night by Pamela Griffin: Boston-bred Ivy Leander despises prairie life. She misses the fancy balls her wealthy grandmother gave and dreads Christmas in the remote town of Leaning Tree, Nebraska, with her mother, new stepfather, and stepsisters. The town's cheerful, teasing blacksmith, Craig Watson, both annoys and attracts Ivy. Will an unexpected holiday blizzard help Ivy discover the genuine worth of family and Christmas—and Craig?

The Christmas Necklace by Maryn Langer: The Chicago fire of 1871 leaves wealthy, pampered Lucinda Porter destitute. Now a maid at the Tillotson prairie mansion, she meets the handsome David Morgan, a law student dreaming of wealth and power. When Lucinda is wrongly accused of theft and threatened with terrible consequences, David helps her escape. Christmas Eve finds them in a stable with a newborn babe. In this setting, will they learn the true meaning of Christmas?

Colder Than Ice by Jill Stengl: Pastor Frank Nelson has met the woman of his dreams—but her heart is a block of ice. Unable to trust even God, Estelle deliberately avoids the perils of love, though she does come to admire the burly country minister. Can Frank convince her that love is worth any risk? Will God thaw the ice storm in Estelle's spirit, or will a jealous rival's spiteful behavior freeze her heart forever?

Take Me Home by Tracey V. Bateman: Kathleen Johnson would have been happy to stay with her large family forever. But when asked to travel thirty miles from home to complete a departing teacher's term, she agrees. Now miserable and alone, Kathleen counts the days until the term ends, her growing affection for Josh Truman notwithstanding. Josh knew the moment he saw Kathleen that God had answered his prayers—now he just has to convince her that home can be anywhere with the person you love. . . .

CHRISTMAS ON THE

Prairie

FOUR ROMANCE STORIES
FULL OF CHRISMAS NOSTALGIA

PAMELA GRIFFIN

MARYN LANGER

JILL STENGL

TRACEY V. BATEMAN

BARBOUR
PUBLISHING

One Wintry Night

by Pamela Griffin

Dedication

A special thank you to all the wonderful women
who helped me by critiquing this book—
Maryn L., Jill S., Paige W. D., Lena D., Anne G.,
Candice S., Erin L., Mary H., and, of course, Mom. Also
thanks to Meredith E., Pamela K. T. (O.),
and Mary C. for helping with the Nebraska
and Welsh information.

To my loving Guide, my Lord Jesus,
who's always been the Light to lead me
through the sudden storms in life.

*Charity suffereth long, and is kind; charity envieth not;
charity vaunteth not itself, is not puffed up.*

1 CORINTHIANS 13:4

Chapter 1

Leaning Tree, Nebraska—October 1871

"Hiya, Boston." With his forefinger and thumb, Craig lazily tipped the brim of his hat toward the pretty brunette.

Indignation shot through her blueberry-colored eyes. Pink stained her cheeks. Instead of answering him, Ivy Leander tossed her dark curls with a little huff and walked right past where he stood on the weathered boardwalk in front of Johnson's feed store.

Old Mr. Meyers rasped out a chuckle before she was out of hearing range. "Might as well forget that one, Craig. She's about as friendly as a pork-ee-pine with all-over body aches. And she don't seem to like you much neither."

The former cobbler from Tennessee might be right about that—for now. But Craig wouldn't let that stop him. He stared after the woman in the gray store-bought dress with the shiny ribbons. He knew the dress was store-bought because of all the gossip flying among the town's old hens ever since Gavin Morgan married Ivy's ma and brought the woman and her daughter to Leaning Tree, Nebraska, this past spring. Then, too, no store-bought dress could be found at the general store, so it must be from Boston. Under Ivy's stylish hat, out of place in this rugged town, spirals of dark curls hung, bouncing along her neck. Most women he knew wore their hair wrapped in two braids around their head or in a bun. Craig liked Ivy's way of doing her hair better.

"She sure is a feisty one," he agreed as he went back to the task of foisting the cumbersome feed sack into the rear of Mr. Meyers's wagon. He shoved the large canvas sack into place next to the farm supplies the old man had purchased.

"Thankee much, Craig." Mr. Meyers rubbed his white-whiskered jaw. "Don't know what I woulda done if you weren't here. Never woulda reckoned that young giant Tommy woulda gone and busted his leg."

"Glad to have helped," Craig said with a sincere smile. Mr. Meyers looked about as brittle as an ice-coated twig and close to being as skinny. Craig hoped the man's nephew Tommy was up to par soon.

A burst of giggling sailed across the muddy road. Craig looked to see two young women, Beth and Sally, strolling along the boardwalk. They whispered behind their hands, staring Ivy's way. Craig also turned to look. A wagon had just rumbled past where Ivy walked, spraying muddy water on the bottom of her gray dress. She stamped her kid boot, her fists pumping once at her sides, and glared at the retreating wagon.

"I hate this town!" The small growl left her throat, but it was loud enough for Craig to hear. She marched forward several more steps and turned to enter the general store. As though she sensed Craig's stare, she looked in his direction.

He dipped his head her way, tipping his hat again. She broke eye contact, slipped her hand to the top of her feathered bonnet to pat it, as if to make sure it was still in place, and marched through the door.

"Yessiree," Mr. Meyers said with a low whistle. "I sure enough do pity the poor fool who takes her for a wife."

Craig eyed the closed door of the general store a few seconds longer, then turned, the grin going wide on his face. "I reckon that'd be me, sir."

"Pardon?" Mr. Meyers pulled at his thick earlobe as if he had wax in his ear and couldn't hear well, though the man was reputed to hear a sneeze in the next county.

"I'm the one who's going to marry Ivy Leander."

Surprise shone from Mr. Meyers's eyes, then pity. He let out a loud guffaw. "The sun must've gone to your head, boy!"

"No, sir. By this time next year, I plan to make Ivy my wife. Or my name isn't Craig Watson." He adjusted his hat, gave a jovial farewell nod, and headed toward the general store.

"Nice knowin' ya, Jim," Mr. Meyers's amused voice came from behind. "Wonder what Ivy'll think of your little plan. Care to make a wager on its success?"

Craig kept walking—not that he had any doubts concerning his claim. He just wasn't a betting man. And even if he were, Jebediah Meyers didn't usually have more than two coins to rub together after a trip to town. It would shame Craig to take money from the old man.

Ivy eyed the sparse selection of goods in the cramped store

with distaste. Even the nicest ribbons and combs and whatnots for sale were a pale comparison to the quality of those found in Boston. Everything in the East was nicer, with more variety from which to choose. The stores were cleaner, too. She skirted a couple of muddy boot prints on the plank floor, scrunching her nose in disgust.

Could the fifty dollars her wealthy grandmother secretly presented to her before she left Boston even be spent in such a place? The dear woman had known how much Ivy dreaded prairie life and told her to use the money for some "little extravagance" but not to tell her mother about the gift. Yet what of that nature could be found here?

Why Mama had to go and fall in love with an uneducated farmer who chose to make his home in the prairie wilds lay beyond Ivy's scope of reasoning. Her young stepsisters certainly didn't add honey to the pot, either. Crystin and Gwen couldn't keep their hands off Ivy's things, despite Ivy's frequent complaints to her mother to have a talk with them and set them straight. Mama quietly explained to Ivy that, being so new a family, there were bound to be disturbances and issues needing to be ironed out, and Ivy should just be patient and let time run its course to fix things.

Ivy had been patient—up until yesterday when she found her gold-filigree garnet brooch with the seed pearls, a gift her beloved grandmother had given her, tromped into the hay-strewn ground near the pig's smelly trough. A tinge of remorse unsettled Ivy at the way she'd lit into eight-year-old Crystin, and she couldn't help but remember the tears that made the child's big blue eyes glisten.

The door opened, and Craig Watson strode inside. A blacksmith by trade, he had the strong arms and hands to prove it. Tall, well-built, with his nutmeg brown eyes often dancing in amusement—no doubt at her expense—he had an annoying habit of calling her "Boston" rather than using the appropriate title of "Miss Leander," as the Bostonian gentlemen of her acquaintance had done. To their credit, a few of the male settlers in this town also addressed her properly, though most just called her "ma'am." But not Mr. Ill-mannered Blacksmith. Oh no. Not him.

"Good morning, Craig," the plump Mrs. Llewynn said from behind the counter.

"Mornin', ma'am." The timbre of his voice poured out like wild honey, smooth and warm. He caught Ivy's stare and tipped his hat, that ever-present, rakish, close-lipped grin on his tanned, all too attractive face. "Mornin'."

Ivy's heart ran a foolish little race in her bosom as it often did when he smiled her way. She snapped her focus back to the bolts of sprigged material lying on a nearby weathered table. Calico. Only poor country folk wore calico. She might as well cut holes in a feed sack and wear that.

She heard his boots clomp toward the counter at the front. Curiosity propelled her to lift her gaze a few inches. From the back, under his hat, thick clumps of wheat-colored hair brushed the bottom edge of his collar. The man was in dire need of a haircut. And a bath. Though the odors weren't exactly offensive, the smell of smoke and raw iron permeated his clothing, and fresh sweat dampened his shirt.

"What can I do for you today?" Mrs. Llewynn asked him with a wide smile, looking up from thumbing through a magazine.

"I need to get a caldron if you have one. Mine sprung a leak this morning."

"Oh, my. I sure don't, but I do have an old washtub you can use."

"I'd appreciate it." Craig tipped his hat back from his forehead. "That your latest issue of *Godey's*?"

"Yes. It just arrived yesterday."

"Excuse me?" Ivy moved forward. "Did I understand correctly? You have a recent copy of the *Godey's Lady's Book*?"

"That I do," Mrs. Llewynn said with a nod before she again looked at Craig. "I'll just go get that washtub." She left her place behind the counter and bustled to the back room. Craig nudged the corner of the magazine with two fingers, pushing it at an angle. He looked down sideways, tilting his head as if to peer at the cover but not wanting to seem too interested.

Ivy stepped up beside him, almost knocking into him in her haste. "Pardon," she breathed as she slid the magazine the few inches her way for a better view. Excited, she thumbed to the first page and soon became engrossed in the illustrations, rapidly shuffling through the pages. Her hand stilled, and she sighed. "Oh, what a simply lovely gown this would make for a Christmas ball."

"I surely wouldn't mind seeing you in it," Craig's amused voice came back.

Ivy's hand froze at the top corner of the next page before she could turn it. Heat flamed her cheeks, and she snapped her gaze from the illustrations of velvet and ribbons and bustles to Craig's laughing eyes.

"Oh, my" was all she could think to say. She wasn't sure which embarrassed her more—his highly personal and improper remark or the fact that in her great excitement to find a link with civilization, she had acted like a hoyden and pushed him aside to snatch the magazine away. Miss Lucy Hadmire of the elite ladies' academy Ivy once attended would be shocked to have witnessed her prize pupil's performance.

"I do apologize," she murmured, snatching her hand from the magazine. "I didn't mean to be rude."

His thick, neat brows lifted in wry amusement, as if reminding her of the irony of that statement, and another wave of embarrassment swept over her. Ever since she'd stepped off the wagon that first day in Leaning Tree, she'd been nothing but rude to this man. Yet such rudeness developed from the dread that he might one day become interested in her, as his looks toward her implied. She could never stoop so low as to marry a farmer, much less a blacksmith! Her husband would be an educated man of considerable means, as her doctor-father had been.

"Well, now, Boston, ladies' magazines aren't exactly of interest to me," he said with another of his irritating grins. "So look as much as you'd like."

That name again. *Insufferable man.*

She turned on her heel. "I'll come back another time." Before he could let loose with another teasing remark, she flounced out of the store.

Chapter 2

Two days after his encounter with Ivy, Craig brushed at the sweat dripping from his brow with the back of one forearm, then set the glowing yellow iron over the horn of the anvil and resumed pounding it into a horseshoe shape. Regardless of the fact that the huge doors of the smithy were rolled open as far as they would go, it was still muggy and unseasonably warm.

He whistled a tune, though the jarring strikes of the hammer ringing off metal blocked most of it. Whistling helped him relax, and he did it for that reason alone. As he worked and the sparks flew, he thought about Ivy. His mind jumped back to the first day he'd met her.

Plump and pretty, she had just stepped off a dusty wagon that rolled to a stop not far from where Craig worked. A thinner woman stepped to the parched ground behind her. She had the same blue eyes and was older by about twenty years. Then Gavin Morgan stretched his short, compact build from the wagon and helped a petite elderly woman to alight. Ivy had stood eyeing her surroundings with a mixture of frank despair and cold disdain. As Craig approached, he could almost feel the thick frost coating her, though the day was about as hot as bacon fat sizzling on a griddle.

"Afternoon, ladies." Craig tipped his hat to the women, then shook his friend's hand. "Gavin, good to have you back." His gaze again settled on Ivy. "Welcome to Leaning Tree."

The younger woman gave what Craig thought might be considered a nod. It was so slight, he wasn't sure.

Gavin presented his new wife, Eloise, and his mother, also referring to Ivy as "Eloise's daughter," then he walked into the general store with the two older women following. Before Ivy could join them, Craig thought up something to say. "So, where are you from?"

She looked down her nose at him. "It really isn't proper for us to converse without first being *formally* introduced. But to answer your question, I'm from Boston. That's in Massachusetts, incidentally."

"Really. You don't say." He felt a grin curl up his mouth at her high-handed approach toward what she considered his ignorance, and he pushed back his hat from his forehead, deciding to play along.

"Well, now, ma'am, 'round these here parts, the most formal interductions sound something like, '*Here, soooo-eeeeee!*' " He let the words loose in a squeal similar to the one he'd heard Mrs. Llewynn use when calling her hogs to their meal.

Ivy's blueberry eyes widened in surprise, and she took a quick step back, almost tripping over the warped boardwalk. She put her gloved hand to the nearby hitching post to steady herself.

" 'Course, that approach only works when you're social-izin' with the hogs," Craig continued matter-of-factly. "When you wanna talk to the chickens, you should say, 'Here, chick, chick, chick, chick, chick, chick!' " He let the phrase jump from his mouth in a rapid stream of bulletlike words, then feigned a look of innocent realization. "But I reckon what you actually was meanin' was a formal interduction with the people 'round these here parts."

"Of course I meant the people," she snapped. "Why should I wish to socialize with the pigs?"

"Hogs, ma'am. They's different than pigs, but prob'ly a whole lot more sociable than mosta the folks here in Leaning Tree." He leaned in close as though about to reveal a secret. "Smarter, too," he confided in a low voice. "Why, ole Stony Jack's hog can count to ten while most people 'round here cain't even read nor write."

She crossed her arms over her frilly, lace-covered blouse, her reticule dangling from one wrist. "Oh, really! Surely you don't expect me to believe such nonsense?"

He crossed a hand over his heart. "Sure as I'm standin' here and the day is warm. Where'd you say you was from again?"

"Boston." She frowned. "Must I write the name on my forehead for you to remember it?"

Craig held back a chuckle. "Oh no, ma'am. I think I can remember it next time around."

And he had—calling her "Boston" from that day on. It fit her, from the top of her sassy, feathered hat to the leather soles of her fancy kid boots and all points between. Still, there was something about Ivy Leander that aroused more than his curiosity. She intrigued him; he'd never met a woman like her. All spit and fire but with a noticeable softness touching her expression when she didn't know she was being watched. And Craig had done his share of watching these past months.

At the harvest dance, he'd even asked her to take a spin with him around the huge wooden platform built just for the occasion. She had snubbed his invitation with a brisk "No, thank you," looking away as if he were no more than a pesky horsefly buzzing about. Yet Craig had made up his mind that he wouldn't let that deter him from his plan to court her. He'd caught Ivy doing her share of watching him when she didn't think he was looking. She didn't fool him one bit; Ivy appeared as interested in Craig as he was in her. Underneath all that lacy froth and those fancy ribbons, he imagined he'd find a woman with a tender heart. At least he hoped so. Everyone from Mr. Meyers to the old doc thought him foolish in his persistence to try to win her affections. Maybe he was, at that.

Seeing that the metal had lost most of its color, Craig stopped his pounding and whistling and twisted around in a half-circle, intending to poke the iron back into the fire blazing yellow in the forge, to get it to the right temperature again. To his surprise, he heard the next notes of his tune faintly whistled behind him before cutting off abruptly.

He spun around in the direction from which he thought the notes were coming in the dim light of his three-walled shop. No one stood there. One hand still wrapped around the handle of his hammer, the other around the tongs, he made a slow circle of the room. In a dark corner, he noticed one of his work aprons crumpled on the floor—then saw it move. Craig thought about the recent theft of one of Gladys Llewynn's chickens.

"You come on out from there," he said, tightening his

grip on the hammer. "I don't want any trouble." He took a step closer. "Come on out, I said."

A stiff rustle of cloth was followed by the sight of a small girl popping her head up, her eyes wide with uncertainty. Beads of sweat trickled down her temples, and wisps of damp hair stuck to her skin. As stifling hot as it was in the smithy, that was no surprise.

Craig relaxed. "Amy Bradford, what are you doing hiding in that corner? You come on out from there. Do your parents know you're here?"

Amy hurried to stand and shook her head, her two corn silk-colored braids swishing against her brown calico dress. "Miss Johnson let us out early today. I'm hidin' from Wesley."

Once classes were dismissed, the brother and sister often played such games on the rare occasions they did attend school. Yet Craig wasn't sure he approved of them playing in his workplace. Before he could answer, a young boy's voice called from outside.

"Amy Lamey, I know you're in there!"

The girl's mouth compressed at the nickname her brother used. "Don't tell him where I am," she whispered, putting a finger to her lips before diving back under the apron and curling into a ball.

Craig blew out a lengthy breath and shook his head. He couldn't find it in his heart to begrudge the two a little fun. Coming from a family of fourteen kids, Amy and Wesley were the middle children, responsible for a good portion of the chores. They barely found time to play. Of course, that was the lot of most prairie children.

"I heard you talkin', so's I know yo a're in here." Nine-year-old Wesley, with his carrot top of curly hair, moved into the smithy as if he owned the place. "Howdy, Mr. Watson."

Craig nodded in greeting. Accustomed to customers milling about the place while they waited on orders to be filled, he heated the horseshoe again, forged a turned-up clip at the front to protect the horse's hoof, then bored eight holes into it with his pritchel tool to hold the nails. After rounding the ends, he doused it in Mrs. Llewynn's nearby washtub filled almost to the brim with cool water. A loud *hissss* escaped, and steam sprayed his face. With the iron now cooled so that he could handle it without burning himself, he hung it over the anvil's horn to join the other three horseshoes there.

"Guess who I saw mailin' a letter today?" the boy asked, reminding Craig of his presence.

"You still here?"

"Aw, come on, Mr. Watson. Guess."

"I wouldn't have the vaguest idea." Craig wiped the sweat and grime from his hands down the front of his leather apron. At present, the schoolhouse shared its space with the postal office—Mr. Owen taking over one corner of the building to conduct his business there.

"Miss Uppity from Boston," the boy announced.

Craig bit back the grin that wanted to jump to his mouth at the boy's nickname for Ivy. He hung his tools on their spot near the bellows. "You shouldn't call her that, Wesley. It's not nice to call people names."

"That's what Ma calls her when she's talking about her to Pa." The boy headed to a hitching post several feet away, where a skittish horse waited to be shod, and hoisted himself up to sit on the wood. The bay whinnied a greeting, and Wesley looped a chubby arm around its neck in a brief hug. " 'Sides, she is uppity. She comes to town 'most every week to look through those fancy ladies' magazines of Mrs. Llewynn's, but she doesn't talk to hardly no one."

"Maybe she doesn't know what to say. You ever talk to her?"

Wesley scrunched up his mouth in a guilty expression. "Naw, but Amy tried today durin' lunch. Miss Ivy got all funny lookin', like she didn't want nobody knowin' her business. She was mailin' a letter but kept lookin' behind her, like she was afraid someone would see. Amy walked up to her and asked her who the letter was for, but she didn't pay Amy no mind."

Craig tucked the words away to ponder later. He donned his hat, picked up his toolbox, and walked out in the sunshine toward the boy. "There's no law that says she has to tell two bean sprouts her business."

Wesley chuckled and began swinging his short legs, as if daring gravity to keep him upright. Craig wondered how come the boy didn't fall, balanced as he was on such a narrow beam.

"Is it true what Mr. Meyers said?" the boy asked. "That you told him you're gonna marry up with Miss Ivy someday?"

Surprised, Craig set his tools down with a bang. "Where'd you hear that?"

"Just around."

Craig grimaced. He never should have told Mr. Meyers his plans. The last thing he needed was for Ivy to hear such news through the town's busybodies. "Know why God gave you two ears and one mouth?"

Wesley shook his head.

"So you'd spend more time listening to the teachings of your elders and less time talking about matters that aren't any of your business." Craig released a long breath. "As long as you're here, put yourself to use. That horse seems to like you, but I've been having trouble with it all morning. When I took the old shoes off, she almost bit me. I need you to hold the halter and talk nice and easy to her while I shoe her."

Wesley's face brightened as he slid off the hitching post. "Does this mean I can be your apprentice?"

Craig's eyebrows lifted. "Where'd you learn such a big word?"

"At school. We was studyin' on colonial times when they had them apprentices. Some of us even had to learn us a poem about a village blacksmith. I'd like to be a blacksmith someday. I learn real fast. So can I be your apprentice?" he asked again.

"Don't know about that. You're a mite small yet." At the boy's downcast eyes, Craig relented. "Give yourself a few more years to fill out, and I'll consider it. That is, if your ma and pa agree. Now hold the horse steady. While I'm pounding these nails in, I don't want her suddenly getting skittish so that I end up missing the horseshoe and hitting my leg instead."

The boy was as good as his word and held the horse while Craig drove the short nails into the holes of the shoes, fastening them to the horse's hooves. The studs on the bottom would give the horse traction over icy roads once the snows hit. Craig had already fitted his own horse with similar shoes and was surprised the town hadn't received any freezing weather yet.

"All done." He removed the hind hoof of the horse from his lap, straightened from his bent position, and turned to face the bay and the boy who held her. "You get on home now, Wesley. Your ma will be worried."

Wesley scratched the back of his curly head. "She does worry an awful lot, don't she? Pa says she's fractious 'cuzza the twins. Bye, Mr. Watson."

Before the boy walked more than five steps, Craig called out. "Wait! Aren't you forgetting something?"

Wesley turned and lifted his shoulders in a shrug. "Uh, don't think so."

Craig raised his eyebrows. "Your little sister?"

"Oh, Amy," he said as if just remembering her name. "I forgot about her."

"That's what I figured," Craig muttered, heading into the smithy. He wondered why Amy hadn't made her presence known before this. Wesley had been at the smithy for the better part of an hour. When he hunkered down in the corner where he'd found her, Craig had his answer. The girl lay fast asleep under the leather apron.

For a moment, he studied her rosy cheeks and the tendrils of light-colored hair sticking to her face. Her expression was peaceful, like an angel's. He hoped to have a little girl like Amy someday—several of them. And a passel of boys, too. He wondered if Ivy liked kids.

Craig put his hand to the girl's bony shoulder and gently shook it. "Amy? It's time to wake up and go home now. The smithy's no place for little sprouts like you."

She blinked her eyes open, then sat up and rubbed them. "Oh, hi, Mr. Watson," she said sleepily. "Is it mornin'?"

"I hope not. Actually, you've been here for almost an hour, since the schoolmarm dismissed you from school anyway."

"Oh!" The girl threw off the apron and scrambled to a stand. "I have to get home and help Ma with the ironin' and cookin'. Bye, Mr. Watson!" She raced out of the smithy, soon catching up with her brother, who was waiting for her on the road. Ivy came into view, walking in their direction. She looked at the children, then darted a glance toward the smithy.

Craig smiled and tipped his hat her way.

Hurriedly she refocused on the road. Skirts a-swaying, she increased her pace and hotfooted it in the direction of her stepfather's soddy. Bottling his irritation at the latest snub, Craig watched her awhile longer, shook his head, then turned back to finish his long list of tools needing forged or mended.

Morning sunshine appeared to illuminate the white-painted, timbered house at the far end of town. Ivy turned wistful eyes upon the two-story structure as she walked past. Modest in size, it was still a lot nicer than any of the other six buildings that made up Leaning Tree. And certainly a great deal more refined than the house of sod belonging to her mother's new husband. Still, it was nowhere near comparable to her grand-mother's stately home in Boston, looming at the end of a tree-lined street.

Ivy halted her steps and further studied the building before her. Lace curtains at the windows. A stone chimney at the side. At least the white timbered house belonging to the Pettigrasses was respectable. People were meant to live in sturdy buildings with wooden floors and pretty rugs. Not underneath earth and grass like bugs and animals.

A petite, brown-haired woman stepped onto the porch and began to shake out a blanket in the direction the wind was blowing. Catching sight of Ivy, she smiled.

"Hulloa, Ivy! You come to town often, indeed," Winifred

Pettigrass called in the lilting Welsh accent that all the Morgans and a few other families in town shared.

"Yes," Ivy called back. With nothing better to do after the morning chores her mother assigned her, she often preferred to spend time thumbing through the pages of the ladies' magazines and perusing the items at the general store, though she still hadn't found anything appropriate to buy. Since her stepfather's homestead was close to town, the walk was short, less than two miles.

"Can you come inside and sit with us for tea?" Winifred called out.

Ivy would like nothing better than to sit in a real chair and drink from a fine china cup, but she shook her head. "I can't. I promised Mother I'd be home to help her with the noon meal."

"Another time, then, while the weather is nice. Go you and tell that dada of yours he must come, too. Never will I understand that man and how his mind thinks."

Her words were cheery. Ivy had been in Leaning Tree long enough to realize what the woman's mood meant. Winifred Pettigrass wanted something from her brother, Ivy's stepfather. How different the two siblings were! Winifred had married a wealthy man who worked for the railroad and originally had come to town as a surveyor, where he'd met Winifred. The spry woman appreciated the finer things in life, as did Ivy, while Ivy's new stepfather was content to live like a mole and toil the earth to produce wheat and corn.

Winifred's mother came through the open door. "Good day to you, Ivy," she said. "You be certain and tell that son of mine I said to come. Three weeks now, I see nothing of him."

"I'll tell him," Ivy called back and continued down the road. Gavin's mother was the initial reason her stepfather had gone to Boston this past spring. Weak from the voyage to America years ago, Bronwyn Morgan stayed with a relative while Gavin settled his claim and built his home in Nebraska.

How unfortunate for Ivy that Gavin chose this past year to collect his mother—and that Ivy's mother had been the one strolling down the sidewalk when Gavin approached asking for directions. Two weeks later they married—scandalous to Ivy and her grandmother's way of thinking, but necessary since Gavin had to return to his homestead and needed a wife and a mother for his two daughters. Eloise Leander had been only too happy to comply, dragging along her only daughter with her.

When Ivy begged to remain in Boston with her grandmother, her mother flatly refused, stressing they were a family and would remain one. And so, one minute Ivy was dancing at a ball with the cream of Boston society. The next she was whisked away and picking up cow patties for fuel with the same gloves she'd worn to the ball.

Ivy sighed at the memory of those chaotic first few months in learning a new way of life. She focused on the road before her. A sea of undulating grass higher than her head flanked both sides of the muddy lane. Skirting the holes filled with rainwater, Ivy was glad she'd given in to common sense last week and had bought the clunky but serviceable footwear at the general store. Her soft kid boots never would have withstood this! At least, underneath her long skirts, the ugly new shoes couldn't be seen.

Hearing a child softly crying, Ivy lifted her gaze off the

puddles and spotted Amy Bradford kneeling at the edge of the road. A bunch of cracked eggs littered the ground in front of the fair-haired girl. Yellow yolks mixed with the clear pool of liquid, which seeped near Amy's threadbare dress.

"Oh, Ma's gonna be so mad at me!" The nine-year-old lifted pale green eyes to Ivy and wiped the backs of her fingers over wet cheeks. "I walked all the way from home and was so careful. But this puddle was deeper than I thought, and I twisted my foot."

Ivy decided not to ask why the child would deliberately step into a puddle. "Are you hurt?" She bent down, careful not to ruin her dress.

"No, but the eggs are. What am I gonna tell Ma? She's already mad at me for stayin' so long at the smithy's two days ago and comin' home late. She needed to stay with the twins—they's awful fractious with the teething—and she told me to take the eggs to Mrs. Llewynn this morning. Ma wants to get Clarence a warm coat before the snows come. And Wesley needs shoes. They ain't got none that'll fit, and Ma's been takin' eggs every morning so's she can save enough money to buy some."

Ivy knew that, with fourteen children to raise, the Bradfords barely had enough to get by. Their sod house was even smaller than the one Ivy was forced to live in with her mother, stepfather, and two stepsisters, and Amy's home contained only one window with a cracked pane.

"How many eggs did you have with you?" Ivy asked.

"Fifteen. One's okay, though." Amy reached in the basket beside her and held up a brown oval that had somehow missed destruction.

Ivy held out her hand for the lone egg and inspected the

shell. It bore a faint, hairline crack. She reached inside her reticule and withdrew a coin. "There you are."

Amy stared at the shiny dime in Ivy's hand as though puzzled. "What's that for?"

"Your egg. I'm buying it."

"But"—Amy's light brows sailed up—"that's more'n Mrs. Llewynn pays for the whole basket!"

"That's all right. I'm fond of eggs."

"A whole dime for one egg?" Amy sounded as if she still couldn't believe it.

Ivy shrugged. "If you'd rather not sell it. . ."

"Oh no." Amy grabbed the dime with dirt-stained fingers. "I wouldn't want ta deprive you of your egg, Miss Leander." She used a version of the saying Ivy had often heard Mr. Bradford use.

Ivy carefully set the egg at the bottom of her reticule. "Good. Then it appears we've struck a bargain."

The child seemed to consider before a sly smile lifted the corners of her mouth. "Anytime you want more, you let me know, and I'll be sure and save you some."

Ivy laughed, the sound trilling through the air. "I'll do that, Amy." The grin was still on her face as she watched the girl gather her empty basket and head for home. Suddenly Ivy noticed a wagon coming her way. As the rider neared, her heart plummeted, then lifted, almost soaring above the clouds like an eagle. She pressed her hand to her bosom in a futile effort to quell the rapid beating and averted her gaze past the wagon.

"Mornin', Boston," Craig said, pulling his horse to a stop beside her.

Despite her desire not to pay him any heed, she darted a

29

glance his way. He tipped his battered brown hat, giving her that lazy smile.

She offered a brief nod in an effort to be polite.

"Can I give you a ride home?"

"We're going in opposite directions."

"It won't be any trouble for me to turn my horse around. And your father's claim is close to town."

"Stepfather, you mean. He's not my real father."

Craig didn't reply. Feeling flustered and wishing she hadn't blurted out what she had, Ivy looked back down the road. "Thanks for the offer, but I'd rather walk."

"You sure?" His voice was gentle.

"Yes. As you pointed out, it's not far, and I enjoy the exercise."

"Okay. If you're sure." His warm brown eyes never left her face, and she felt the blush rise to her cheeks. His look reminded her that she was an unmarried woman and he was an unmarried man. A rather attractive unmarried man, even with that slight bend in his nose and his untamed hair, which grew a little long over the ears.

"I–I have to go now," she said quickly, moving away as she spoke. She set off at a walking-run for the first several feet, then slowed to a more moderate pace. However, her heart didn't slow one bit.

What was she thinking? She could never be interested in anyone from this godforsaken little town tucked away in the middle of nowhere! Even if the man wasn't a farmer and did hold what her mother had informed Ivy was one of the most respected trades in the township, Craig Watson still lived like a pauper in one cramped room adjoining his shop. He didn't even own a decent home—not that she could think of the soddies that most people from these parts lived in as decent. Yet they *were* houses with windows and doors.

With each step she took, Ivy's resolve strengthened. She would keep as far away as she could from the town blacksmith.

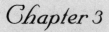

Chapter 3

The wind howled outside the soddy as Ivy concentrated on helping her mother hang the wash over the clothesline extending from one end of the dirt-brick wall to the other. Cold weather had hit with a vengeance, and this week's washing needed to be done inside the crowded front room. The family's faithful guard dog, Old Rufus, snoozed at his usual place near the cookstove, and Ivy had to step over the old hound more than once as she went about her task.

"'Under a spreading chestnut tree, the village smithy stands,'" Gwen suddenly quoted as she scrubbed a shirt on the washboard. "'The smith, a mighty man is he, with large and sinewy hands; and the muscles of his brawny arms are strong as iron bands. . .'"

"Must you recite that now?" Ivy asked her stepsister, perturbed when an image of Craig Watson breezed past the shuttered door of her mind. It had been difficult to bar invasive thoughts of the man ever since she'd last seen him, when he offered her a ride home in his wagon. Now the poem brought vivid pictures to mind.

The eleven-year-old turned solemn blue eyes Ivy's way. "I'm supposed to know Henry Wadsworth Longfellow's poem by tomorrow, when Mr. Rayborne will make me stand up in front of class to recite it. I have to practice." She began scrubbing again. "*His hair is crisp, and black, and long, his face is like the tan; His brow is wet with honest sweat, He earns whate'er he can. . .'*"

"I'm going outside to get some air," Ivy muttered, grabbing her woolen cloak.

Her mother's gentle gaze met hers from across the room, where she stirred lye-water in a kettle heating over the fire. "While you're out, please gather more fuel, Ivy."

"Yes, Mama." Ivy grimaced in distaste but wrapped a scarf around her head, pulled on her discolored ball gloves, and reached for a nearby basket. She despised this chore above all others, but the fire was getting low, and she was the only one available to do it.

A bitter, cold wind chapped her face and bit into her, almost sweeping her the rest of the way outside. She struggled with the door to close it. Searching the frozen ground for the brown lumps, she walked a short distance until she found some. Scarcity of trees in the area made this type of fuel a necessity. Wrinkling her nose in distaste, she picked up the hardened cow patty with gloved fingers and quickly dropped it into the basket. She'd kept her old ball gloves for just this purpose. She wouldn't dream of touching the disgusting things with her bare hands as her stepsisters did!

Soon her basket was filled, and Ivy straightened. Her lower back had cramped from bending over so much, but she wasn't about to rub the ache out with the glove she'd just used.

As she trudged against the wind and back to the sod house built of "Nebraska marble," as the locals were fond of calling the earthen bricks, she critically appraised it. Even prettying the name didn't change its appearance, making Ivy certain that the man who had coined the phrase did so out of a warped sense of humor. Their home was dirt with dead, brown grass growing on its roof. And the fuel for their fire was dried cow manure. If her grandmother could see the depths to which her only granddaughter had fallen, she would likely have a fit of apoplexy.

"Well, I think she's horrid!" Gwen's voice coming from around the other side of the soddy brought Ivy up short. She hesitated at the rear of her stepfather's home, wondering if she should make her presence known or keep quiet.

"I hate her," Gwen added, her words emphatic. "She thinks she owns the world and everyone's supposed to wait on her."

"She does do her part of the chores," Crystin reminded. "And Dada says it's not right to hate."

"Maybe. But just by looking at her face, you can tell that she clearly thinks all work is beneath her. And she doesn't do half of what she should. Miss Ivy, queen of Boston society." Her voice took on an affected tone. "You, girl, iron my gloves and darn my stockings. *I'm* going to the ball!"

Crystin giggled. "You can't iron gloves, Gwen."

"I know. But if she had her way, she'd probably give the order to have it done. She's so mean and bossy. The way she yelled at you when her stupid old brooch went missing is proof."

"But I did take it to look at it." Crystin sounded both repentant and puzzled.

"Yes, but she has so many fancy things. She could share instead of flaunting them in our faces like she's better than us. Not everyone has a mother or grandmother who has pretty things to give."

"You mean us?" Crystin's voice was solemn. "Was our mama poor when our dada met her?"

"She had the riches that counted. Inside beauty is what Dada called it. Sweetness of spirit."

"Do you remember her?"

"Some. Not a lot."

"Me, either." There was a short pause. "Gwen, do you like our new mama, even if she is from Boston where the rich people live?"

"She's a lot nicer than Ivy. Yeah, I like her."

It was a moment before Crystin spoke again. "Is our dada poor?"

"No, leastways not poor like we were in Wales when we lived in the mining camp. But you were too young to remember those days. Now then, cheer up, Crystin. Who needs Miss Uppity's old Boston things anyway?"

The girls' voices grew stronger, and Ivy ducked around the opposite corner before they came into view. From her hiding place, she saw that between them they held a large pail and were headed in the direction of a nearby stream. Probably to get more rinse water.

"I think she's sad," Crystin said. "Because she don't fit in. That's what Maryanne says."

"She could fit in if she wanted to," Gwen shot back. "She just doesn't want to."

Although the words were accurate, they cut Ivy to the quick. She never entertained any doubts that her new

35

stepsisters held anything but dislike for her, though the little one seemed to like her a bit. She'd taken up for her, anyway. Yet why should Ivy care?

She stiffened her back and walked to the front of the soddy, against the wind, letting it dry the few unexplainable tears that teased the corners of her eyes. The girls were right. She did not belong. So maybe it was time to go back to where she did.

Craig worked the lever of the huge bellows, fanning air over the fire to get it hot enough to repair a plow. His mind went to thoughts of Ivy. Weeks ago when he'd seen her on the road, after delivering an order to an old farmer who didn't get around as well as he used to, Craig had been touched to watch the encounter between her and Amy. It didn't take a lot of figuring to realize what must have happened. Craig had perfect vision and hadn't been so far away that he couldn't spot the cracked eggs and overturned basket at the side of the road. He had watched Ivy take an egg from Amy's outstretched hand, then give her something in return.

The girl's jubilant face afterward as she turned in his direction and ran for home—like a shining sunbeam parting the gray sky—made it obvious that Ivy had paid a handsome price for the hen offering. Ivy *did* have a good heart underneath all those ribbons and furbelows. He'd known it all along. And hearing her laughter caress the chill air, Craig's own heart had soared within his chest. Her laugh reminded him of small tinkling bells and produced a smile on his face, a smile that stretched his lips even now.

Seeing by the white color of the fire that he'd made it

too hot, Craig stopped fanning the flames and grabbed his washer. He immersed the bundle of tied-together twigs in water, then flicked the drops over the blaze to bring it down to a steady yellow glow. Thinking about Ivy was breaking his concentration, and that could prove dangerous. Besides, he had another busy day ahead.

Craig had finished up five of his orders when young Wesley ran into the smithy. "Mr. Owen said to tell you something came for you today by freight wagon," he blurted, out of breath. "I have to get home now, or Pa'll tan my hide."

Before Craig could respond, Wesley was gone. Craig eyed the sawhorse table along one wall, holding the orders still needing to be filled, then looked at what he'd accomplished that afternoon. Deciding it wouldn't hurt to take a short break, he put his tools away, exchanged his leather apron for his coat, and settled his hat firmly on his head.

Once outside, he moved against the cold wind toward the opposite edge of town that held the school and post office. The sky was blue and clear, and the sun gleamed off the windows of the modest-sized building. Inside and to the right, a colorful blanket hung from the ceiling. Through the gap, empty benches revealed that school was out, though the young teacher still sat behind her desk. To Craig's left, a customer stood in front of Mr. Owen's counter, and Craig's stomach did a little rollover when he saw who it was.

"Miss Leander," Mr. Owen patiently stated, "you should cut some words from that telegram to make it shorter. I charge by the word, you know."

"Yes, I know. However, every word is essential to the message."

"I understand that, ma'am, but, well, for example, this

part: 'It is imperative that I hear from you before the snows begin to fall and travel becomes difficult. I am most eager to return to Boston within the next two weeks.' Well, now, ma'am. That's repeating something you said in the first sentence."

Craig's heart dropped to his boot tips. Ivy was leaving?

He shuffled his foot, unintentionally gaining her attention. She looked over her shoulder. Her eyes widened when she saw him, and her face paled.

"Hello, Boston," Craig said quietly.

"How much of that did you hear?" Her blue eyes were anxious.

"Enough to know that you plan on breaking your poor ma's heart."

Her mouth thinning, Ivy faced Mr. Owen. "I want the entire message telegraphed. I can pay for it."

The bearded man shook his head but didn't pursue his arguments. "There's a package over there for you, Craig. For some reason, it got dropped off here instead of at Mrs. Llewynn's."

Craig nodded his thanks and went to retrieve what he saw was a crate. His new caldron must have arrived. Seeing it was too big to carry, he decided to come back for it with a wagon later. He'd already settled all accounts with Mrs. Llewynn, so the caldron was his. After giving a solemn nod to Mr. Owen along with a brief explanation that he'd be back soon, then a nod to Ivy, who hesitantly turned to glance at him, Craig exited the building.

Ivy concluded her business with the postal clerk. Taking a

deep breath, she stepped outside. She'd half-expected Craig to be waiting for her, so she wasn't at all surprised to see him leaning against a hitching post, his arms crossed. What did surprise her was his somber appearance, so much different from the usual one with the expression lines ready to stretch out in amusement.

She moved down the road, intending to ignore him.

"Why are you leaving us, Boston?" He straightened as she walked past, his long legs easily matching her stride.

"I don't see that it's any of your business."

"Maybe not. But you're going to hurt a lot of people by your decision to go."

"I do not belong here. This isn't my home and never has been."

"Do you really think you've given it a decent enough try?"

Needled by his words, she stopped walking and spun to face him. "Just what difference does it make to you, Mr. Watson? I should think you'd be glad to see me go. I haven't exactly been sociable toward you—toward anyone here."

A boyish grin lifted the corners of his mouth. "Not even to the hogs or the chickens?"

She felt her own lips lift upward in a smile, surprising her. She wanted to remain annoyed with this man but found it difficult to do so. "No, definitely not to them. Incidentally, I discovered you were right about Mr. Stony Jack's hog being able to 'count.' Although my stepfather explained away the incident as Mr. Stone teaching his animal to fetch objects rather than the hog itself being intelligent. Still, I suppose I do owe you an apology for that first day we met. I was upset and weary from the train ride, and I, um, acted rather supercilious toward you."

"Oh, now I wouldn't have gone and called you conceited, exactly. More sure of yourself and everybody else than anything." His grin widened.

The man was a scholar? Amazing. Ivy hadn't reckoned on him having enough schooling to possess any knowledge of the word she'd used to describe her bad behavior. "Then I'm forgiven?"

"I don't hold grudges."

"Thank you." She hesitated. "About what happened in there just now—I would appreciate it if you'd keep this our little secret. I don't wish for anyone to know of my plans."

"You planning on running away in the middle of the night?"

"Of course not! I simply want to approach my mother with the news when I feel the timing is appropriate."

He studied her a long moment. Uneasy, she glanced away from the steady look in his eyes. "I'll keep your secret," he finally said, "but on one condition."

A sense of misgiving made her gather her brows. "What condition?"

"That you let me take you to the church meeting next Sunday and go on an outing with me afterward."

"Church meeting?"

"You hadn't heard? A preacher is coming through here next week. We'll meet in the schoolhouse for services."

"No, I hadn't heard." Ivy thought quickly. A few hours with the man seemed a small price to pay for his silence. "All right, I'll go with you."

The warmth of his smile took her breath away. "I'll be looking forward to it, Boston. Well, I should get back to work now. I have orders to fill. Afternoon." With a quirky tip of his dusty hat in farewell, he headed down the road to his smithy.

Ivy continued to stare after Craig until he reached the huge doors of the building, then she realized what she was doing. With a frown, she shook herself out of her trance and walked in the direction of her stepfather's claim.

Chapter 4

I doubt he'll come. The snow is too much like ice for a wagon."

At Crystin's solemn words to Ivy, she looked out the window again, all hopes fading. The light from the morning's gray skies revealed a world clothed in a blanket of white stretching as far as the eye could see. Crystin was right. It was doubtful Craig would show. Ivy smoothed the skirt of one of her best dresses, a rich maroon brocade embellished with black ribbons matching the one she'd woven into her hair. Around her neck she wore her garnet brooch on another black velvet ribbon, and her fingers went to the stone, tracing its square outline. She told herself that she was relieved Craig hadn't shown, that this released her from their agreement. Yet the feelings coursing through her were not those of gladness.

"Never mind, Ivy." Her mother's soft voice broke through her thoughts. "We have each other, and we can read from the Holy Bible as we always do."

Ivy glanced at her mother, and concern replaced disappointment. She didn't look at all well. Her face was drawn, and her eyes had lost the luster that usually made them shimmer like precious sapphires.

Ivy went to kneel beside her chair and took her hand. "Mama, aren't you feeling well?"

"Of course, I'm fine. Just a little stomach upset. Hand me my Bible, dearest."

Ivy did so, and her mother opened the gilt-edged book she'd brought with her from Boston, reverently touching the pages as she skimmed through them. Her stepfather couldn't read English, though he spoke it, but he also often spoke in Welsh to his girls to keep their language from dying. Still, Ivy noticed that he seemed to derive great satisfaction from listening to Mama read the English words in her soothing voice.

" 'Behold, how good and how pleasant it is when brethren dwell together in unity. . . .' " As her mother continued to read the passage from Psalms, Ivy inwardly squirmed, though outside she remained as still as she'd been taught. Afterward, her mother closed the book, and no one spoke for a moment.

"Dada, when will Uncle Dai come to see us?" Gwen asked.

The question surprised everyone and seemed to hang in the air. Ivy knew the girls had been taught not to speak unless they were spoken to. She glanced at her stepfather to gauge his reaction. His face grew red, and he looked away toward the cookstove. "He chose the road to take. No one forced it upon him."

"But can he not just come see us?" Gwen insisted softly. "Nana says the same thing Mama does—family is important. Won't you write a letter to Uncle Dai and ask him to come, like Nana wants? He can stay with Aunt Winifred, since they're making their home into a boardinghouse."

"Gwendolyn! That is enough. I will have no more talk on the matter."

Ivy jumped. Even Old Rufus lifted his head off his paws to look at his master. Ivy had never before heard her step-father raise his tone in anger, and she studied him curiously. Just what kind of man was this Uncle Dai to get such a rise from Gavin?

"I'm sorry, Dada." Gwen's lower lip trembled, and her eyes grew moist. Gavin held out his hand to his daughter, and she went to hug him.

Before Ivy could dwell more deeply on the subject of Uncle Dai, the sound of faint bells came from outside, growing louder. Old Rufus pricked his ears and padded to the door, fully alert, his tail wagging. He let out a bark. Crystin darted to the window.

"It's Mr. Watson!" she cried. "And he's in a sleigh!"

Ivy quickly rose to see, Gwen right behind her. Sure enough, Craig sat inside a sleigh being pulled by his dark gray horse. Bells rang from the harness, and Ivy wondered if Craig had made them.

Crystin turned excitedly. "Can we go, Mama? Can we?"

Ivy's mother smiled and nodded. Amid many squeals, the girls grabbed their coats and shrugged into them, pulling scarves about their necks and hats over their ears. Ivy also went about the ritual of preparing to face the outside cold, but she did so more sedately than the girls.

Inside, her heart mocked her with its rapid beats.

Ivy met Craig at the door. "Hello," she said, feeling at a strange loss for words. She motioned to Gwen and Crystin, who appeared at her side. "My sisters are coming with us."

"Of course they can come." The smile he gave them was genuine. He bent down to scratch Old Rufus between the ears. "There's room, but you two children might have to snuggle close like fox cubs."

At this, Crystin giggled. To be on the safe side, Ivy planned the seating arrangement so that the slight Crystin was sandwiched between her and Craig, and Gwen sat behind them. The ride to town was filled with the little girls' excited chatter and Craig's patient answers to their questions.

Due to the nasty weather, the schoolhouse wasn't crowded, but Ivy was surprised to see among the townsfolk there a family who owned a claim a few miles away. The Reverend Michaels was young with bushy red eyebrows, long sideburns that swept down his jaws, and a decidedly Irish accent. He had a way of spearing a person with his intense blue eyes, and his words were full of something that convicted Ivy's heart. The passages he read from 1 Corinthians about love seared her conscience, and she thought back to what her mother had read earlier.

Perhaps Ivy never had tried to exhibit Christian charity or goodwill toward anyone while living in Leaning Tree and only expected to be treated kindly by others. Yet had she truly expected even that? She wasn't sure what she'd expected; she'd been so angry with her mother and new stepfather those first few months after she'd moved here. Yet the anger had begun to subside at some point without her realizing it. When had that happened?

After the rousing service, which lasted all morning, the people visited. Winifred pulled Ivy aside and asked how her parents were. Ivy explained that her mother wasn't feeling well, and both Winifred and Bronwyn shared a smile. "It will soon pass," Winifred said. "Give her tea with mint. It has helped me." She blushed.

By their reactions and words, Ivy felt a stab of dread. Oh no. Her mother couldn't be in a family way!

"It is the way of things," Bronwyn said, her blue eyes wise. "She is still young and strong. She will be fine."

Ivy nodded, though inside she felt like a newly broken wheel cast aside from the stagecoach whose destination promised a better life. How could Mother do this to her? How could Ivy leave Leaning Tree now?

"Are you all right?" Craig asked when they returned to his sleigh. Both Gwen and Crystin ran ahead and jumped in back, leaving Ivy no choice but to sit beside Craig. She did so stiffly, and he pulled up the bristly fur lap robe over their legs. She shivered when his arm and leg inadvertently pressed against hers in the confined space.

"Cold?" He pulled the lap robe up farther before taking the reins.

The warmth surging through her blocked out most of the chill.

"How did you get this sleigh?" she asked, raising her voice above the wind that resulted from the vehicle's movement once it was in motion. If they talked about inconsequential matters, she might be able to concentrate on those issues and not on the man sitting so close to her.

"A customer asked me to fix it for him last year, but he ended up moving back East. When I reminded him about the sleigh before he left, he told me that if I could fix it, I could have it. It was in bad shape when he brought it to me. It had hit a tree, and the runners were twisted."

"Did you make the bells on the horse's harness, too?"

"My cousin did. He's a silversmith who I'm trying to convince to move here. He's considering it. The town is growing, and by this time next year, I'd be surprised if the population hasn't doubled. We even have our own doc now."

Doubt edging her mind, Ivy looked at the ramshackle town. Either Craig had high aspirations or she was blind.

"Still doubt that Leaning Tree amounts to much?" he asked.

She shrugged, deciding it best not to comment. When he didn't steer the sleigh left at the turnoff leading to her stepfather's soddy, Ivy looked at him. "Where are you taking me?"

"To a little piece of the future."

"Where?" Her brows shot upward.

"You'll see. Relax, Ivy. You did agree to an outing after the service, and we do have the girls along as chaperones."

Some chaperones. A glance over her shoulder revealed that Gwen and Crystin had their heads tucked underneath their lap robe. Occasionally, a giggle would escape from beneath the fur.

"All right. I suppose," she gave her grudging consent.

Craig steered the sleigh by a copse of trees growing along the stream. White coated any remaining leaves and branches, and the water lazily trickled under a thin crust of ice.

"See that?" Craig pointed to a tree whose trunk leaned at an angle toward the water. "That's how the town got its name."

Ivy was interested despite her resolve not to be. She'd never been in this area before. Where her stepfather lived, there wasn't a tree in sight, though a scant few grew on the outskirts of town. She'd recently heard her stepfather and Winifred's husband discuss a man named J. Sterling Morton, who'd proposed an idea for everyone in Nebraska to plant a tree next spring. He felt the economy would benefit from the wide-scale planting. Ivy looked over the vast land of untouched white that the sleigh now faced. It would take a great many trees to make that happen! She tried to imagine all that empty white being broken up by forests of trees or even a small wood.

"What do you see?" Craig's voice caught her attention.

What did she see? "Um, snow, and a lot of land. Gray skies above."

"Know what I see?" She shook her head, and he continued, "I see opportunity. A land that's ready for growth and is just waiting to be farmed or used in other ways for the good of the community, even the nation. Miles and miles of rich, fertile soil ready for the first touch of that plow."

She turned her head to look at him. "Are you planning to trade in your anvil and become a farmer?"

He chuckled. "No. But where there are farming tools, mules, and horses, there's a need for a blacksmith. And where there's virgin land, there's a need for people with enough courage to carve out a promising future. People who won't say no to a challenge, who keep on when all they want to do is quit." His gaze briefly swept the land again. "And I believe you're one of those people, Boston. I believe you've got what it takes."

Ivy jerked in surprise. "Surely, you're teasing me."

"No. You've got gumption. I noticed that the first day we met. While it's true you weren't happy to come here and felt forced into it, you made do and adjusted the best you could. I have a feeling that if you'd also adjust your thinking and try to see some good in this town, you might find that this could be more of a home to you than Boston ever was."

"I sincerely doubt that."

He shrugged. "Just don't close your mind to the possibility. It may be that you coming here was all part of God's plan."

His words irritated her, and she looked away to the sweeping vista. "Please take me home, Mr. Watson."

"Don't you think you could learn to call me Craig?"

"Only if you'll stop calling me Boston!" The words shot out of her mouth before she could stop them.

Craig laughed, a rich, exuberant sound that warmed her clear through and brought two small heads from beneath the fur lap robe. "I can't promise I'll always remember," he said. "But I like the name Ivy, so I'll surely try."

That wasn't what she'd meant—she'd meant for him to address her properly by her surname. She opened her mouth to tell him so, then snapped it shut. Oh, what was the use? From what she knew of the man, Craig Watson would likely do as he pleased. Moreover, she did notice that the people in Leaning Tree weren't big on formality. So maybe no one would make anything of it.

Another pair of giggles brought her sharp focus to the girls, who quickly ducked their heads back underneath the blanket.

Ivy watched her mother pull the flat iron from the top of the cookstove and continue to press the wrinkles out of Gavin's shirt. She turned back to her own task of kneading bread dough. Since Winifred and Bronwyn had spoken to her after Reverend Michael's message three weeks ago, Ivy had kept a close eye on her mother. Mama hadn't told her she was expecting, but that was little surprise. Such things weren't discussed in polite society, and her mother had been raised in Boston, too. What had happened to make Mama forget that? Why would she wish to leave behind a life filled with every luxury imaginable to marry a poor farmer?

At the other end of the table, Crystin painstakingly used a pencil nub to write out a short essay on the discarded brown paper that had been wrapped around a parcel from the general store. By the light of a kerosene lamp, Gwen read the book on colonial life her teacher had lent her. Outside, the night was still and not as cold as it had been. December proved to be milder than Ivy expected, with few scattered snows. Yet she'd been warned that January had the teeth of a wolf—and being snowbound for days or weeks wasn't an improbability.

"What are you working on so diligently, Crystin?" Ivy's mother asked.

Crystin looked up from her paper. "We must write an essay on what we like most about Christmas and then tell what's most important." She looked in the direction of the sleeping quarters of the two-room soddy. "Will we go to Aunt Winifred's and pull taffy, Dada?"

Gavin walked into the room and sat at the opposite end of the table. He pulled a handmade pipe from his mouth and turned his blue eyes to his youngest daughter. "Much will depend on the weather."

"I hope we do," Crystin said wistfully. "That's one of the things I like best about Christmas."

"I like the *Mari Lwyd*," Gwen said, putting down her book. She turned her gaze toward Ivy, who stood less than a foot away. "That's where a big horse's skull knocks on your door to ask a question, and if you get it wrong. . ." She mashed her elbows together, hands wide apart, then brought her palms to connect with a loud smack directed Ivy's way. Startled, Ivy jumped.

"Snap!" Gwen continued gleefully, a smug look in her eye. "Off with your head."

"Gwendolyn, I will have no more of such foolish talk," her father said sternly. "Or perhaps you shall not get the pink sugar mouse in your stocking this Christmas. You are too young to remember the customs practiced in the old country."

"Did the horse's skull really bite people's heads off?" Crystin's eyes were wide.

"No." Gavin directed another severe look at Gwen before explaining. "The *Mari Lwyd* was an ancient ritual for luck the townsfolk played among one another, a game of wits. No one was hurt."

"What's your favorite Christmas memory, Dada?" Crystin asked.

Gavin's eyes grew misty. "I remember going with my brother, Dai, to the *Plygain,* since the time we were young men. It is a service where the townsmen sing carols and songs and read from the Bible. Always, it takes place in the dark hours of Christmas morning before the dawn."

"While the women pull taffy!" Crystin inserted eagerly. "Nana told me that."

"Yes." Gavin's word came softly. He stared into the distance, and Ivy wondered if he was thinking about his brother.

"What about you, Ivy?" Crystin suddenly asked. "What's your favorite thing about Christmas?"

Ivy stopped kneading the dough, surprised the child would ask but heartened that she had. She thought back to happier Christmases. "In Boston my grandmother gives a festive party and a grand ball during the Christmas season. Everyone of importance is invited, from the mayor to the wealthy ship merchants to the doctors and their families. People come from miles around to enjoy one of her affairs. There's dancing until all hours of the night and lavish banquets with roast goose and plum pudding. Among the many pastries she has her chef make are lady fingers, since she knows how much I fancy them."

Crystin looked horrified. "You eat ladies' fingers?"

Ivy shared a smile with her mother. "They are thin white cookies the size of a woman's finger. That's how they got their name, I suppose. You dip them in chocolate, or they have chocolate spread over them. I've eaten them both ways."

"A cookie with white sugar? I can't remember the last time I had white sugar."

"Brown sugar is just as good, Crystin," Gwen said, a sting in her voice. She ducked her head back toward her book before her father could see, but the look she shot Ivy spoke volumes.

Ivy knew the white variety was expensive because it was scarce. Most settlers used brown sugar instead. Seeing Crystin's wistful expression, Ivy wished she hadn't spoken.

She pounded the dough, placed it in a pan, then covered it with a towel and left it near the warmth of the stove to rise. Thankfully, this time she hadn't forgotten the yeast. Last time she'd made bread, her thoughts had been centered on Craig instead of the contents she mixed in the bowl, and she had omitted that most essential ingredient. Gwen had teased her mercilessly about her flat bread, and Ivy had bitten her tongue so as not to respond sharply.

She recalled the last time she'd seen Craig, in late

November when he'd taken her for another ride in his sleigh before that first snow melted to mush. He'd told her then that he also had a stepmother and stepsister, and adjustments had been difficult for him, too, at first. None of them were able to get along, so he could sympathize with Ivy's plight.

Then he'd said something to make her think. He told her that one day his stepsister went missing. During the search, Craig realized he didn't actually want her gone, as he'd often thought after one of their rows. The dread he'd felt until they found her safe in the tall grasses helped to dissolve the distance between them, and he was able to open his heart and see that his stepmother and stepsister weren't quite so bad as he'd thought. In fact, according to Craig, they had formed a caring relationship before the women had moved with his father farther west to California.

Ivy wondered why Craig hadn't also gone but was glad he'd decided to stay. To her amazement, she'd found him good company.

Ivy looked at Gwen and Crystin. They could be a trial at times, especially Gwen, but Ivy wouldn't wish evil upon either of them. Again, memory of Craig's words during that first sleigh ride revisited her—that if she would only adjust her thinking, she might find some good in Leaning Tree. Ivy pondered the idea and recalled the past months of living on the prairie.

She hadn't been fond of the inch-long worms that appeared on the walls, ceiling, and floor after a hard rain months ago. Nor did she like the dirt that sifted down and once landed in her bowl of fried corn mush. And she detested the snakes that liked to hide in tall grasses—and the one that preferred the soddy this past summer and had suddenly dropped down from the inside wall, landed at the foot of her cot, and frightened her silly. She had jumped out of bed and run outside screaming, while Gwen had doubled over laughing. Still, Ivy had to admit that the little sod house stayed warmer in winter and cooler in summer than a wooden one, and since her stepfather had plastered and whitewashed the inside walls, the place even seemed somewhat cheerful.

She enjoyed the huge canopy of sky that was often a rich, robin's egg blue and stretched on endlessly without any buildings or trees to mar it. Wildflowers in spring dressed the grass with abundant splashes of crimson, gold, and purple, pleasing to the eye. And when she stood outside and looked in all four directions at the miles of windswept grassland, an exhilarating feeling of freedom sometimes surged through her.

That was the sole thing about Boston that Ivy didn't like. Sometimes she'd felt confined. Here, anytime she felt the need to leave the cramped soddy, she could walk outside for miles with nothing but the constant, whispering wind for company—and Old Rufus, when the hound chose to trot beside her. The hard work that resulted from living on the prairie and all the walking she'd done had trimmed her figure and given her muscles a strength they'd never before had. Town wasn't so far away that she couldn't visit, and often she did, though she had yet to make friends. Unless she could count Craig Watson as a friend. . .

A rush of warmth tingled through Ivy, and she attributed it to standing so near the cookstove. She stepped over to the window and parted the curtains made of flour sacks embroidered with green flowers. A thick frost covered the ground, and a half moon provided little light. She might not want to admit it, but she was growing accustomed to living in this place.

"Gwen, Crystin, come with me to tend the animals," Ivy's stepfather suddenly said.

"Yes, Dada," they both replied.

Once the three left the soddy with Old Rufus trotting beside them, Ivy watched their trek to a smaller soddy that her stepfather had made to house the cow, the horse, and the chickens in winter.

"Ivy, a word with you." Mother's soft voice bore a trace of sobriety, and Ivy knew she must have signaled Gavin to leave with the children so that the two of them could speak privately. She turned to face her mother.

"I know life has been difficult for you here and that you miss Boston a great deal," her mama began. She sat down on the bench and laid one work-worn hand over the other on the table, then stared at them. "To understand why I wouldn't allow you to stay with your grandmother, as you asked of me, I would have to recall the past and speak of issues I long to forget. Suffice it to say, my mother and I had opposing views as to what was important, and I didn't want you under her sole influence."

Ivy took a seat across the table, waiting for her to go on.

"I love my mother, but we see things differently. She wasn't pleased when I married your father. She wanted me to wed someone wealthier, though your father wasn't poor. When he died, I was devastated and chose to move in with her. You were only six at the time."

Ivy knew this already but nodded in acknowledgment.

"Wealth and position are of paramount importance to my mother. It's true that I enjoyed many luxuries while growing up in my parents' home, but your father helped me to see that there were more important matters in life, such as God and family." Her mother reached across to take hold of Ivy's hand. "I wanted you to learn this, too. Your father would have wanted it."

"I know, Mama," Ivy said, her voice a wisp.

"You will soon be seventeen," her mother said. "A woman of marriageable age. I know I cannot keep you with me forever if you wish to go, but I ask that you remain here until early summer. You see," a faint blush touched her face, "I am expecting and will need your help. Mother Morgan told me that you knew."

Ivy looked at her lap and nodded. She'd never spoken of that first telegram she'd sent to Grandmother but wondered if Mama might have somehow learned of it. Once Ivy found out about her mother's delicate condition, she'd sent another telegram, this one telling her grandmother that she would have to delay her travel plans until after the baby came.

"I only want what's best for you, Ivy, and I considered it best to bring you with us to Nebraska. I wanted us to be a family. If I erred in that respect, forgive me. I don't want us to drift apart as Gavin and his brother have done."

Ivy's head snapped up. "Oh no, Mama!" She moved off the bench to hug her mother. "I could never feel any ill will toward you. I know that you love me."

Her mother smoothed Ivy's hair, much as she had done when Ivy was a child. "I spoke to you of this because you're old enough to understand such matters now. You've matured in the months we've lived here, and I thought it time that you know the lay of things. However, your grandmother loves you as well, Ivy. It is not my wish for you to bear any ill feelings toward her."

"I don't, Mama." Ivy thought about the money her grandmother had given her with explicit instructions not to tell her mother. Grandmother often did things like that, allowing Ivy to have anything she wanted against her mother's wishes and without her knowledge. As Ivy grew older, she'd felt uneasy about the duplicity. Perhaps she should tell Mother of the fifty dollars.

"Well, then!" her mother exclaimed, her voice light, signaling an end to the serious discussion. "If I'm to learn how to make a pink sugar mouse, I must find a way to do so with the ingredients I have. I shall make one tonight once the girls are asleep."

Ivy pulled away. "A pink sugar mouse?"

"A Welsh custom. I don't want Gwen and Crystin to be disappointed on Christmas morning when they look into their stockings."

"Can't Winifred or her mother do it, since they likely know how and we plan to be at their house on Christmas Eve?"

"Winifred has enough to do preparing for the social that she plans to hold for anyone who will come. It will be the last gathering before she turns her home into a boarding-house this spring."

"Still, Christmas is a week away."

"Yes, but I need the practice. I've never made anything remotely like a sugar mouse." Her mother smiled. "Will you help me?"

"But, Mama, you know I haven't yet learned to cook without burning what I do make!"

"I know. Yet this can be something we learn together. We can help one another. Mother Morgan told me some of how it's done, but I've no idea how to make the mouse pink! Berry juice from preserves perhaps? What do you think?"

Ivy smiled. "That might work." Suddenly she felt light-hearted and looked forward to the event. Who would have thought the idea of making a pink sugar mouse with her mother could give her such joy?

"Will all the townspeople come to Winifred's on Christmas Eve?" she asked.

"All have been invited. Whether they will come or not is another matter." A gleam lit her mother's eye. "Was there anyone in particular you were inquiring after?"

Ivy rose from the bench to sort through the freshly pressed laundry and collect her things. "Of course not." Yet when thoughts of Craig visited, she realized that wasn't entirely true.

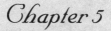

Chapter 5

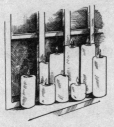

Christmas Eve arrived cold and windy with a few inches of new snow. Yet the weather wasn't bad enough for Gavin to cancel their outing to his sister's place. They bundled up for the ride in the wagon. Before they could leave the soddy, Old Rufus barked and ran to the door. Soon the jingling of bells alerted them to company. Ivy hurried to the window to see, as did Gwen and Crystin.

"It's Craig, and he's in his sleigh!" Crystin announced.

Gwen threw open the door. "Hulloa!"

For a moment, Craig seemed uncertain. "Hello. I came to ask permission to take Ivy to the social."

Ivy felt her face warm while her stepfather seemed to mull over the request. From the twinkle in his eyes, Ivy wondered if this was the first he'd known about Craig's invitation. "I think you'd best ask Ivy," Gavin instructed.

"Ivy?" Craig looked her way, his brown eyes hopeful. "Will you accompany me?"

She hesitated, not wanting to seem too eager, then nodded and walked toward his sleigh. She did enjoy his company, even if considering him for a husband was out of the question. Instantly he scrambled from the conveyance to help her into it.

"Can we go, too, Dada?" Ivy heard Crystin ask from behind.

"Not this time. There is a pout; now then, I'll have none of it," he said a little more sternly. "Or you will have no taffy pulling this night."

"Oh no, Dada, I'll be good," Crystin hurried to say.

As though afraid he might indeed change his mind, both Gwen and Crystin scampered in the direction of the wagon, which sat hitched up and waiting by the barn. Gavin chuckled and nodded to both Craig and Ivy before he and Ivy's mother set off in that direction.

The sleigh whizzed over the snow the short two miles to Winifred's, while the wagon bumped over small drifts at a much slower pace. Ivy noticed that the Bradfords' wagon was coming from the east, from the direction of their claim, and also headed toward town. All sixteen of the Bradfords appeared to be packed inside.

"I'm surprised they're taking the time to go to something like this," Ivy mused.

"A social is good enough reason for everyone to put off work for a few hours," Craig explained. "They're few and far between, especially this time of year. I worked extra hard this week at the smithy getting orders filled so that I would have today to enjoy with my neighbors."

Despite the chill air blowing on parts of her face not covered by the woolen scarf, Ivy's skin and insides warmed with embarrassment. She hadn't reckoned on Craig hearing her observation about the Bradfords. The man must have the hearing of a hound! Yet she was glad that he would be there—just as a friend, of course. Ivy certainly had no other reason for desiring his company.

Sleigh bells ringing, they soon arrived at the white timbered house. A curl of gray smoke rose into the sky from the chimney. Craig took care of the horse and sleigh, while Ivy hurried up the wooden steps. Thankfully, they weren't coated in ice.

Winifred met her at the door. "Hello, Ivy. I'm glad you could make it! But. . ." Her brow creased, and she looked behind Ivy in the direction of the road. "Where are my brother, your mother, and my nieces?"

"They took the wagon. Craig brought me." Too late, she realized the slip of using his first name in public.

Winifred smiled. "Come in and get warm."

Ivy did so, though she left her cloak on. It was cold inside even with the fire to warm the parlor. From what Ivy knew, the Pettigrasses were the only people in Leaning Tree to own a genuine parlor, but then, Winifred's husband was wealthy, though not as wealthy as Ivy's grandmother. As Ivy drew nearer to the blaze, she noticed wood didn't burn there but the usual "Nebraska coal," as her stepfather chose to call the cow refuse. She looked toward the corner where someone had chopped down a wild plum bush to use as a Christmas tree and had decorated it with strings of popcorn.

"Greetings, Ivy," Bronwyn said, coming from another room, a fine china cup and saucer in her hand. "Have some wassail to warm yourself." She offered the steaming cup to Ivy, who gratefully took a short sip. Piping hot apple, cloves, and cinnamon teased her tongue while delicious warmth filled her.

The door constantly opened as more people arrived. A few were Welsh immigrants who'd also settled in Leaning Tree like the Morgans. It appeared that everyone who lived nearby was making a showing, and the parlor soon felt cramped and warm. Men and women talked and visited. Older children rushed outdoors to amuse themselves, while the younger girls sat in a circle to play with the corncob dolls they'd brought from home.

As the afternoon progressed, some of the families left the gathering early. Mrs. Llewynn's husband, Milton, brought out his fiddle, and lively music filled the place. A few men, including Craig, circled the baldheaded fiddle player. They clapped their hands and stomped their feet to the frenetic melody while the women flocked together and chattered away like magpies who hadn't seen each other for an entire season. The topic was the second theft of one of Mrs. Llewynn's chickens just that morning.

"Well," Mrs. Johnson, the feed store owner's wife, said, "I think it's just horrendous. And on Christmas Eve, besides. Whoever would do such a thing? A definite ill-bred churl, if you ask me." Her gaze speared Mrs. Bradford, and Ivy felt the look was deliberate. Did Rowena Johnson suspect one of the Bradford children of being a chicken thief?

"I'll be thankful when we get a sheriff for this town," Mrs. Llewynn said. "As well as a preacher." Suddenly she was all smiles. "I hear, dear Winifred, that the men of Leaning Tree asked your husband to act as our first mayor."

"Yes," Winifred said. "It is all so exciting."

"Then he has agreed?" the doctor's wife, Adella Miller, asked.

Ivy's attention was diverted to Bronwyn, who offered

each of the guests their choice from a platter layered with fancy iced cookies and sliced fruitcake. Ivy had never seen Crystin's eyes go so round as they did when her grandmother held out the tray toward her. The child moved her small hand in the air over each item, as though uncertain of which to take, then opted for a slice of fruitcake. Ivy took a cookie. It was brittle, but it wasn't bad.

"Your mother tells me of the pink sugar mouse and your attempts to make one for my granddaughters," Bronwyn said, eyes twinkling.

Ivy felt the blush rise to her face and was thankful no one was within hearing distance. Crystin had taken her cake and moved toward one of the Bradford children. "Yes, and sad attempts they were, too. They crumbled to nothing."

Bronwyn chuckled. "Tonight, after the girls sleep, I will show you both how it is done. Pleased I am that your mama tries so hard to be a good mother to Gwendolyn and Crystin. The Lord smiled the day Gavin met your mama. Before she came, lonely were the girls to have no mother."

Ivy saw the truth of what the elderly woman said, though her poetic way of speaking was a bit difficult to follow at times. Ivy's mother was kind and unselfish, wanting only the best for her family. She had adapted to this wild prairie life and was a good wife to Gavin, too.

"It is also well to have you as part of our family, Ivy," Bronwyn continued. "There is kind, you are, to be a good sister to the girls. To you as an example they look."

If Ivy wasn't well trained in social etiquette, she might have gawked or allowed her cup to clatter to the saucer. Gwen definitely didn't regard her as a friend!

Bronwyn seemed to read her thoughts. "Gwendolyn is

like my youngest son, Dai. Stubborn he is, with a strong will. The voyage to America and losing her mother years later to fever made troubles for Gwendolyn. She was made to tend Crystin much, and she, only a child herself. She is angry but does not dislike you. Many times I see her watch and imitate what you do. As she does now." Bronwyn smiled and barely nodded to a corner of the room.

Ivy's gaze followed. Gwen stood, adopting the same well-postured stance as Ivy, with her little finger in the air as she sipped her tea and smiled politely at those nearby.

Suddenly Ivy heard raised voices, and she looked to see that the Bradfords were leaving. Mr. Bradford, his face flushed, said something to Wesley. The boy grabbed the hand of one of his young brothers and hurried outside. Two of his sisters followed. Had Mrs. Bradford been offended by Mrs. Johnson's remark or the taciturn look she'd given? She didn't look happy. Nor did Mr. Bradford.

Bronwyn rushed toward the couple to offer her farewells, Ivy assumed. As the front door swung open, she noticed that the sky had grown murky and a heavy snow fell. The Johnsons and another couple gathered their outer wraps, making for home as well.

"Will you also need to leave since the weather's taken a turn for the worse?" Craig's voice came from near her elbow.

Ivy managed to keep her grip on the saucer, though her cup gave a telltale clatter. She hadn't heard him come up beside her. Perhaps there was a disadvantage to having a carpet cover the floor.

"No," she said. "My mother and sisters and I plan to stay and take part in the late-night taffy pulling. My stepfather will return to the soddy to tend the animals. He'll come back for us in the morning."

Craig nodded. "I imagine this isn't anything like the fancy socials you're used to. But admit it, Ivy—you did have a good time today, didn't you?"

Why his words should irk her so, especially since there was a ring of truth to them, she didn't know. She raised her chin a notch. "Why should you think that?"

"Because your cheeks are glowing like summer-ripe strawberries, and your eyes are sparkling like blueberries after the rain." His grin was teasing, his gaze admiring.

Ivy felt the hot blush spread toward her ears and down her neck. She lowered her voice to a whisper so only Craig could hear. "If my face is glowing and my eyes are shining, it's due to annoyance regarding your improper behavior, Mr. Watson. Kindly desist from further talk of comparing my features to fruit."

Craig let out a loud laugh, bringing a few glances their way. He shook his head, still grinning. "Boston, you are the only woman I know to get offended by a compliment. But in the future, I'll keep your wishes in mind."

"Miss Ivy." A child's voice spoke to her right.

Ivy swung her gaze in surprise to see Amy Bradford standing there.

"Do you know where my mama is?"

Alarm filled Craig as he looked at Amy, whose tousled golden hair and heavy-lidded eyes suggested she'd been sleeping. "I was hidin' from Wesley, but he never came and found me. I don't see none of my family here, neither."

Craig quickly bridged the distance to the door and

opened it. Behind him the fiddle playing stopped. The wind blew the snow harder, and some of it swirled inside. He could see the Bradfords' wagon in the distance, slowly making its way home. He closed the door and strode to the fireplace. Winifred had joined Ivy, who had an arm around the girl's shoulders. Amy now looked wide-awake, her eyes uncertain and a little afraid. Apparently she'd just learned that she'd been left behind—again. Why the Bradfords couldn't keep track of their children, Craig didn't understand. Fourteen kids was a lot for any couple, but this kind of situation happened far too often to be called accidental. More like negligent.

He hunkered down in front of the child and smiled. "Ever ride in a sleigh, Amy?"

She shook her head no.

"Would you like to? We can catch up to your folks in no time."

Her eyes began to shine. "You mean that sleigh with all those pretty ringin' bells? Oh yes, Mr. Watson. I'd like that awful much."

"Then let's hurry."

While Craig shrugged into his outerwear, Ivy buttoned Amy's threadbare coat, which looked a size too small. "Is this all you have to wear, Amy? Have you no hat or scarf?"

The girl shook her head.

"I'll just go upstairs and get a quilt to wrap her up in," Winifred offered.

The wind raised its voice, an angry foe, and now Craig could hear it shrieking through the eaves. "Better make it fast, ma'am. I want to get back before the weather gets worse."

"You think it will?" Ivy asked, concern edging her voice.

"Are you certain you should risk it then? I'm sure Amy's parents will know that she's here and safe with us."

He grinned. "You worried about me, Boston?"

"Me worried? About you?" Pink stained her cheeks. "I've never heard of anything so vain. Why would you think such a thing? My concern was solely for Amy."

He chuckled. "Methinks the lady doth protest too much," he teased under his breath so Amy couldn't hear. "Shakespeare. *Hamlet.* And yes, I can read, too."

The pink swept up to cover Ivy's entire face. Winifred returned with the quilt, and Ivy quickly claimed it, kneeling down to wrap the child inside. "Merry Christmas, Amy. Mr. Watson will see that you get to your family safely."

"Thank you, Miss Ivy," the little girl whispered.

"I will be back shortly," Craig said to Ivy. Maybe he shouldn't have teased her, but he hadn't meant the words in a negative way. He had only positive feelings with regard to Ivy. Yet he was beginning to wonder if she would ever feel anything for him. Eight months of trying to win her favor was a long time. Maybe such an effort really was wasted, as he'd been told often enough, and he should just give up.

Craig bent to scoop the bundled child in his arms. He could feel her tremble against him.

"Still cold?" he asked as he headed for the door.

"No. I'm just hopin' Pa won't be mad about this fix I'm in."

"It'll turn out all right. It wasn't your fault you got left behind." Sensing that she was still upset, he added, "Know what I do when I'm nervous or scared?"

"Pray to God to make it all better?"

"That, too. I also whistle. It relaxes me. Shall we whistle?"

She grinned and nodded. Yet, as they stepped outside,

the angry wind snatched their cheerful notes from their pursed lips, and Craig fought the wintry beast all the way to the sleigh.

❖

Staring out the window at a world of white, Ivy stood with folded arms and rubbed them. Craig had left with Amy some time ago. Not long after his sleigh took off in the direction of the Bradfords' homestead, the wind increased to gale force, whipping snow first one way and then the other. Only for periodic snatches of time had Ivy been able to see farther than a few feet past the porch. A short time ago, the storm calmed some, though the snow still blew in whirls. At least she could see for a much greater distance than before.

Why had she snubbed Craig yet again when he'd asked her if she was worried about him? True, she'd been embarrassed that he'd so accurately discerned her thoughts. Regardless, she shouldn't have treated him so shamefully.

"Ivy, come away from that window," her mother gently commanded.

Ivy turned. "He should have been back by now."

"Perhaps he went home. The smithy is only across the road."

"No, he told me he'd be back shortly. Something's happened. I just know it." She glanced toward the window again, as if by doing so she could summon Craig back.

"Worrying won't help matters, dearest. All it will do is put wrinkles in that pretty forehead of yours. Now come here and let's pray."

Ivy did so, and her mother took her ice-cold hands in her own. "Father, we ask that You protect all Thy children out there. Help everyone to reach safety, and—"

Her mother's prayer was cut off as Ivy's stepfather and Winifred's husband walked into the room. Doc Miller and Mr. Llewynn were right behind them. All the men wore coats, hats, and mufflers. "We've talked it over, and we're going to look for them," Gavin explained quietly. "There is no way the Bradfords could have reached home in time. And Craig cannot have gotten far."

Ivy's mother rose to hug Gavin, and Bronwyn did the same to her husband. Mrs. Llewynn wrapped the scarf a second time around her husband's neck and fussed with his coat. Then they watched the men walk outside into the dancing snow. Ivy moved to stand beside her mother and slipped her hand into hers, both to take comfort and give encouragement. "Heavenly Father," she said, taking up the prayer where her mother had left off and trying not to let her voice shake, "we earnestly ask that Thou wouldst be a guiding light and protect our husbands and fathers and friends so that they may find and help any who are in need."

Ivy's mother squeezed her hand gently. "Amen," she whispered.

Chapter 6

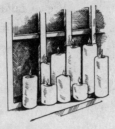

Minutes after Craig left the Pettigrasses, the blizzard had started in earnest. Though he wore thick gloves, he had ceased feeling his hands long ago. The unforgiving wind whipped stinging particles into his eyes, the only part of his face exposed to the blinding snow. He couldn't tell if the constant, faint ringing he heard was in his head or from the sleigh bells. The wind drowned out most other sounds. He should have listened to Ivy. If he had, Amy would be safe by the fire right now instead of curled up in fear under the lap robe beside him.

If only he could sense direction; if only he could see something around him besides a curtain of white. He hadn't driven that far before the storm worsened, so he'd turned back in what he assumed was the direction of town. Now they were struggling against the wind.

Father, my own stupidity got me into this mess. I was so sure I could beat the storm. Please don't let a little child's life be lost because of me. Show me where to go.

Traveling blindly on in a foreign world of nothing but

white, Craig urged the horse forward. If they stopped, the horse might freeze. He might freeze. With that thought, he moved his limbs to try to keep the blood flowing while taking care not to drop the reins. Amy's thin arms suddenly clutched him tight around his waist. He couldn't blame her for being scared.

"Help, please."

Craig blinked. Did his ears deceive him? Had that been a human cry for help? He strained to hear against the forceful wind.

"Help."

Sensing the call was coming from his right, Craig directed the horse that way. He pulled down his muffler from his mouth. "Call again so I can find you." The wind snatched his words from him the second they reached the air, and he doubted he could be heard.

"Over here!" The reply came, stronger this time.

A shift in the wind made the dancing snow seem to stop and swerve. In that instant, Craig spotted a sod house with light coming from inside. He remembered it as belonging to a family who'd moved back East two summers ago after a prairie fire destroyed their crops.

Craig guided the sleigh less than a foot from where a boy stood in the open doorway. A lamp glowed inside the run-down one-room house, devoid of all furniture except for a small bed and table. Craig questioned the intelligence of leaving Amy in the sleigh, even for a short time, but he did not know what he would find when he entered the soddy.

"I hear the bells and know help has come." A boy of perhaps eleven with shoulder-length black hair, brown skin, and liquid-dark eyes looked up at him. "Please to help my mama,"

71

he implored in broken English. "She very sick."

Craig stepped inside. No fire burned, though a flame steadily shone in the lamp's glass globe. Chicken feathers littered the earthen floor and table, and what was left of a stew sat in a pot. Craig would guess that he'd just discovered the identity of the chicken thief. Across the room a smaller boy sat on the cot, upon which a young woman lay stretched out, fully clothed. A baby nestled beside her.

"I am Roberto, and that is my brother, Paulo," the boy at the door said. "Mama sick many days, since my sister, Carmelita, come two months ago."

"Where is your father?" Craig asked.

"He died when we come West. We find this place, me and Mama, and stay here now."

Craig moved forward. "Are you all right, ma'am?"

The huge, dark eyes of the beauty surveyed him, but she didn't answer.

"Mama speak no English."

"How is it that you do?"

Roberto smiled. "Boys in wagon train teach me some. Other words I learn after we leave our band."

Gypsies. That explained it.

"And did you learn to steal chickens, too?"

The boy's eyes glittered in defense. "The store owner has many birds. My mother and brother are hungry. I am head of family now." He puffed his small chest out. "My duty is to feed them."

Craig decided this wasn't the time for reprimands. Realizing the situation wasn't dangerous, he went to collect Amy from the sleigh. Roberto's eyes widened when he saw the girl in Craig's arms, and his fascinated gaze focused on her snow-covered fair hair. Craig set Amy down, shut the door, and searched for fuel to make a fire. He must get the place warm. Then he would figure out what to do next.

"Put a table by the front window," Bronwyn ordered a few minutes after the storm worsened and the wind increased again. "Fill it with every candle and lamp in the house. Do the same with the upstairs window, Winifred."

Her directives caused the women to hurry into action. Soon a yellow blaze lit up the rattling pane from the inside, and the aroma of honey from many beeswax candles filled the room. The rest of the house was dim, but if sacrificing light with which to see might help bring the men home safely, Ivy wasn't going to complain.

She prayed nonstop for Craig and the Bradfords, for the search party, and for her stepfather. She was surprised that she felt so strongly about her stepfather's safety and realized she didn't dislike him at all. Now that she was being honest with herself, she silently admitted that she approved of her mother's husband even though he had chosen to make his home on the prairie. He took care of Ivy and never ceased to treat her as one of his daughters despite how she behaved. She burned with shame when she thought of the caustic remarks she'd flung his way upon her arrival in Nebraska. He wasn't her own dear papa, but he was a good man, a strong man, and he obviously loved her mother. Ivy owed him her respect.

When her thoughts returned to Craig, she forced her hands to any task that presented itself to help her forget. She couldn't think of him right now or she might cry. It had taken a blizzard to make her realize she loved the man. She didn't know what she would do if Craig were killed, if she never saw his sunny smile or heard his warm, teasing words again. How she wished she could retrieve every occasion on which she'd acted indifferently toward him or ignored him outright.

As they waited, Bronwyn took the chair beside Ivy and began to speak of her son Gavin and of how proud she was of what he'd achieved. Her reminiscences brought up the conflict between Gavin and his brother, something about which Ivy often wondered. Ivy's heart ached for the brothers and their mother, who felt torn by the anger between sons. Gavin, the oldest, strongly felt the responsibility for his family and had worked hard to keep them together. Upon reaching America, his brother had other ideas. Gavin assumed Dai would help him stake his claim during the five years necessary to possess the land, but Dai had not wanted to be a farmer. Harsh words arose between them, ending in fisticuffs, before Dai stalked off, angry. That had been seven years ago, and to this day, Gavin and Dai had not seen one another or written to each other.

"I pray for them, every night, to end their quarrel," Bronwyn admitted, tears trickling freely from her eyes. "I miss my Dai. There it is. Only the Almighty can work in my sons' stubborn hearts."

Ivy thought about Bronwyn's words as she took her mother some tea with mint. "Winifred said this will help ease the sickness, and it might help to calm your nerves, too."

Her mother took the saucer. Ivy noticed how her hand trembled and the small amount of liquid that sloshed from the teacup.

"Mama, please don't be upset. We've prayed, and now

we must trust. We mustn't worry, as you said. My stepfather is an intelligent man; I've seen this. He's not one to make foolhardy decisions."

Her mother laid a palm against Ivy's cheek. "Bless you, dearest. Thank you for being such a comfort to me."

Ivy took her mother's hand—a hand that had once been so smooth and pale but was now rough and brown—and kissed the inside of her callused fingers. Then she moved around the room to serve tea to the other women. She found that she enjoyed helping by doing what she could; it gave her a sense of purpose and helped to keep her thoughts off Craig.

"Ivy," Winifred said, "in the spring when the weather warms, the women will meet for a quilting bee each week. We would like for you to join us."

"Thank you, but I don't know how to quilt." She felt embarrassed to admit it.

"We will teach you," Winifred said with a faint smile. "It will be a time for us to encourage and pray for one another's needs also. As we are doing this day," she said more softly.

Ivy felt tears prick her eyes at the sense of unity she suddenly felt toward these women. "I'd like that."

"Listen!" Adella Miller lifted her head of tight curls higher. "Do I hear bells?"

"It must be Craig!" Forgetting etiquette, Ivy set the platter holding the tea pitcher down with a bang and rushed to the door, throwing it open. The snow didn't swirl as heavily. The icy wind sucked the breath from her lungs, but its effect didn't compare to the breathlessness she felt at the sight of a sleigh drawing closer.

"Craig," she whispered, clutching the doorframe.

He awkwardly exited the conveyance and picked up a long bundle. As he drew closer, Ivy could see he carried a woman. Amy and two other children hurried behind them, bent over as the wind half blew them to the porch.

"Hiya, B–Boston," Craig said stiffly from between blue lips as he moved across the threshold. "Miss me?"

The gripping emotion of wondering if he were dead, then seeing him alive—with a strange woman in his arms—was almost Ivy's undoing. She couldn't respond. She stared at him for a few quick heartbeats, then gave a short, abrupt nod and switched her focus to Amy and the two boys.

Ivy helped to get the children out of their snow-encrusted coats, hats, and mufflers and noticed Bronwyn and Winifred doing the same for Craig. Ivy's mother and Adella were tending to the woman, whom Ivy could now see clutched a baby to her chest. Mrs. Llewynn took the child. When Ivy felt she could face Craig again, she shifted her gaze to where he'd taken a seat in a chair nearby. He was wrapped in a quilt, and icy particles of snow still clung to his eyebrows, hair, and eyelashes. His skin looked pale, his brown eyes serious.

"You really d–did miss me," he said, his words still stilted from the cold. They didn't contain any of their usual teasing but were filled with amazement.

"Drink your tea," she ordered, noticing that he held a cup someone had given him.

As he lifted the steaming cup to his blue lips, Ivy decided to be honest with him. After her telling actions upon his arrival, she couldn't very well pretend differently. Nor did she want to. "Yes, I did miss you. I was worried about you and continually prayed for you—and the others."

Craig frowned. "What others? The B–Bradfords?"

Ivy nodded. "And the men who went searching."

Craig clumsily set his cup and saucer on the floor. "I must help them."

To his obvious amazement—and hers—Ivy pushed him back in the chair with one hand. "Oh no, you mustn't! You might get lost again, out there all alone. Look at you! You resemble a walking snowman. And your teeth are still chattering. You must get warm before you can even think about going back out there. How ever did you find your way?" She switched the topic, hoping to detain him.

He drained his tea. Winifred appeared, quickly refilled his cup, and moved away again to tend to the woman. Craig then related to Ivy what had happened and how he'd found the gypsy family. "When the wind stopped blowing so strong, I kn–knew I had to get Juanita to the doc."

"Juanita?"

"Roberto's mother. I prayed I was d–doing the right thing and took the risk once the storm died d–down, figuring out which direction to go from their s–soddy. I knew that town was to the w–west. While I was still a ways off, I saw a light and was sure God was leading me home. That was a smart thing you women did, putting those c–candles and lamps in the windows."

"It was Bronwyn's idea." Ivy hesitated. "Is Roberto's father away? Is that why he didn't come?"

Craig took another large swig of tea. "He died on their journey West."

"Oh. Then Roberto's mother is a widow." Ivy glanced her way. The exotic-looking woman was wrapped in a colorful blanket and seated before the fire. The baby was nestled at her bosom. "She's quite lovely."

"Not as lovely as you."

Craig's low words sped up Ivy's heartbeat. She blinked his way. The steady look in his eyes sent warmth trickling through her, and suddenly she didn't mind the cold so much.

"Miss Ivy," Amy said, walking up to her. She still trembled. "Are my m–ma and p–pa going to be okay? And my brothers and sisters?"

Ivy hugged the girl close, rubbing her arm to help warm her. "We can pray that God will keep them safe, as we've been doing since this started." Noticing the concern on Gwen's and Crystin's faces as they kept casting glances toward the door and window, Ivy came up with a plan.

"Bronwyn, didn't you tell me that one of your traditions is to put on a Christmas play?"

"Yes, every year in the old country we hold a play of Christ's birth."

"Then let's have one now." Ivy ignored the shocked looks sent her way by the rest of the women. She thought that if they engaged in such a play, it might help lighten the atmosphere as they waited for their men to return.

Winifred looked at Ivy and nodded, lending her support. "Yes, this will be a good thing."

Ivy smiled her thanks at her stepfather's sister. "Amy, you be Mary. And Crystin, you can be the angel. Gwen, you shall be the wise man, since you're the eldest."

"Who will be Joseph?" Crystin asked.

Amy pulled on the older boy's arm. Ivy had noticed how he tried to edge out of the room during her announcement of the play. "Roberto can be Joseph—and we even have a baby to play Jesus!"

"But Carmelita's a girl!" Roberto protested.

"That's okay," Ivy assured him. "No one will be able to tell. If it's all right with you?" Ivy looked at Juanita for permission.

Roberto spoke in rapid Spanish to his mother. The woman looked mystified but nodded. She handed the baby to Roberto, then with another uncertain nod accepted the tea Winifred handed her.

"Perfect." Ivy smiled at her small cast of characters. "We shall need costumes."

Winifred smiled. "I will help. I have dresses I can no longer wear." She blushed, then hurried upstairs. Soon she returned, her arms full of ivory-, blue-, and peach-colored dresses, sheets, and a gold-topped walking stick that belonged to her husband. She handed the contributions to Ivy, then excused herself to make coffee.

Roberto folded his arms across his thin chest and absolutely refused to wear a sheet for his costume. However, he did accept the fancy walking stick to use for a staff. Crystin looked adorable in a white satin dress, though it was much too big for her; Winifred was petite like her mother, yet the dresses still hung on the girls.

Someone fashioned a "halo" from a ring of lace and set it atop Crystin's dark curls. Amy's thick, golden hair shone against the oversized, pale blue gown. The glow on her face and the brightness of her eyes as she stared at the baby in the manger—the cradle that would be used for Winifred's child—made her appear peaceful and awed, much like the Virgin Mary must have been. Ivy noticed how often Roberto stared Amy's way.

"Are we ready to begin?" Crystin asked. "Shall I make my announcement to the shepherd now?" The shepherd was Paulo, and he looked lost wrapped up in a white sheet with only his nut-brown face showing.

"Not quite," Ivy said. "There's one item we've overlooked." She undid the velvet ribbon from around her throat that held the garnet brooch and approached Gwen. "Why don't you wear this, since a king—or in this case a queen—would wear jewels?"

Gwen's mouth opened, but no words came out. Crystin gasped.

"Here," Ivy said, "I'll fasten it around your neck." Once she did, she stepped back to look. "Perfect." She smiled.

"Thank you," Gwen whispered, awkwardly fingering the square jewel and seed pearls.

The old irritation rose up, but Ivy squelched it. Her sister's fingerprints couldn't harm the brooch, nor could she hurt it if she squeezed the stone too hard. The truth was, Ivy had thought up that and any other ridiculous notion as an excuse to be selfish with her things. *Dear God, forgive me for being so self-centered*, she prayed when she saw Gwen's joy at wearing the brooch. The genuine smile the girl sent Ivy did her heart good. Perhaps they really could be friends someday.

The children began their rendition of Christ's birth. Roberto walked with Amy from the top of the stairs to the parlor to reenact the journey into Bethlehem. Carmelita gurgled from her place in the wooden cradle off to the side, awaiting her debut appearance.

"I am tired and hungry, Joseph," Amy said, putting one arm across her stomach and draping her other hand across her forehead. "I need rest."

"I will find us a chicken," Roberto proclaimed.

"That's not what you're supposed to say," Amy hissed.

Mrs. Llewynn raised her brows, and Craig leaned toward

her. "I have something I need to tell you later," he whispered, the effects of the cold no longer affecting his speech.

"I think I know." The woman looked at the skinny boys, then at their sickly mother wrapped in quilts and leaning weakly back against her chair. A smile replaced Mrs. Llewynn's frown. "Never mind. I'm sure we can work this out to benefit everyone. I could use a strong boy like Roberto to help at the store. As you said, we will discuss this later."

Ivy decided that she also wished to discuss a matter with Mrs. Llewynn when she could get the woman alone—the purchase of a doll with a real china face for Crystin and of a leather-bound book of children's stories for Gwen. She remembered seeing such items in the general store. Add to that the beautiful oak cradle she'd also noticed—a cast-off from a family who'd returned back East—that would make a perfect gift for a new baby sister or brother. She should have enough of her fifty dollars left over to buy several yards of material for both her and her mother to have spring dresses. And gloves. She simply must buy herself new gloves.

Ivy mentally created her Christmas list. Hopefully the gifts would impart the message she wished to convey: that she now considered them all her family.

"You look like the cat that got away with the mouse," Craig whispered to Ivy as Gwen, the wise man, moved forward bearing a plate with an iced cookie and a piece of fruitcake to use as a gift for the baby. Roberto eyed the offerings hungrily.

Ivy winced and glanced at Craig. "Please, don't talk to me about mice," she whispered. "Not after our failure with the pink Christmas mouse."

"That sounds like it could be an interesting story," he

mused. "A pink Christmas mouse? Still, I have to wonder what would cause your face to glow like that, as if you'd just swallowed one of those candles. Pleased with yourself and the play, maybe? A great success, by the way. The women's minds are off their worries for the time being. And the children are having the time of their lives."

Ivy smiled. It was true. "I just came to the realization that this is where I belong. Being here finally feels right, as if I fit in now."

A couple of heartbeats passed before Craig spoke. "Ivy, look at me." His tone was serious.

She turned to stare into his steady brown eyes.

"Are you telling me that you've decided to stay in Leaning Tree?"

"Yes, Craig. This night has helped me to discover what's truly important, as well as shown me how foolish I've been."

Before she could explain further, the door blew open. Four white-crusted figures stiffly clomped inside, followed by fifteen more shivering forms.

"Ma!" Amy cried, abandoning her role when she caught sight of her mother. She almost tripped over the borrowed dress in her haste to get to her. The women jumped up from their chairs to embrace their frozen husbands and help them and the others out of icicle-laden coats and mufflers. Roberto dove for the slice of cake and crammed the entire thing into his mouth, his smile wide.

"It w—was a miracle we f—found the p—place before we f—froze to death," Ivy's stepfather said, his teeth chattering. "Their w—wagon was stuck. W—we had to w—walk, and I th—thought all w—was lost when the s—storm started up again. Then, w—we saw that light in the w—window."

"Thank God you're safe," Ivy's mother said, briskly rubbing on the blanket that she'd draped around his stocky form. "Come closer by the fire."

Mrs. Bradford hugged Amy, and her father put a hand on her shoulder.

"Miss Ivy took care of me and helped us put on a play," Amy enthused. "I'm Mary. Will you watch me, Ma? We can start over."

The woman's grateful gaze met Ivy's. The look in her pale green eyes said what words couldn't. Ivy smiled and nodded in understanding. "I'll just go and get some coffee for everyone."

"I'll come with you." With the quilt wrapped around his shoulders, Craig stood to his feet.

Ivy darted a glance at the others as he walked on ahead of her. Everyone was so wrapped up in their loved ones' return and getting them warm again that Ivy didn't think she or Craig would be missed. Laughter, tears, and thanks filled the parlor, and she silently added her own prayer of gratitude. Strange as it might seem, this Christmas had been one of the best—and most challenging—she'd ever known.

In the kitchen, a cookstove burned, and the coffeepot simmered. Sweet spice scents of cinnamon and cloves lingered in the air, along with the aroma of rich coffee beans.

Craig abruptly turned Ivy's way. She jerked in surprise, her skirts brushing the wall. Her heart began a lilting cadence at the intense look in his eyes.

"Tell me again," he said. "I'm not sure I heard right the first time. Do you plan on staying in Leaning Tree?"

"Yes."

"For good?"

"Yes."

He raised one brow. "Do I dare hope your decision might have something to do with me?"

At least two-thirds of it does. "It might," she said. It was one thing to be remorseful for needlessly slighting him in the past; it was quite another to throw herself at the man.

A slow grin curled his mouth. "I've got enough money saved up to build a house come spring—the kind you like with wooden walls and floors and a roof. If you'd consent to be my wife, Ivy, you'd make me the happiest man in all of Nebraska."

"Craig Watson!" Exasperated, she shook her head, though her heart beat triple time at his words and she couldn't prevent the smile that stretched her cheeks. "Before introducing the subject of marriage, don't you think you should at least ask to court me properly?"

"Would you agree?"

A sudden case of shyness hit. "I might."

"To both?"

"Yes," she whispered.

Craig whooped in delight and cast the quilt from his shoulders. Sliding his large hands about her waist, he twirled her once around the confined space. She squealed when his leg knocked against the table. Dishes clattered, silverware clinked, and she laughingly protested that he put her down before someone came into the room and saw them. He set her gently on her feet, his brown eyes rich with amusement and warmth.

"I'll always love you, my proper Boston girl. I knew it from the first day I saw you stepping off that dusty wagon with your chin a mile high in the air."

Before she could think to be indignant about his teasing remark, Craig dipped his head and tenderly kissed her, and Ivy forgot all else but him.

BOSTON'S LADY FINGERS

Adapted from an old prairie cookbook, this recipe is for thin, biscuit-like chocolate-frosted cookies—perfect for a Christmas tea or small party.

3 egg whites	½ teaspoon vanilla
5 tablespoons powdered sugar	½ cup flour
2 egg yolks (well beaten)	¼ teaspoon salt
	Powdered sugar for coating

Beat egg whites until stiff. Add powdered sugar. In a separate bowl, beat yolks. Fold into mixture. Add vanilla. Fold in flour and salt until batter is well blended. Line a cookie sheet with waxed paper. Press the batter through a pastry bag and onto cookie sheet, forming strips approximately 4 inches long and 1 inch wide. (I use a plastic freezer bag with one tiny section snipped off at a bottom corner for a pastry bag.) Sprinkle with powdered sugar. Bake at 350 degrees for 10 minutes. Edges should be light golden brown. Remove from oven. After a minute, while cookies are still warm, slide spatula underneath to loosen them from waxed paper. Frost or dip in chocolate when cool. Makes approximately 24 cookies.

CHOCOLATE FROSTING/SAUCE:

Stir over low heat 1 cup powdered sugar, ½ cup semisweet chocolate chips, and ⅛ cup water until rich and creamy. As it cools, it thickens and makes a sweet frosting to spread over cookies. Or put back on low heat and add several drops more water until thin enough to use as a dipping sauce.

PAMELA GRIFFIN

Pamela lives in North Central Texas and divides her time among God, family, and writing. Her main goal in writing Christian fiction is to encourage others and plant seeds of faith through entertaining stories that minister to the wounded spirit. Christmas is her favorite time of year, and she enjoys writing stories centered on the season. She has contracted over twenty novels and novellas and loves hearing from her readers. You can visit her at: http://users.waymark.net/words_of_honey/.

The Christmas
Necklace

by Maryn Langer

Dedication

With gratitude to the talented writers
who helped me in so many ways with this book:
Pamela G., Patti D., Terry M., Sandy S., Robin H.,
Michael M., Nicole C., Shirley P., and always, Ken. Also
thanks to Ray B. and Loraine and Gayla A.
for giving the Christmas story the right setting.

To my beloved Savior, Jesus Christ,
whose birthday this story celebrates,
for being my Comforter and loving Teacher.

Now therefore put away. . .strange gods
which are among you, and incline your heart
unto the LORD God of Israel.

JOSHUA 24:23

Chapter 1

Chicago—October 8, 1871

A rumble like the sound of an approaching train rolled through Lucinda Porter's dream, growing louder and louder until the roar enveloped her. It continued to roar, not lessening, not moving on. Lucinda rolled onto her back and worried herself awake. *Trains never sound that loud for this long.*

She jerked off her sleeping mask and sat up, puzzled by the crimson light filtering into her canopied bed. She tore open the brocade bed curtain and stared in disbelief through the wall of windows across the room. Flames licked at bare branches of the ancient sycamore. Black smoke seeped in around the window frame.

From outside her room came a rattling, a pounding on the door. "Mistress! Mistress!" The lock gave way and Pearl, nanny of her childhood and now beloved personal maid, rushed in with two serving girls. Lucinda bolted out of bed, grabbed a velvet dressing gown, and struggled into it.

"Hurry, Mistress," Pearl pleaded. Strong hands rammed satin slippers onto Lucinda's feet.

The sycamore exploded into a giant torch of white light. Windows blackened and cracked. Smoke came from everywhere and filled the room. Coughing and with eyes streaming, they stumbled toward the hallway. Blistering heat enveloped the room, and the roar of red-yellow flames swallowed up all other sound.

Terror muted her, muted them all. They gripped hands to make a human chain and rushed, stumbling, choking, into the hallway. Lucinda, Pearl, and the loyal serving maids staggered half seeing down the grand staircase to the foyer. They stepped onto the marble tile and fumbled their way through the smoke across the foyer, down the back passageway, and out the servants' entrance into the cool October evening. Lucinda took her first deep breath and stopped. Pearl wrapped her arm around Lucinda's shoulder and guided her to safety.

Lucinda twisted about in time to see the home of her childhood, sanctuary in her widowhood, haven after the sudden loss of both parents, and one of the most beautiful houses in Chicago collapse into a great bonfire. She searched for voice to scream her pain but found none. Her lungs burned, her heart hurt, her legs buckled.

Peoria, Illinois—December 22, 1871

A heavy hand shook Lucinda. "Lady, wake up," a weary

voice said. "It's mid-morning and train's about to leave Peoria. You ain't got a ticket to go beyond."

Lucinda Porter jerked awake and blinked up into the furrowed, mocha-colored face of the uniformed conductor. "What? Who?" *How dare he speak to me in such a familiar manner.*

"You almost missed your station."

Where is Pearl? I can't miss my station. Why didn't she wake me? Lucinda shook her head to clear the confusion. Slowly, the heartbreaking reality of Pearl's leaving settled in again. She had departed two months ago, but Lucinda still couldn't fully accept that she wasn't there. Forcing the painful memories back into hiding, she sat up and slid forward on the wooden bench. She pulled her ill-fitting, secondhand coat tightly about her and glanced down at serviceable, over-the-ankle brogans. Impoverished and alone, the finality of her situation sent a chill that rattled her bones.

During this past week, she had been reduced financially to a class lower than that of the conductor. She felt ill at ease in his presence, but she forced a tremulous smile. "Thank you for your concern. I must have been exhausted to fall asleep so soundly," she managed to say.

Apprehension registered in his eyes as he waited.

"My experiences of the past two months have left me fatigued." Her words were mumbled, hurried. The conductor raised his eyebrows. "The Great Chicago fire destroyed my home and everything in it."

Why should he care? Their lives would likely never touch again. Daily he would keep his train on schedule, and she, by early afternoon, would become a kitchen maid at the Tillotson mansion outside Peoria. At least there, though she was not of that world any longer, she would be tucked away in familiar circumstances. She could lick her wounds and try to put her life back together.

"Ohhh, I see," the man said. "Mrs. O'Leary's cow what kicked the bucket burned ya out, so you've come to Peoria to spend Christmas with relatives, have you?"

Lucinda gathered her worn carpetbag and stepped into the aisle. "I have no relatives, here nor anywhere. I've come to Peoria as a domestic at Judge Marshall Tillotson's country estate." *There, you have my pathetic story in one sentence.* Hearing her own words forced her to finally accept the hard truth of her new station in life. She couldn't pretend anymore that this new life was a bad dream and would go away.

"I'm sorry that you have to go out in the storm. It's comin' straight across the prairie. Nary a tree to break the wind." Gently, he held her arm and moved her along the aisle and down the steps to the platform. "This storm's gonna be a real humdinger. You got someone to meet you?"

She looked up and studied his eyes, his face. He knew little about her situation yet seemed genuinely anxious for her welfare. *Amazing. Why should he give me a second thought?* It had never occurred to her that, with the exception of Pearl, her servants and others of the serving class truly cared about her comfort and well-being. This notion needed some more pondering.

"I'm sure my transportation to the Tillotsons' will be along." At her weak smile, the conductor's face relaxed somewhat, and he climbed the steps. Over the clanking and grinding of the train into motion, he shouted, "Have a merry Christmas."

His well-meant words stabbed her heart. This Christmas

would not be merry. No magnificent tree in a foyer that was larger than many homes, no welcoming candles lighting twenty-three sparkling windows. There would be no teas, no balls, no banquets, no Christmas Eve service with her parents in the family pew, no expensive gifts spilling from under a tree whose top star reached the second-story balcony. This Christmas she would not accompany her mother in directing the preparation and delivery of baskets heaped high with food and clothing for the unfortunate.

A year ago she had become a widow before she reached her twenty-first birthday. Last July she was orphaned, and this December she was left completely without means. Even Pearl was living a pampered life with her wealthy sister while Lucinda had become one of those unfortunates.

Shivering in the oversized coat and ugly blue and yellow striped cap, she watched the caboose sway off down the tracks. Not until the train became a distant blur did she remember that her small trunk had not been put off. Except for her sweater and nightgown in the carpetbag, everything she owned was in that trunk.

Her heart lurched, and her hand flew to her chest. Hidden beneath her navy wool dress, the precious antique necklace with flawless emeralds the color of her eyes was still there. It was the first and last Christmas present from her late beloved husband, the seventh earl of Northland. Lucinda pressed her hand against the precious gift and fought back tears, thankful she had fallen asleep wearing it on the night everything burned.

Hopeful, she looked around the platform. Except for the stationmaster in his little box of an office, the station was deserted. Remembering her new class in life, it dawned on her that a servant of such lowly rank wouldn't likely have someone waiting to convey her. Those charged with the transport of common serving maids weren't known to be prompt or polite. Sent on more errands than one, picking up the new kitchen help was probably last on their list before they left for home.

She crossed the street in front of the station and stood where she would be visible to any passing conveyance. The street corner offered no protection from the wind; gust after gust swept over her, biting through her coat. Shivering, she pulled the collar tighter about her throat and moved back into a warehouse doorway, looking up and down the empty street. At last, the smart *clip-clop* of horses' hooves broke the silence.

"Oh, thank you, thank you," Lucinda whispered. A large enclosed sleigh came into view. She rushed into the street where she could more easily be seen. The sleek team drew alongside. The driver gave her nary a glance and raced on, leaving a miniature blizzard behind. Fine snow settled over Lucinda and marked the departure of the only transportation to have traveled that way.

"They aren't coming for me." She wilted against the building, her courage draining. "Maybe they don't expect me. Maybe I don't even have a position." A tear she couldn't contain slid down her cheek and froze. Lucinda found a clean handkerchief and wiped her nose. "Oh, Pearl, I miss you so. You would know what to do." It then occurred to Lucinda that she should have asked the stationmaster for advice before she stepped into this freezing, awful wind.

She limped on numb feet back across the street to the little building and related her situation to the old man. The stationmaster shook his head. "Mistress Tillotson don't furnish transport coming or going. You get out there the best way you can, and it's mighty hard to leave once you're there."

"But I'm expected to arrive by early afternoon, or I shan't have a position. What am I to do?" She blinked back threatening tears.

"Best I can suggest is you go over to Main Street. Maybe you can catch a ride on a farm wagon. They come along that way all the time. With it being the last Friday before Christmas and a storm coming in, if you hurry, you might find one."

Lucinda thanked him. Fighting against a blend of panic and misery at being so helpless, she limped away through the blowing snow toward Main Street.

Chapter 2

David Morgan stood in the hall outside the sitting room of Mistress Rosella Tillotson's townhouse and adjusted his cravat. He removed his mouton Cossack hat and ran a hand along the sides of his blue-black hair in a futile attempt to smooth it. Calling on Mrs. Tillotson before noon probably wasn't the wisest thing he had done in his life, but time was running out. The Tillotsons were leaving in two weeks for an extended trip to Paris for the winter season.

I must find the good judge today. Remind the kindly old man to write the referral letter he promised.

He shucked off his overcoat and knocked with a firm rap on the ornately carved door.

"A pox on your generations. It's not yet ten," called a woman's voice, deep and gravelly. "Who's the degenerate cur who can't tell time?"

"David. David Morgan, Mistress Tillotson."

"David?" Her harsh voice changed to beckoning satin. "Since when have you started knocking?"

What is that supposed to mean? I always knock.

"Come in this minute and explain why you've been neglecting me, you naughty boy."

An unremarkable girl in a gray uniform opened the door. David entered the sitting room and handed her his hat and coat.

Though professional decorators had tried to create elegance, Rosella's taste for heavy furniture upholstered with bold textured fabric overpowered the classic objects of art the Tillotsons had collected from around the world.

Rosella fit with the surroundings perfectly. Society matron of Peoria, wife of renowned Judge Marshall Tillotson, she reclined in a regal pose on an elaborately carved chaise lounge. She was robed in a white satin dressing gown and propped amid plump pillows in burgundy satin cases. Mistress Tillotson laid aside a large hand mirror and smiled a coquettish welcome to David. "Come. Sit and tell me what is happening in the outside world." She sat up and patted the foot of the burgundy velvet chaise.

He ignored her command. "I've come hoping the judge was here."

"I suspect he's in the country. We are having a Christmas party this evening, you know." She patted the chaise again.

He deliberately walked to the fireplace. Nodding toward the newly hired maid hovering in the doorway to the bedroom, he asked, "What happened to Gigi?"

"Gigi, that ungrateful wench! She ate her way into a waddling, shiftless mountain of fat. Cost me a fortune to keep her in uniforms. Three days ago, without a second's notice, she up and left. Disappeared. Vanished without a trace." Rosella's eyes, an unusual autumn green with gold flecks, glared at him as though this disaster were his fault.

David shook his head. *The woman is impossible. No wonder Judge Tillotson stays away.*

She picked up the mirror and pursed her lips. "What a pity I don't rouge my lips. I could wipe them clean and add another touch to my invalid's ruse." She looked over the top of the mirror at him, eyes twinkling. "Can you not see, David, how very ill I am?"

He folded his arms. "Why, may I ask, are you playing the invalid?"

"I must look sick enough to convince Marshall that I am unable to attend that wretched dinner he insists on having in the country this evening."

"Why did you agree to have it if you didn't want to attend? I fail to understand the need for the charade. There's a storm predicted for today. And coming in on this *particular* day, you could just say that you don't feel well enough emotionally to cope with such an affair."

Her eyes narrowed. "You remember what day this is?"

"How could I forget? You've reminded me every December twenty-second for the past five years. But you've never gone to this extreme to celebrate your grief."

Rosella drew back her hand and flung the mirror at the wall. David jumped out of the way of scattering shards that fell like ice crystals onto the oriental carpet. "Mistress Tillotson, throwing things is going too far."

She didn't acknowledge his scolding. "I wonder why Marshall doesn't remember? Meghan was his daughter, too. The fact is, the way he doted on her sickened me."

"Of course he remembers, but he needs friends to help him through the pain."

Rosella's expression softened. "Meghan would have been twenty-two today." Her voice trembled. "She's been gone twenty years—a lifetime." Rosella reached for her linen handkerchief and blotted the tear threatening to streak her powder. "To this day, I cannot believe someone could creep into the house and snatch a sleeping child from her crib without leaving a trace. Not a clue could the Pinkerton detectives find. Two years of searching and they never found how she left Peoria." Rosella buried her face in the handkerchief.

David watched the performance and felt a churning start in the pit of his stomach.

Rosella dabbed around her eyes and snapped her fingers. "Girl, get me another mirror."

The maid quickly handed a replacement to Rosella, who ignored David and checked her makeup for damage. David pulled out his pocket watch. The morning was slipping away. "I must—"

"I'm really glad you dropped by this morning. I'd like for us to have a little visit before lunch." Rosella stood and walked slowly toward him.

He edged away from the fireplace. "What do you want to visit about?"

"Your going to Paris."

"Paris! I don't want to go anywhere close to Paris," he said bluntly. "What I want is to go west, not east."

She shuddered. "West? Have you lost your senses? The West is unfinished. Nothing but sagebrush, Indians, and other wild things."

"The far West is new territory. A man can get a foothold. Become anything he wants to."

"That's nonsense. What is it you want to become that you

can't achieve right here in Peoria? After we get back from Paris."

He was amazed at how innocent her smile appeared, how convincing her eyes. "Before *you* get back, I shall be gone."

Rosella's mouth took a cunning twist into a half-smile that he had learned spelled danger.

"David," she said ever so sweetly, "I've given the past five years to turning you, a raw Welsh immigrant, into a gentleman with the savoir faire to be my escort in Paris. And I just spent a king's ransom on my wardrobe and yours."

"Rosella, you've been telling everyone you and the judge are going."

She wasn't listening. *She's already plotting her revenge.*

Her thin smile sent a shiver down his spine. "That is no way to repay the kindness I have extended you. That makes me very unhappy. And Marshall won't be happy, either."

"That sounds like a threat, Rosella. I repeat, you've told—"

"About a month ago, Marshall decided he couldn't go. Too many court cases on the docket, or so he says. So, David dear, because I am going and I will not go without an escort, you *are* going."

"No, Rosella, I'm not." He turned to the maid. "Please bring me my coat."

Fury darkened Rosella's face. "Hear me well, my young friend." Her eyes sparked a look he had seen turned on others. Never on him.

Her hand shot out, lightning fast, and grabbed his wrist. Rosella stared hard into his face. "If you think you can run away on a whim, think again. If you even consider such a thing, I shall tell Marshall you took advantage of my disturbed state during this upsetting time of the year—Meghan's disappearance—and you forced yourself on me."

"You would be lying and would have to prove those accusations in court, Mistress Tillotson." David clamped his jaw tight, revealing none of his own rage.

"Ha! Don't you worry about court. Have you any idea what Marshall would do to you? You'd be ruined!" Her evil smile suddenly turned sweet. "But enough of this. Look over there, dear." She waited until he looked. "See the lists on my desk? I have a million things to attend to."

He started to speak, but she cut him off with a wave of her hand.

Her mood shifted, and her voice was now light and happy as a child's. "Your wardrobe is ready at the tailor's. Pick it up, and I'll send word so you can accompany me to the country."

David grabbed his hat and coat from the maid and left without a word. He stormed down the stairs, jamming his hat on his head and his arms into his coat as he went. Propelled by fury, he scarcely noticed the storm or the stately homes he passed as he stalked toward Peoria's downtown and his boardinghouse across the tracks.

Rounding the corner of Jefferson and Main, he came face to face with an ill-dressed waif. They collided, and she went spinning toward the street. He grabbed for her, managing to get a grip on her coat, stopping her fall. Angry and frustrated, David forgot both when he looked down into her eyes—clear green with flecks of gold, framed by long, smoky lashes. Her eyes. . .they reminded him of someone.

Little else of her face showed between the striped woolen cap pulled down to just above her eyes and the large coat collar covering her cheeks. But the eyes: He couldn't help staring. They held him captive, nearly drowning him in the sorrow reflected there. Only once before had he seen such deep sadness. When his father was killed in the coal mines of Wales, his mother's eyes never lost that look. *What has happened to you, little mud lark, to scar you so?*

He let go of her coat and stepped back. "I'm so sorry. Are you hurt?" She shook her head, and an auburn curl escaped from her cap. Her coat was soaked, and snow spilled over her shoe tops. "You are not properly dressed for such weather. You must get inside at once."

"Indeed, I shall avail myself at the first opportunity."

He smiled. She might look like a poor waif, but her speech was that of a lady. Interesting. He wondered what she looked like without that unsightly cap. He gestured at the three-story brick structure across the street. "The Pinkney Building is a good place to get warm. The bakery there is the best in town."

She thanked him, and he watched as she slipped and slid her away across the street. The bakery would be warm. They would give her a free sample of the day's special. Once in front of the three-story building where Judge Tillotson had his offices, she looked back at him, nodded, then disappeared inside.

Alone on the empty street, David's frustration returned. With every step, he seethed at Rosella's cunning entrapment. Indeed he had escorted her through five years of social events, but it was at the insistence of her husband who never seemed to be available. *Now I know why. She's demented,* he thought.

By the time David reached his room at the boarding-house, he could see no way to gracefully disentangle himself except to flee far and fast. He knelt before the steamer trunk given to him by his mother. Taking out the little coffer locked away inside, he counted the money he had saved. Eighty-four dollars, after the payment of his room and board. Enough to take him west if he guarded his spending.

He decided to accept the suit Rosella promised him. The tailor shop was in his neighborhood, so he hurried over. There, to his chagrin, he found a complete wardrobe waiting. A month ago when he went in to be fitted for one suit, he had no idea what Rosella had planned. It took two trips for David to carry his new wardrobe to his room.

From the mountain of items laid neatly on his bed, he chose the tuxedo for the dinner at the Tillotsons' prairie mansion. His mind raced as he carefully folded the items of clothing into his soft-sided leather case. "I know one thing. I am not going to the country with Rosella. Or anywhere else."

David snapped the case shut and changed into his riding clothes. "I shall stop over at the judge's office and write the referral letter. Then all he'll have to do is sign it, and I'll be out of Rosella's clutches before tomorrow dawns."

Chapter 3

Inside the spice-scented bakery, Lucinda sat thawing her nearly frozen extremities and sampling immodest amounts of oatmeal cookies, lemon custard pie, and cherry cobbler the owners urged on her. Business was brisk, but in the dim corner where she was seated on a crate near the ovens, no one paid her any mind. While she ate, she took stock of her situation.

For the first time, she allowed herself to review the events of last Wednesday. Was it only two days ago that she had still thought of herself as the wealthy Countess Lucinda Porter, fresh out of widow's weeds? Though her house and buildings had burned to the ground, she did own the ground. Her father's business partner, whom she called Uncle, took care of the legalities. After the fire, she had stayed in his lavish home and been treated with great kindness but not allowed to look at the books. Wednesday last, he had sat her down and told her the whole story.

Papa always assured Lucinda and Mama that they would always be well cared for. Never did anyone dream he would be temporarily deep in debt and both parents would die in a carriage accident before the debts could be paid. Uncle tried everything he knew to save her estate, he said. But even with the infusion of her inheritance, there was only enough money to pay off half the loans. However, he assured her he would gladly assume her debt if she would marry him. Uncle was a man twice her age, pompous and demanding. She quickly understood she would become his hostage until the debt was paid. She signed over her property to him.

Having chosen poverty, here she was in Peoria.

Lucinda's reverie was interrupted when a tall, thin woman dressed in calico and moccasins walked into the bakery from the interior darkness of the back hallway. Long dark hair pulled into double braids down her back framed her furrowed bronze face. Taking no notice of Lucinda, the woman began checking the contents of the ovens. When she finished, she straightened up and walked over to Lucinda.

Lucinda blushed at having been caught in her silent examination. Clear, nearly colorless blue eyes stared at her with an intensity that felt to Lucinda like they pierced her soul. She felt a deep connection to the old woman and, with it, a tremor of anticipation.

"I am known to all as Yarrow Woman. You are a stranger here." Her voice enfolded Lucinda like a warm blanket. She hadn't felt this safe since before the fire.

"Yes. I'm seeking transportation to the Tillotson estate. I'm expected this afternoon to assume duties as a kitchen maid."

The old woman looked deep into Lucinda's eyes. "I have been prayerfully searching for some answers about my future, and I now have the feeling you and I are going to be bound together somehow." Taking Lucinda's hands, she examined them. "You have never served."

Lucinda looked and saw what Yarrow Woman saw—hands soft and manicured. She shook her head.

Yarrow Woman let go of Lucinda's hands and continued to study her. "You will serve the Tillotsons scarcely any time at all and then never anybody else." Her words were soft, her tone reassuring.

Lucinda felt the blood drain from her face. *I cannot fail in my first position. Where will I turn?*

Yarrow Woman's expression softened. "I apologize for upsetting you, but God moves in unexplained ways, and on occasion I receive impressions about a person's future. I give all praise to the Lord and take no credit unto myself." She waved a work-hardened hand in a gesture of helplessness. "I am not usually this forthright, but I could not seem to contain this message."

Lucinda's heart skipped a beat.

The woman stood quietly, her eyes fixed on Lucinda. "I have never been to such a place, but I see beyond great mountains of granite, across a desert of death, to a city built by silver."

Lucinda shivered and closed her eyes.

"Do not let your necklace be seen. Keep it hidden and in your possession at all cost."

Lucinda's eyes flew open. She felt for the outline under her dress. "Ho—how do you know these things?" she stammered.

"From childhood I have been gifted with second sight. It is not a thing I control. In the Sioux tribe, I was a wise woman. Now that I know Jesus as my Savior, I receive only that which He chooses to give me." She turned and started back toward the shadows.

Lucinda jumped up. "Do you see when I shall go to that far-off land?"

"You will begin the journey tonight, of course." The words were spoken matter-of-factly as she entered the dim hallway.

"Surely not tonight. How will that happen?" Lucinda called, but Yarrow Woman continued down the hallway.

Lucinda felt warmth deep in her chest, yet at the same time she shivered at Yarrow Woman's words. To consider that she could be out of work by tomorrow was frightening. She had no place else to go. Her fingers trembled as she dusted crumbs off her clothes. She wouldn't consider the possibility of being let go. *I must work hard to please and make myself so useful that they will find me irreplaceable.* She thanked the bakery owners and let herself out, vowing to waylay any conveyance that might be moving upon the prairie toward the Tillotson mansion.

Lucinda walked along Main Street's crowded sidewalk, clutching her valise in one ungloved hand and the collar of her coat tightly about her throat with the other. She mulled over her experience in the bakery and decided that people of the working class were kind and honest. She liked them. Surely one of them would give her a ride.

She approached several kind-looking shoppers, but they gave her sharp looks and continued on their way. Desperation drove her to walk in the street, where she hailed sleighs, carts, wagons, any conveyance moving and some that were parked, but all she received were blank stares or curses for her trouble.

The wind picked up, building the drifts ever deeper until

the shoppers gave up and vanished, leaving the streets deserted. "Oh, please, dear Jesus, help me find a ride. Please."

Before the noon church bells chimed, the storm retreated inside low-slung gray clouds. Still, she trudged up and down Main Street, around and through the drifts, battling mounting despair. She kicked at a drift of snow blocking the sidewalk. The more discouraged Lucinda became, the more she clung to Yarrow Woman's words. *She said I would serve scarcely any time at all. But she did say I would serve. That must mean I will get to the Tillotson mansion somehow.*

She walked into the middle of the street and looked both ways but saw no wagons. Not even a rider. What was she to do? She turned her back to the wind and began to cry, no longer able to hide her despair. It was then she heard hoofbeats pounding hard and fast. Before she could move from the center of the street, he was upon her.

He reined the charging horse to a skidding stop. "Excuse me," a deep voice said, "are you or are you not going to cross the street?"

She whirled around and found herself staring up into the face of the fine-looking man who earlier that morning had directed her to the bakery. Now he sat astride a magnificent chestnut stallion that refused to stand still.

With eyebrows knit together, he asked, "Why are you still out in this weather?"

"Ahh. . .my. . .the train left with my trunk on it. I only have what is in that carpetbag." She gestured at the shabby bag resting on the curb. "And I must. . .I am trying to. . ." *Lucinda, you're babbling.* She took a deep breath. "I have the promise of work as a domestic at the Tillotson estate, but I can find no transportation to take me there."

She said a silent prayer of thanks that her voice sounded strong and clear. "I must be there by early afternoon if I'm to claim the position." She kept her unwavering gaze on his face. His skin was a weathered brown common for farmworkers and did not match the gentleman his riding habit and coat suggested. His eyes focused on her with a force that made her uncomfortably aware of how common she must look. Covered with a dusting of snow, peering out from under a boyish woolen cap, the rest of her buried inside the giant coat, she must look awful.

Swallowing hard, she continued to stare at him. His broad shoulders were covered in a stylish long coat layered with a cape buttoned high around his throat. He had a regal tilt to his head, accented by a Cossack hat that gave him the appearance of an English nobleman, a scowling English nobleman. Then he flashed a wide smile that lit his face.

Even in her misery, Lucinda smiled back. Was he as kind as he looked? Had her prayer for a ride been answered? "I would pay you to take me to the estate." Her voice filled with hope, and she opened her palm to show twenty-five cents. "I know this isn't much, but perhaps we could work out an arrangement where I might pay you later. . . ."

His laugh cut her off. "You're not familiar with money, are you?"

She shook her head. "I was served by a woman who took care of all the details of my life."

"You have offered far too much." The horse tossed his head and gave an impatient stamp. "Kambur says it is time we were off. My name is David Morgan, and you are. . . ?"

"Lucinda. Mrs. Lucinda Porter, late of Chicago."

He nodded at the introduction. "You are fortunate, Mrs.

Porter. I'm traveling to the Tillotson estate. Put your money away. I shall be happy to deliver you to your destination if you have no objection to riding astride and double."

Dumb with gratitude, she shook her head and picked up her carpetbag. He removed his foot from the stirrup and reached out his hand. "Let me have your satchel." She handed it up to him, and he hung it from the saddle horn opposite his own fine case. She hiked up her skirt, slid her square-toed brogan into the empty stirrup, and let herself be pulled up behind him. Ladies generally rode sidesaddle, but she wasn't going to point that out.

"Put your arms around my waist and hang on," he ordered. "I don't relish being out in this weather longer than necessary."

Gingerly, she reached around his waist.

"My dear lady, this is no time to be shy. I mean to ride hard, and if I cannot feel your arms, you'll probably land in the road at the first corner. Now slide closer so your face rests against my back, and lock your hands together in front." His brusque voice left no room for argument.

Lest she be left behind, Lucinda positioned herself tight against his back and clasped her hands around his waist. Even from the back, this man radiated power, someone to be reckoned with.

"That's better," he said and flicked the reins. The horse leaped forward. They whirled away up the steep incline and out onto the prairie.

As they flew along, she silently repeated his name, David Morgan, an important name she must not forget. When she was sure she would not forget his name, she began to wonder just how much twenty-five cents was. It must be a goodly sum. She must learn about money.

All she had to her name was contained in the small trunk left on the train and the well-used carpetbag—and of course, her necklace and the clothes on her back. She reminded herself that she was probably going to be known as Lucy Porter, household servant, hoping to arrive at the Tillotson estate in time to serve other people's lavish Christmas parties.

She sighed and let her thoughts drift to this man she was clinging to. She was certain that the likes of David Morgan would not normally give the current version of Lucinda Porter a second glance. That he did said much about him. But such a man was bound to have a beautiful lady waiting at the Tillotsons', most likely his wife. *If he isn't married, Lucinda, he's far above your station now.*

The sky lightened the farther into the country they rode. Lucinda studied the beautiful homes on expansive grounds. A majestic red brick house, clearly visible at the top of a rise, caught her fancy. It cheered her when they turned up the wide road that led toward the front entrance guarded by thick white columns—the Tillotson mansion. However, they veered to the left onto the tradesmen's narrow lane that ran alongside the house. She had never entered a house through the servants' entrance. Once more she was reminded of who she had become.

A hedge of tall yew, pruned to unnatural perfection, screened the lower windows of the house. At the back, the lane widened into a cobblestone yard that separated the kitchen wing from the carriage house and stables. David stopped at the kitchen door. Lucinda held still as he swung his leg over Kambur's neck and landed on the ground at her feet. He offered up his hand. She took it, and their gazes locked for a moment. Quickly, she came to her senses and concentrated on getting off the horse with some degree of grace.

David carried her satchel and ushered her up the steps. "With the dinner hour drawing near, there's such chaos in the kitchen that a cannon blast would go unnoticed. They'll never hear you knock." Handing her the carpetbag, he pounded on the door with no success. He shrugged and said, "Just go on in."

He looked intently into her eyes. "I hate to leave you like this, but three days ago, the good Andy Henderson, head groomsman, and his wife left in the middle of the night. I'm sure the stables are in a muddle since most of the guests are already here. I owe it to the judge to set things straight." He gave her hand a slight squeeze and, with easy grace, swung onto Kambur.

"Thank you," she called and waved. David returned her wave before he rode on to the stables.

He didn't really squeeze my hand, did he? You're imagining things. A combination of emotions raced inside—unexpected attraction to Mr. Morgan and pure terror of facing an unfamiliar kitchen from the servant's side of the fanning doors.

Cautiously, Lucinda tried the latch. It lifted, and the heavy door swung open on silent hinges. A rush of hot air filled with a mix of savory aromas swept over her as she stepped inside.

Chapter 4

How she wished for Mr. Morgan's comforting presence as she stepped into an unfamiliar kitchen for a job she had never done. She stared in disbelief at the sea of humanity running in all directions. To keep from getting trampled, she huddled in the corner and surveyed the kitchen. At the far end of the room and up seven stone steps were the fanning doors that separated the main house from the kitchen and service pantry. Serving maids wearing toadstool-shaped hats bustled in and out through the doors, carrying linens, trays of flatware, and condiments.

They would be bringing in empty plates and carrying out the next course if the meal had begun. Relief surged through her; she had made it in time. Very soon she would be one of those servants, indistinguishable from the others unless someone looked closely. No one probably would unless she did something inappropriate.

Lucinda had never studied formal dinner preparations in the detail she did now, but she knew these girls would keep their harried pace until long after the dinner hour. Guilt sprang up when she remembered her uncaring attitude in the past toward those who served her. Especially Pearl. *I was so ungrateful. I took her for granted. Now she's gone, and I have to fend for myself. I deserve this fate. I truly do.*

The kitchen was almost as large as the one in her English manor house, and the floor and the walls were tiled bright red. Against the outside wall stood a copper sink with water piped directly into it. The Tillotsons must truly be rich to afford such a luxury. Young servant girls stood on stools before the sink, elbow-deep in dishwater, scrubbing endless stacks of pots and pans. From the wood range, Lucinda caught the aromas of burning fruitwood and tantalizing spices. It had been many hours since she had eaten, and her mouth watered.

The kitchen was sweltering. The large cook, autocratic ruler of her domain, mopped the sweat from her face with a Turkish towel round her neck. She was in the process of hoisting a huge baron of beef from the oven onto the chopping block in the middle of the room.

She looked up from testing the roast and spotted Lucinda. She pointed at one of the maids. "You, Molly! Come." Molly came running down the stairs. "See who's hiding in the shadows by the door. If it's a dirty tramp begging food, lay this frying pan across his back." She grabbed up a heavy black skillet and thrust it into Molly's small hands.

Lucinda hadn't thought of herself as looking like a tramp, and she wasn't going to cower in the corner. She moved out of the shadows and watched Molly cross the kitchen.

At a safe distance, she stopped. "Mrs. Kidd, do I . . ."

"Get on with it, girl."

"Yes, Mrs. Kidd." Molly straightened to her full five feet and raised the pan over her head. "Get out, you ruffian! Get out afore I split yer skull." Her voice squeaked like an adolescent boy's and made a mockery of the threat.

Clutching her satchel, Lucinda pushed back her cap and began walking toward Molly, never taking her eyes from the skillet. *If I don't assert myself right now, I'll become the goat for the entire staff.* She brushed by Molly and said in a firm voice, "I am the new maid Mr. Button engaged. Please let him know I have arrived."

Not used to such boldness, the other servants stopped in their tracks and gawked at Lucinda. *Good. They shall not know how frightened I am. Let them think I'm a trusted colleague of the mighty Mr. Button.* From managing her own house, she knew that the butler was the person to watch out for. He ran the staff upstairs and was absolute dictator below.

Mrs. Kidd was first to recover her composure. "Well, goose, go fetch him," she thundered.

Still clutching the frying pan, Molly fled past Lucinda, up the stairs, and through one fanning door as Mr. Button entered the kitchen through the other. His cherubic face remained calm, but round eyes, partially obscured by bushy black brows, narrowed as he drew closer to Lucinda. "Ah, you are Mrs. Porter?" he asked in an adenoidal voice.

The effect of the imperious Mr. Button bearing down on Lucinda caused her to stand tall and tip up her chin. Then she remembered her position and lowered her eyes as became a domestic servant.

"So you have deigned to finally honor us with your presence. Early afternoon, as you promised, would have been much preferable. However, we're a bit short of help, so I won't throw you out with the chickens just yet."

They needed her, so she could afford to establish herself a bit higher in the pecking order. "Circumstances prevented an earlier arrival." She spoke firmly.

"I see," said Mr. Button. "I understand your experience is limited."

"I have had no experience in this country. In England, however, I spent two years with the earl of Northland." She stopped short of mentioning that she spent it as his wife. "I worked with the staff of a very large manor house. I am capable of serving in any area where I am required."

He cast a jaundiced eye over her from head to foot.

Lucinda knew her worn coat and cap certainly did nothing to validate her claims. "All I had in this world was destroyed in the great Chicago fire last October. I have been forced to accept the generosity of others for my needs."

He sniffed and nodded. "Are you sensible and literate as your papers state?" His left nostril twitched in time to his words.

"The papers are correct," she said, giving an autocratic lift to her words. "I am both sensible and literate. Trained by the royals of England, I remain today on the most intimate terms with Lady North."

"Yes, yes, you come highly recommended. Have you brought sufficient aprons in good repair for housework? And suitable apparel for your afternoon off, if you are found worthy to be granted one?"

"I did. However, my trunk was not put off the train."

"Late and no aprons. Not an auspicious beginning. What are you called?" he asked sharply.

"My name is Lucinda. Lucinda Porter, sir," she said over the steady chug of the water pump in the background. When she pulled off her cap, auburn curls tumbled over her shoulders. She lowered the collar away from her face and bobbed a curtsy.

His eyes widened, and his left nostril twitched violently. "Yes, well. . ." He cleared his throat. "A bit pretentious, I'd say. Lucy seems more appropriate."

Lucinda debated with herself but a moment. "Perhaps Lucy is more appropriate for a serving girl, sir, but Lucinda is my name, and I prefer it."

Mr. Button smiled. "A girl with spirit has a place. However, I hope, Lucy, you know the time and place."

He turned toward Mrs. Kidd. "Though the mistress has not yet arrived, Judge Tillotson says we are to serve dinner. And you, Lucy. . ."

Lucinda winced at the name but held herself in the best servant stance. "Yes, sir?"

"You will be assigned a post in the dining room. We shall assess the quality of your work while you serve dinner. Molly, take Lucy into the press for a fresh white apron and cap and show her how they are to be worn."

Lucinda followed Molly down a dim hallway and into the laundry press. Her back to the entrance, a lone woman stoked wood into the small, cast-iron range. Half a dozen irons of different sizes heated on the top of the stove, and a wrinkled sheet lay on the ironing board to press. Molly walked over and placed her arm around the woman's shoulder. "I've brought the new girl in for an apron and hat."

The woman straightened and gave Molly a tired smile. "You know where they're kept. Help yourself." Molly scurried away. The frail woman wiped her hands on a towel and returned to the ironing board with a fresh iron.

Lucinda studied the piles of laundry neatly arranged by color near the washtubs. *I hope I never have to work here. This has to be the hottest, hardest work in any house.* "Do you do all this work alone?" she asked.

The woman looked up. Her face paled. "Oh, my," she gasped and rushed to shut the door into the linen keep.

"Pearl?" Lucinda cried out in disbelief, and they flew into each other's arms. "Oh, Pearl, I can't believe it's you. What are you doing here? You told me you were going to live with your rich sister."

"Lucinda?" Pearl stepped back; her expression looked as though she would faint. "Is Molly getting the uniform for *you*?"

Lucinda touched Pearl's cheek. "Why are *you* here in the laundry press? Where is the rich sister who needed you to come be with her?"

"I am living in my rich sister's house. But no matter. I want to hear about you, my dearest child. Why are you here?" Pearl studied Lucinda. "You look. . ." Her eyes filled with tears. "What has happened to you?"

All that Lucinda had bottled up came out in a tumble of words. "Wednesday last, Uncle announced it was his unpleasant duty to tell me that I was no longer wealthy. In fact, I was deeply in debt. Papa had unfortunate financial reverses, so he took on many loans. When Mama and Papa were killed, all that indebtedness fell on Uncle's shoulders. He said he must repay these huge loans or the business was doomed. And there was no hope of rebuilding my home. Uncle assured me that my only option was to declare bankruptcy."

"But what happened to your settlement from Lord North's estate?" Pearl asked. "That was substantial."

"It all went to pay off loans, according to Uncle."

Pearl's brow creased. "But if it was your money that cleared the loans, shouldn't you own the land?"

"I did own it, but there's no money to pay off the other loans. Uncle handed me sheaf after sheaf of papers. After I scanned them, I signed away everything."

Pearls eyes widened. "Not your necklace." She spoke in a whisper.

Lucinda shook her head and put hand over her heart. "Uncle finally let me keep it." She glanced anxiously at the door into the linen keep, certain that Molly would be returning soon. "He said he had to sell his house and all he could scrape together to put against the debt or the business would fail. He had no money and suggested that I visit an intelligence service to find work as a domestic. So here I am."

Pearl wrapped Lucinda in her arms and crooned, "Your papa was a fine businessman, but I knew there had been financial reversals. I had no idea they were so severe. Only a few days before. . .the Fourth of July, I heard him tell your mama he had made an exceptional sale that would clear all their debt and permanently assure their financial future. Oh, my poor girl." She released Lucinda. "Hurry, tell the rest."

"I must have looked stricken, because Uncle offered me money to tide me over until I could locate work. I thanked him and told him that I would get on just fine."

Pearl caressed Lucinda's cheek. "So you went to the

intelligence office and found work with the Tillotsons. But how did you get from the train station to here?"

"Mr. David Morgan was kind enough to bring me." The mere mention of his name made her glow inside.

Pearl nodded. "A fine young man." She held Lucinda at arm's length. "Is the mistress home?"

"I don't think so. I overheard it said that we are to serve dinner without her."

"Then some quick words, my dear. Listen carefully. Stay out of sight as much as possible. Never turn your back on your betters, and never meet their eyes. Speak clearly but only as much as is necessary."

"Thank you, Pearl. I will be respectful in all ways, but I don't plan to spend the rest of my life as a domestic—"

Molly threw open the door and bustled into the press. "Land, Pearl, you had the aprons on the top shelf, and I liked never to have found one her size. Come, Lucy, take off that coat, and I'll help you with the apron. Thank goodness you have a decent dress on." Molly worked as fast as she talked, helping Lucinda don the apron and hat. "Now you look like a proper servant. Step lively, now. We're to be in the serving pantry."

Pearl glanced toward Molly. "I need a moment with Lucin. . .Lucy. She'll be right out."

Molly shrugged a shoulder and hurried down the hall.

Pearl tucked a copper curl inside Lucinda's mushroom-shaped hat. "For your own sake, keep your head down, your hair covered, and remain in the background. If the mistress arrives, stay as far from her as you decently can. Now hurry off. You'll do just fine."

Reluctantly, Lucinda left the comfort of Pearl's company.

Fighting back tears, she walked slowly down the hallway, mindful of each step that took her farther from her predictable past into an unpredictable future.

"Lucinda? We seem to have a tendency to run into each other," a deep velvet voice said.

She turned quickly, her gloom lifting. "Mr. Morgan? Whatever are you doing in the servants' wing?"

"I needed to see if you were all right. I dumped you off like a sack of potatoes and left you to fend for yourself. I've felt guilty ever since. The least I can do is apologize for not seeing you safely inside."

With a faint smile, she asked, "What exactly is your position here, Mr. Morgan?"

He laughed. "You're a courageous one, aren't you?"

"Are you avoiding my question?"

"On the contrary, I was buying time while I tried to determine what exactly my position is. First of all, please call me David. I am uncomfortable with being Mr. Morgan to you."

That wouldn't be difficult since she had been thinking of him as David all evening. "David it is. And I'm Lucinda, even though Mr. Button has christened me Lucy. He feels Lucinda is an uppity name."

David laughed again. "Yes, Button, as he is called on this side of the fanning doors, would consider that a threat to his dominion."

"Your position, David?" she reminded. She was desperate to know more about him. Even in the short time she had known him, she had become acutely aware that he was a mighty man. It showed in the way he moved, quick and powerful as the horse he rode. It showed in his eyes, bright and respectful—a rich navy blue she could see now in the light of the corridor. He seemed to know what she was thinking even when she did not speak her thoughts. It showed in his voice, deep, full, to match his speech. He was not given to needless words or courtly phrases but came to the point of things. Yes, she very much wanted to know more about this man.

"Well," he began with some hesitation, "during the past five years I've been a law clerk in Judge Tillotson's office, read for the law with him, escorted Mistress Tillotson to various social events when requested to do so, and shoveled out the stables when the need arose." He pursed his lips. "That pretty much sums up my position."

"You will be a lawyer one day?"

"I think that day may be upon me very soon."

Lucinda's heart sank. "Does that mean you'll be leaving?"

He studied her as though reading her story. "Yes, right away. But now it won't be by choice, and I shall regret having to go."

"You will?"

"I will. Very much."

Molly's worried face appeared behind David. "Lucy, please come. You're going to be in terrible trouble if Mr. Button comes back and you're not in the serving pantry."

David took her hand. "I know this is unacceptably sudden, but I can't bear to think of leaving you just when I've found you. Perhaps later this evening when you have finished your duties. . ." He paused and looked deep into her eyes. "Could we talk? I feel I must know more about you."

"Lucy! Come!" Molly was running toward them.

"Yes, David. You will find me?"

"I will find you."

Molly grabbed Lucinda's arm and guided her away. She looked back before she was propelled through the fanning doors. David stood in the middle of the hall, his eyes focused on her.

Chapter 5

D avid arrived outside the drawing room as Button was ushering the men from the library into the Tillotsons' elegantly appointed drawing room. The ladies, resplendent in low-cut evening dresses, greeted them. David slipped inside and mingled with the assemblage. The men brought with them the fragrance of bay rum and the pungent scent of smoke from the thick cigars and cheroots that most in the library had smoked. Mixed with the women's heady perfumes from Paris, the aroma was unusual but pleasant.

Then, as was his habit, David retreated to an inconspicuous corner to observe. Though the women wore different colors and fabrics, all wore long skirts drawn back, bunched into an elaborate arrangement at the hip and, over a supporting bustle, draped into a train that swept the floor. No doubt the latest Paris fashion. He imagined Lucinda in such a gown.

He jerked himself up short. He must keep his wits about him if he was to get the judge's signature tonight. He forced himself to stay in the present by studying the gentlemen's attire. They wore flowery waistcoats, impeccably tailored. Most were embellished with watch chains from which jeweled charms dangled. Precious stones anchored wide, colorful cravats. Black or dark blue swallowtail tuxedo jackets, the rage this winter, hung over fawn-colored pantaloons. He couldn't help but notice that in most cases they stretched across ample stomachs.

David ran his hands over his own black frock coat. Thanks to Rosella's excellent tailor, it fit perfectly. He imagined Lucinda next to him, promenading gracefully across the room. A waltz played in his head, and he could feel her in his arms as they pirouetted around the floor. He became so lost in his fantasy he almost missed Judge Tillotson motioning him to join a small group of community leaders.

The judge was short and ruddy of complexion. He had one badly squinting eye, which he habitually kept closed, and his head was oversized for his body. His thick white hair was his best feature. Tonight its sheen glowed in the lamplight like a halo. On the judge, however, the halo effect missed being regal because he had been forced since birth to hold his head stiffly inclined toward his left shoulder. His detractors said his head was askew like a cow with horn-ail. David, on the other hand, thought that Judge Tillotson had a fine presence, giving the impression of a successful and happy man. That is, until one caught him off guard and looked deep into his eyes. Behind the judge's pleasant, summer blue eyes lurked a chained darkness writhing to break free. David had only looked there once.

He came to stand with the group. "Good evening, Judge Tillotson," he said and nodded to the other gentlemen.

"Glad you could join us, my lad. I want the boys to meet a first-rate new lawyer. You'll be hearing of this young man, gentlemen."

David could feel heat rise above his cravat to his cheeks. He clasped his hands behind his back and squared his stance, ready to listen to the judge's current monologue.

Instead, the judge said, "Please excuse us, gentlemen. Business never takes a holiday." He put his strong hand around David's back and guided him to the side of the room. "David, I must admit, I've never worked with a lad that I've enjoyed as much as you." He took a long swallow from his glass of sherry. The judge usually drank nothing stronger than watered wine. Was this his attempt to ease the pain of this day?

The judge continued. "You know that I've come to care about you. Your quick wit and diligence have touched a chord in me. You're a young man with a future."

David flushed again, realizing that praise was harder to handle gracefully than criticism. "Thank you, sir."

"I'm sad to think you'll be moving on soon."

His words caught David off guard. He started to protest, but the judge held up his hand. "Nothing to be ashamed of, son. Be ashamed if you didn't want to strike out for yourself. Besides, you're ready. Where is it you're thinking of going?"

"Well, sir, I do have an article about the possibilities." He pulled a newspaper clipping from his tuxedo pocket, but before he could unfold it, the dinner gong sounded. The judge glanced around the room and then gave David a pat on the back. "I don't believe Mistress Tillotson has arrived yet, but we will be dining without her. Excuse me, David, perhaps we can talk later. Right now I must claim my dinner partner."

"Of course." David mumbled something about finding his own partner. Without Mistress Tillotson, the table would be short one lady. This was not the first time he had waited at the back of the line, ready to escort a neighbor hastily invited.

The double doors to the dining room swung open. Under the scrutiny of the well-organized Mr. Button, the judge and his lady led the guests in to dinner. The table, set for twenty, created a forest of French crystal and English bone china. Holly and evergreen cascaded down from a regiment of tall silver cones spaced along the center. Kerosene lamps on the sideboard, along with rows of candles down the center of the table, gave off a romantic glow. A pair of footmen hired for the occasion stood at attention at the head and foot of the table.

David's dinner partner had a difficult name he never seemed able to recall, a great many large teeth, not to mention arthritic fingers that occasionally gripped his arm or twisted a long rope of pearls. David braced himself for an evening of her nonstop conversation. She immediately launched into the intimate details of how she came to be unmarried.

The woman seated on the other side of David managed to engage him in conversation. But each time David's dinner companion sensed the slightest break, she skillfully turned his attention back to her story, beginning precisely where she had been interrupted. She did not require answers, making it possible for him to contemplate Lucinda. She had the most unusual eyes and a square chin with a delicate cleft. She was captivating yet with a disturbing resemblance to Rosella Tillotson as she must have looked in her early years. That connection gave rise to all manner of speculation.

Thinking about Lucinda was not wise. She so completely took over his concentration that David lost track of the table conversation. He must keep an eye on the judge and anticipate when he would be approachable to sign the referral letter.

To occupy his thoughts, David tried to plan the best route across the prairie in the morning. He tried to think what to take with him. He tried to envision all the things he had to do. He tried, and all he saw was Lucinda's face, Lucinda's smile, and the sadness in her eyes. He could easily drown in the emerald depths of those eyes. He longed to let his fingers trace her delicate forehead and high curving cheekbones, the straight nose, and her full mouth. His hands flexed with the urge to feel her chin with its intriguing cleft and the smooth line of her throat. *Is she the woman for me?* He thought about the circumstances of their meeting. *Is there a divine plan behind this day?*

He scolded himself. This was not the time to be thinking such things.

Just at that moment, across the room from David, a door opened noiselessly. Half-hidden by a carved wooden screen, a maid emerged wearing one of those absurd English caps. She delivered a large silver tray into Button's hands. He in turn passed the tray to the footman to begin serving.

David forgot all else when he recognized the maid. It was only a glimpse before Lucinda vanished behind the screen, but he knew well that intense, pale face with a copper-bright lock of hair escaping from the cap. His heart leaped, and he remembered the feel of her small, soft hand in his. *She speaks like a lady; her hands are soft and manicured. What is she doing*

130

here? Why is she a serving maid? Questions reeled in his head.

"Excuse me, sir."

Dazed, David blinked up at the footman who served the fruit compote, then discreetly slipped a piece of paper into his hand and moved on.

David excused himself politely and left the table. Once in the hall, he read the note. *Meet me at the servant's entrance immediately.* No signature. He burned with curiosity as he hurried along the hallway. How very odd. Was it Rosella? No, she would never step foot near the servant's door. Lucinda, perhaps? David reached the back hallway. In the dim light he could see a figure in the shadows.

A frail little woman stepped forward to greet him. "Thank you for coming. I apologize, but this is a desperate situation. I have no one else to turn to, and they say you are a just man." The woman bowed her head. "My name is Pearl. Lucinda told me that you brought her from town this afternoon. I am Rosella's sister."

"Rosella's sister? I can assure you, madam, all between us has been most proper in every respect."

"I am in no way suggesting otherwise, Mr. Morgan."

"Then may I inquire how it is that you know Lucinda?"

"All I can say at this moment is that I am Lucinda's friend. I apologize for taking you from dinner, but time is of the essence. You are a stranger to me and Lucinda, but I understand you are well thought of by the judge and my sister. Lucinda is in danger, and I am helpless to do anything."

David came to full attention. "Danger? How? She arrived not two hours ago."

"The story is long and tragic. I shall try to give you only the briefest details. Please understand, sir, that Lucinda knows nothing of what I am about to tell you. For years, I thought it best she never know. Now my deceit could cost Lucinda her life."

She took a breath and hurried on. "Rosella and Marshall had a daughter, a beautiful child named Meghan that Marshall was so taken with he failed to give Rosella the attention she demanded."

The frail woman looked stricken. "Twenty years ago today, at Rosella's insistence, I secretly spirited that child away to New York to a wealthy family who was desperate for a child. The couple paid a huge sum of money for her. They made Rosella a rich woman, so rich she didn't mind not knowing any details of the transaction. I became nanny to that child, Meghan. The couple renamed her Lucinda. As she grew, she looked more and more like Rosella. Certainly you have noticed the strong resemblance. Twelve years ago, the family moved to Chicago, and for Lucinda's safety, I told them the truth. It frightened them, so they took Lucinda to England. She married the earl of Northland, and just over a year ago, he died. Lucinda and her parents returned to Chicago."

Pearl paused and wiped the tears streaming over her cheeks. She hastily summed up the story of the fire and Lucinda's financial situation. "Left with nothing, Lucinda chose to make a new beginning. Do you understand the danger of her being here? If my sister recognizes her. . ." She looked up, pure terror reflected in her eyes.

David stared. He most certainly understood the peril. If Rosella so willingly sold her child, then how far would she go to keep her secret? "What do you want from me?"

"I have no plan, sir. But Rosella is no fool. Even disguised in that horrid uniform, Lucinda's identity will be obvious.

Rosella loves Marshall, but she is beauty to his beast. She will not allow anyone or anything to come before her. Lucinda inherited her mother's great beauty, and Rosella will make certain Marshall does not see his daughter. Ever."

Icy fingers of dread squeezed David's heart. The torment hiding in the judge's eyes finally made sense. So did the melodrama Rosella had staged on this date every year since he had known her. David's first inclination was to dash into the serving pantry, grab up Lucinda, and flee far and fast.

He spoke in an urgent whisper. "A new storm has begun. I can't take her away tonight without someplace to go. So how do we keep her hidden until morning?" David chastised himself. Ordinarily he could solve any predicament with a logical plan. But he had never faced a problem of this magnitude. His thoughts tumbled over each other and refused to be ordered.

Pearl's look told him she had no answers. "You must get back, now." She touched his arm before she scurried along the hall and disappeared through the fanning doors.

David started back to the dining room, his mind churning. What if the judge wasn't as drunk as he pretended? David was a successful lawyer because he seemed to have a sixth sense. Maybe he felt the unrest in the house. He had been uneasy all evening but had chosen to ignore it. Now he had to get Lucinda hidden. But where? How?

Entering the dining room through the serving door, he returned to his seat. At the end of the table, the judge was deep in conversation; he didn't look up, but David had the distinct feeling he had been missed. His dinner partner immediately turned to him and launched into a new story as though he'd never left. David glanced toward the drawing room. *Please, Rosella, don't come through those doors.*

Lucinda spotted David halfway along the table, sitting with a coquettish older woman who never seemed to stop talking even while eating. The princeliest man at the table, David had on a beautifully tailored tuxedo that showed his broad shoulders to their best advantage. Though Lucinda tried subtly to attract his attention, he seemed unaware of her efforts. His faraway look told her that his thoughts were elsewhere. Reluctant to leave, she picked up a tureen and backed through the door to the hall, only to bump into Molly. "Lucy, you best get a run on. Cook's screaming for your scalp." She rolled her eyes.

Lucinda rushed toward the kitchen, the aromas of food filling the hall. Unexpectedly, hunger overwhelmed her. Her knees started to buckle; she caught her balance against the wall inside the fanning doors. In a lightheaded moment, she saw herself seated as David's dinner partner. Felt his eyes warm and loving as he lifted a spoon of soup to her lips. Their gazes linked and the warm soup trickled onto her tongue. . .

"You, be quick with this platter of lamb!" Mrs. Kidd screeched, shattering Lucinda's dream. She deposited the tureen on the mountain of dirty dishes and, under Mrs. Kidd's eagle eye, raced to lift the enormous silver platter. Concentrating, Lucinda picked up the platter without sending the slightest shimmer through the delicate rope of mint jelly decorating its edges. She caught the cook's slight smile of approval.

"Now hurry along," Mrs. Kidd added in a much kinder

voice, but Lucinda had already cleared the top of the stairs, rushing as fast as her burden allowed toward the dining room. There, David waited to be served. And after dinner they would meet. Quivers of anticipation lightened her spirits.

Chapter 6

Mr. Button took the tray from Lucinda. "That will be all in the dining room tonight, Lucy. Molly will show you the way to the card room. Polish the furniture one last time. Then see that the tables are prepared for playing whist." He looked hard at her. "You know about whist?"

Lucinda curtsied. "Yes, Mr. Button," she said and groaned silently. She hadn't eaten since this morning, but there was no mention of food. She remembered those who had served her so faithfully and lamented that she had been raised to think of servants as having few needs. When she was again in a position to be served, she vowed to be a different mistress.

While she polished the Chippendale tea table until it gleamed in the candlelight, she thought of David. How, when, where would they meet? She placed whist cards and score sheets on each of the five gaming tables and arranged the chairs into more suitable conversation groupings. She surveyed her handiwork and, satisfied that all was in readiness, pulled the bell cord that signaled Mrs. Kidd in the kitchen. Soon Molly arrived with a Sheffield tray of teacups and a heavy silver teapot. She dashed back to the kitchen, leaving Lucinda to set out the tea service. That done, she scanned the room once more. Numerous candelabra and wall sconces cast a warm glow over the brocades and velvets, all in shades of golden peach. The fire in the large marble fireplace burned in silent and smokeless perfection. The slight fragrance of oriental incense added a hint of mystery. Everything was as ready as she knew how to make it.

In the Florentine mirror, Lucinda reviewed her appearance and looked carefully at her apron to be sure it was still clean. At least she had been allowed to wear her blue wool dress instead of a gray, shapeless maid's frock. She tucked the stubborn lock of copper hair under the giant mushroom cap and made sure her hidden necklace didn't show. Satisfied she was presentable, she turned from the mirror. Were those lights in the lane? Mistress Tillotson's coach perhaps?

Hurrying to the window, she pulled aside heavy lace curtains and stared into the dark. *Oh my, that coach is having a sorry time in this snow and wind.* The coach and four, battered by the storm, drew up before the house. Down from the driver's box vaulted a dark figure carrying a ship's lantern to light the way. He leaned into the wind and struggled to reach the broad front steps of the baronial house.

Disregarding the driving snow, a woman called from the coach window. "Button! Where are you? Is there no one to answer the door?" Her voice shrilled above the wind.

The staff was busy serving dessert, so Lucinda went to answer the summons. She had survived dinner without being thrown out with the chickens. Could she now please a mistress who came late and screamed for assistance? She set her face in a smile and, with quick, efficient steps, hurried down the stairway to the front door. All the while the mistress was caterwauling at the top of her lungs.

Lucinda held the oversized door open enough to see the footman leap from the box. He opened and steadied the coach door against the wind. A second footman lifted Rosella Tillotson from inside the coach. Carrying her, he staggered against the driving snow and deposited her at the top of the steps.

Judge Tillotson came hurrying down the hall and pulled the door wide open. The wind swept inside, blowing out the lamps and casting everything in darkness. Stepping into the doorway, the man with the lantern held it high to furnish light. The judge braved the storm and stepped outside to meet his wife. The wind flapped the tails of his long black coat and rearranged his cravat and hair. Mistress Tillotson, standing erect and as tall as her husband, presented her cheek for his kiss. His lips brushed the general vicinity as he reached to take her arm. She pushed him away.

His expression remained pleasant, but Lucinda noticed a muscle working along his jaw. He ushered Rosella into the foyer, but it was so shadowed Lucinda could see little of the large woman except for a square chin under the bill of the bonnet.

David came striding along the dark hallway with Mr. Button and Molly at his heels. Immediately, the butler ordered the candles in the wall sconces relit. He looked straight at Lucinda.

David stepped beside her. "I'll show her where the safety matches are, Mr. Button." With the briefest of nods at David, Button turned his full attention to the Tillotsons.

Taking Lucinda's arm, David set a breathtaking pace down the hallway and into the dimly lit drawing room. He sat her in a large wing-backed chair facing the fireplace. "Stay here while I take the matches to Button." And he was gone.

Lucinda stared in the fire. What in the world made David whisk her away like that? If he didn't have a good reason, they were going to have words. Just because she was a servant girl didn't mean she would allow such treatment. She had been assigned to the game room, and she was going to be on duty there whether David liked it or not. Dinner would soon be over, and the guests would be adjourning to the game room. What would Mistress Tillotson do when no one was there to serve? As Mr. Button threatened, Lucinda would be out with the chickens for sure. She was ready to leave when the door opened and closed.

"Lucinda?" David whispered.

She leaned around the chair so he could see her. "I'm here, but now that you're here, I must leave."

"I've brought Pearl to see you."

"Pearl?" Lucinda started to stand.

"Please, sit down." David's words were gentle as he pulled up a chair for Pearl and knelt beside Lucinda. "Pearl has something she needs to tell you. It will help you understand many things."

"What is going on? David, I won't be ordered around like this."

Pearl took Lucinda's hand and gave her a weak smile. "I'm so sorry. I should have told you years ago, but I never imagined anything like this would, could ever happen."

Chills ran up Lucinda's spine. "I don't think I want to hear this."

Pearl looked deep into Lucinda's eyes. "And I don't want to tell you, but you must know." When Pearl finished her story, Lucinda sat silent. "I hope you can forgive me." She hung her head and stepped back beside the fireplace.

Lucinda felt as if she had been pitched off a cliff and sent spinning toward huge rocks at the bottom. She gasped, but her lungs refused to fill. David rubbed her back. "Breathe in," he said softly. "That's right, another breath." She heard his voice as from a distance until her breathing stabilized and she could speak. "This is going to take time to sort out, Pearl. But I love you and hold nothing against you."

Pearl kissed Lucinda and held her for a moment. "I must get back to the laundry. David is a good lad. He'll see to your safety."

The door clicked shut, and David moved to the chair Pearl vacated. "The problem is keeping you safe through the night until we can put together a plan for getting you away from here."

"No matter if Rosella does recognize me, she'll be as shocked as I am. I'll be safe for a while yet." She slumped back in the chair. "Could I rest just a minute before I go upstairs?" Her eyes drooped from weariness.

He nodded, and her lids closed.

When voices filtered into the room from the hall, Lucinda woke. She felt brittle, as though if she were touched she would shatter into myriad slivers of glass. She felt the urge to scream and to go on screaming until she broke. Instead, she stood, her hands balled into fists at her side, and willed herself to complete the task at hand. "They are on the way to the game room. I must go."

"Come with me," David said. "I'll show you a way to the

140

card room that will keep anyone from noticing your arrival."

Holding her hand, he led the way to a large mirror on the fireplace wall. He touched the heavy gold frame, and the mirror swung open. Lucinda gasped. "What, how. . . ?" she stammered.

"This house was used to hide runaway slaves during the War between the States. This is the hidden stairway they used." He helped her through the opening, closed the mirror, lit a small lamp, and led her up stairs that eventually came out at a panel in the library next to the card room.

"You go in. Busy yourself like you've been there all the time. I'll go back down and come up the main stairs."

When Lucinda arrived in the card room, Mistress Tillotson was waiting across the room at the top of the main stairway. She had changed clothes and wore a peignoir of white satin, flounced at the throat and covered with heavy lace at the waist. A double rope of pearls and diamonds lay across her ample bosom. Her amber hair was locked in a careless chignon held in place by a white net. *So, that is my mother.*

Thankfully, the mistress couldn't see her. Lucinda picked up a tray of champagne, and, staying as far from the woman as possible, began passing it to the guests. Mixing among them, she felt safe until she felt a tap on her shoulder. Keeping her head down, Lucinda turned. Rosella tipped her face up. The attempt to stifle her gasp failed. She continued to stare with a look of unclothed astonishment little different from those registered by David Morgan and Mr. Button. *She recognizes me!*

Lucinda kept her face frozen. "Champagne, mistress?" Her voice sounded normal, the English accent firmly in place.

Rosella, on the other hand, turned deathly pale, and her

chest heaved for breath. "What is your name?" she gasped through trembling lips.

"Lucinda, ma'am." She carefully balanced the tray and curtsied. Over Rosella's shoulder, she saw David's eyes widen. He turned as pale as Lucinda felt.

Rosella's eyes narrowed. "Come," she said in a shrill voice and led the way to a card table. Her hand trembled as she picked up the deck of cards. "Now, my dears," she said to the three men present, "if you don't mind playing with my personal maid and secretary, we can begin."

Lucinda gasped. "Mistress, I–I. . . ," she stammered.

"You do play whist, do you not?" Her tone was sarcastic.

"I have played some," she said quietly.

"I do not wish to play this evening," Rosella announced. "You will be the fourth at my table."

The looks on the men's faces told what they thought of the idea. "Really, Rosella, this is too much," one of the men objected. "We came to play with you." The others at the table echoed his sentiments.

Mistress Tillotson ran an unsteady hand over her brow. "Very well, gentlemen, but don't expect much of me. It has been a long and most trying day." She looked squarely at Lucinda before she sat down and began shuffling the cards. "Lucinda, put that tray down."

"Yes, ma'am." Lucinda curtsied and handed off the tray.

"Make yourself useful in the library." Rosella began dealing the cards expertly, watching Lucinda all the while. "There are newspapers there. Find some bits of scandal to amuse me tonight when you prepare me for bed. See if you can find a novel, a love story, something set in India." She had regained her color and her voice, but her smile was brittle, her eyes hard. "And David, you are a poor player. Sit at my elbow and learn."

He sent Lucinda a look of resignation and seated himself beside Rosella.

Lucinda managed to stuff the feelings aroused by knowing that Rosella was her mother, but her movements were too sharp, too quick. She smiled at the right times and answered politely, but she was off-key, like an out-of-tune piano. She could tell David was worried. His eyes were overly bright and, to the detriment of his attention to the card game, he often gazed after her. That made her task more difficult because she wanted to look at him, but she forced herself to concentrate on the black print. In the *Peoria Review* and *Chicago Democrat* she found items she thought might interest Rosella. She finished her task, but the card party showed no sign of ending. After building up the fire in the card room's fireplace, Lucinda again moved to the library and examined the shelves for a novel to fit Rosella's description. Attracted by the title *The Ganges by Moonlight,* she drew a volume from its place. As she did so, a leather pouch hidden behind the books slid out, scattering its contents.

Lucinda stood stock still, staring at the floor. "What is this?" Her heart leaped at the sight.

A handful of cut, unset jewels—emeralds, sapphires, two large rubies, and diamonds of various shapes and sizes—splattered over the Persian carpet. She stooped and was gathering them up when Rosella Tillotson came into the room with David at her heels, his face creased with concern. Rosella's eyes instantly focused on the sparkling stones in Lucinda's hand.

The briefest of smiles brushed Rosella's lips, then the

expression vanished and her face became unreadable as she walked with firm steps across the room to where Lucinda stood, her trembling hands cupped around the jewels.

"How fortunate that you found my little gems. I had quite given them up for lost." Rosella's hands closed like icy claws over Lucinda's and grasped the stones. Her red mouth smiled, but her eyes were dark and hard.

Chapter 7

I t was well past midnight before the guests were bedded and Lucinda was able to light her own candle to carry up to her attic room. The flame flickered in the sudden drafts and sent writhing shadows over the unfamiliar stair walls. She closed the door at the foot of the attic stairs and slid the little lock into place. Her room under the eaves was directly above Rosella's dressing room.

Though there was a bell to call for service, Rosella insisted on this arrangement because she preferred to rouse her maid during the small hours of the night by throwing a shoe at the ceiling, Lucinda had been told. She was ordered to listen for the thud beneath her bed and consider her position at the mansion to be dependent on her instant response to such a summons.

From kitchen maid to personal servant to the mistress— her mother. So much had happened this day.

Lucinda stumbled with weariness on the last step and pitched the candle forward onto the splintered floor. It guttered out. The storm had passed for now. Through a single dormer window set in the slanted roof over her bed, moonlight flooded into the tiny cubicle and fanned across the tied patchwork quilt. Kneeling on the bed made from a knotty plank, she let the moon bathe her in white light. Warmth from an unseen source seemed to envelop her, bringing with it a longing for the way things were before catastrophe became an almost constant companion.

Thoughts of Rosella tried to rise, but Lucinda forced them away. She was far too weary to examine the latest blow to her life. *I never dreamed I would be grateful for such poor lodgings, but tonight I am. I am gifted with my own room.* The other maids slept in a long room under the eaves of another wing of the house. There were two rows of beds and no privacy.

Lucinda sat on the bed and caressed the platinum heirloom fastened around her neck. This was her only physical tie to her past. The memories it kindled would help her through the rough places. Surrendering to a consuming weariness, she scarcely managed to hang her apron and hat neatly on the peg beside her coat and cap. She brushed out her hair but chose to sleep in her dress in case she was summoned in the night.

Just when exhaustion should have sent her slipping under the quilt, she became caught up by a strange sensation she could neither capture nor dismiss. In that moonlit moment, Lucinda knew that she would not be a servant all her days. One day she would again have her own mansion filled with servants. And she would be waited on as she had served others tonight. *Is this the vision Yarrow Woman had of me?*

She eased her aching body under the quilt and onto a harsh covering over a thin horse blanket used for a mattress.

The narrow bed might have been as soft as eiderdown for all she noticed. Staring up into the night through the window, her mind drifted away to mingle with the stars that shone like the jewels she had held in her hands. One day she would again have piles of beautiful gemstones. She thought about how Mistress Rosella, her mouth twisted, her eyes hard, had snatched the jewels and clutched them to her bosom. Lucinda would not clutch her jewels. She would have so many she could be, would be, generous.

Her thoughts turned to David Morgan sitting beside Rosella in the card room. *He was looking at me, only me.*

Lucinda's mind slipped further into the stars and saw that David stood alone on the veranda of a silver mansion glittering in the noon sun. She advanced toward him, bearing a heavy ornate tray. On it, instead of drinks, was a lumpy sack of silver and a neat stack of papers, stark white with black writing and large official seals. He helped himself to a stack and motioned to her to do the same. She set the tray down and took a few papers. He shook his head and handed her the whole stack. She fanned the sheets. They turned to silver coins falling like snow on the floor until she stood in a knee-deep drift. For no apparent reason, she woke up.

Her heart altered its pace and pounded a different rhythm in her ears. Her eyelids would not stay closed, fluttering instead like insistent moths. Nothing in the house below suggested an intruder, yet she believed someone to be about. She thought of the door at the bottom of her stairs. The simple lock would keep no determined soul out, but it would sound its own rattling alarm were someone to set hand to it.

Lucinda tensed and listened and knew with an unexplainable certainty that somewhere in the bowels of the sleeping house someone was awake and abroad. She slid from beneath the quilt and rose to her knees, searching for the latch on the slanted window over her head. Her fingers found and flipped open the latch. She broke the seal on the frame and tried to avoid the shower of dislodged grit and dead flies. Standing on her bed, she thrust back the window and straightened into the opening.

The air, tinged with the smell of evergreens, hung unmoving. Chimney pots belching occasional wisps of smoke stood over the house in rigid ranks like guards. Yes, she could climb out onto the roof and escape if it became necessary.

Relieved, she slid back through the window. Her feet, freezing now, found the bed below. She pulled the window closed and twisted the latch shut. Brushing off the debris and curling into the quilt, she shivered, not so much from cold as from the disturbing feeling that would not leave. At last, exhaustion overtook her and she slept.

For the second time that night, Lucinda sat bolt upright. A thud beneath her bed had wakened her. She struggled to remember where she was and finally realized Rosella had summoned her. Still caught in the web of a dream she could not remember, she moved as if in a trance across the cold, splintery floorboards toward the stairs. In the blackness of the stairway, her bare feet found their footing.

Loosed from its efficient knot, her curly hair tumbled over her shoulders and down her back. At the foot of the stairs, she twisted the lock, tripped the cold latch, and pushed open the door. Her bare feet sank into the oriental carpet runner along the hall leading to Mistress Tillotson's bedroom suite. Her hair blew across her face as air currents from the hallways below rose past her and into the attic.

A beam of moonlight struck the face of a floor clock. The time stood at three.

Lucinda turned the corner and entered an unlit hallway. She moved slowly along the corridor until she felt the doorframe and realized that she faced Mistress Tillotson's sitting room door. Her heart pounded in her throat, and her mouth dried with fear. She reached for the knob.

Someone came unheard from behind, and a hand gripped her shoulder. Lucinda's mouth opened to scream, but only a pitiful whimper escaped. *I shall be murdered,* she thought with terrifying clarity as the soft hand with fingers like steel bands tightened on her shoulder near her throat.

The black hallway seemed rent by screams, but when the man spun her around, she realized the sounds were all in her head. The dam in her throat prevented any communication. His hand easily held both of hers in a vise behind her back, and he pulled her to him, half-smothering her against his chest.

The sleeve against her throat was silky, and he smelled of sweet pipe tobacco. His cheek rested against her temple. "Oh, my beautiful one," he whispered. "Please don't fight me. I only want to hold you. I would never hurt you. Never. I will protect you. Care for you. Love you." A hand closed behind her neck, beneath her flowing hair. "Such magnificent hair, such perfect features." He caressed the flowing strands. "Do not be afraid. No one will hurt you. I promise."

Who was this man? Lucinda could not force her eyes open to look, shut tight in terror as they were. *None of this is happening.* Her exhausted mind and body refused to function further. She sank into a stupor, too stunned for thought or prayer, too frightened to call for help.

Then, as suddenly as he came, he vanished without a sound.

Tears flooded her cheeks. Lucinda's shaking hand gripped the chair molding along the hallway, and soundlessly she started back along the corridor. Before she turned the corner, she looked back. In the deep shadows, she watched a short man open the door to Rosella's bedroom. He stood for several seconds silhouetted in the glow cast by fire from the hearth of the bedroom fireplace. Then, as though having been invited, he stepped across the threshold into Rosella Tillotson's bedroom and carefully shut the door.

Lucinda fled up the narrow stairs to her attic and curled into her bed. With cold, trembling fingers she sought the comfort of her necklace.

It was gone.

A sob escaped, and a stupefying emptiness swept over her. Yarrow Woman's words drummed in her head, "*Never* take it off or let anyone else take it from you." Yet Lucinda could not bring herself to go back down those stairs. Even though her mistress summoned her, she could not go. A deep moaning sob escaped, shook her body. She knotted her fist at her throat and cried over her loss until she fell into a deep sleep.

Chapter 8

Lucinda woke with a startled cry, roused violently from more violent dreams. Strong hands muffled her mouth as someone ripped the quilt from her trembling body. She struggled against her assailant and fought for breath.

"Hush, Lucinda!" a strong, deep voice pleaded urgently. "It's David Morgan come to save you. Stay still!" The hovering form removed his hand from her mouth.

Shouts and the clatter of the bolted door at the foot of the stairs rent the night.

"What are you doing here?" she gasped. "What do I need to be saved from?" It was then that the scene in the hallway spun up through her exhaustion-fogged brain. Was that awful person trying to get at her again? How would David know?

The sound of wood splintering meant the door was giving way under the assault. He shoved her feet into the brogans. "Hurry! Up through the window. Those shoes are bound to be slick. Watch your footing on the roof."

His voice was rough as he helped her into her coat and hat and hoisted her through the opening. Far below, the yard was still darkly quiet, but footfalls pounded on the stairs behind them. David crept out onto the roof and stood beside her. Lucinda burrowed into his sheltering arms and pressed her face hard into his chest as though he could make the terror go away.

"Stay low," he said softly. Hugging the shadows, he steered her along the roof. Her shoes slipped on the cold tiles, but David held her tight and kept her moving.

"Watch your step on the ladder," he whispered. "I'll go first and guide your feet onto the rungs." He pried her hand from his, and the parting wrenched her heart. With the greatest care, he placed each foot on the rung, but still she never felt more gratitude than when she stepped onto the ground. He pulled her into the deep shadows of shrubs next to the house. "Wait here."

Taking down the ladder, he laid it against the foundation and came back to her.

Lucinda fought tears. "David, can't you tell me what's going on? Who are those men? Why are they chasing us?"

He motioned her to silence and rushed them through the shadows along the side of the house.

A horse whinnied.

He pulled her to her knees and knelt before her, shielding her body from any eyes. "Catch your breath. I know you didn't do anything, but we have to keep you from that pack of ruffians the judge has set on you. Do you understand that?"

"No, I don't understand any of this, but I trust you." She set her lips in a line and swiped two large tears tracking down her cheeks. David stood, wrapped her in his great arms, and pulled her to her feet. "The entrance to the secret stairs is inside the yew hedge." He glanced right, left, and behind like a cornered fox. "All right, run!"

They fled across the lane and inside the thick hedge. He took a branch and swept away their footprints, then lifted the trap door. Once inside the tunnel, he struck a safety match and lit the small oil lamp. "This is used often by servants returning late." He grinned. Making sure the trapdoor was secured, he led the way through the tunnel and up the hidden stairway inside the house.

It seemed an eternity before she was once again sitting in the drawing room, now dark except for what was left of the fire's faint embers casting a glow on the area directly before the hearth. David spread a lap rug over her. "I'm hoping this is the last place anyone would think to look for you. I need to get my letter and money."

"Please, David, I don't understand any of this."

"I'll be right back and will tell you everything."

Lucinda heard the door latch click shut, and her heart sank. Too tired and frightened to think, she stared into the embers of the hearth for what seemed hours until once more the door opened and someone—no, more than one— came into the room. She held her breath. Footsteps came toward the fireplace. *Dear Father in heaven, help me, help me,* she prayed over and over.

"It's David," he whispered. "And Pearl." He set his leather case beside the fireplace.

"Did you say 'Pearl'?"

Pearl came into view and set two small bags beside David's. She bustled over to Lucinda. "You need looking after, and I don't want to spend the rest of my days in the laundry press. I'm coming with you." She stood bundled inside her coat.

Lucinda looked at the bags. "Where are we going? Please tell me what's happening. I can't imagine why I'm being pursued."

David knelt beside her. "Earlier this evening Mistress Tillotson was found assaulted in her dressing room. The gemstones she took from you are missing. The judge said she was clutching a shoe in one hand and your antique necklace in the other. Thus, my dear Lucinda, it is you they are seeking."

Lucinda's hand flew to her throat. Panic rushed over her. "I had it on," she cried. Her heart raced, and she felt sick. "How did the judge get it?" Then, she remembered the man who accosted her in the hallway. She told David the story.

"Your account of the man who waylaid you describes the judge. He must have taken the necklace from you and later placed it in Rosella's hand. I wondered how he even knew about it." David reached in his pocket and laid her necklace, the emeralds gleaming, on her lap.

Lucinda caressed the jewels. "David, how did you get this?"

"It was on my bed wrapped in a silk handkerchief like the ones the judge carries."

"I don't understand."

"I think he figured out that Rosella arranged for you to be kidnapped twenty years ago. He confronted her with his suspicions. Whatever she said or did made him so angry that he grabbed the poker and hit her, though he didn't kill her. Afraid for you, he planted the necklace he took, knowing that would force you to flee. She is still unconscious, but Pearl overheard Rosella tell the judge she'd take care of you herself this time and know the job was done right. Since he saw us talking together earlier in the salon, I suspect he counted on

Pearl and me helping you to get away. It's snowing hard, and our tracks will soon be covered." He checked his watch. "Things are finally getting quiet, but dawn will soon be here. We don't have much time."

Lucinda's thoughts were spiraling. "Where are we going?"

"To Yarrow Woman."

"Why to her?"

"Her name is Mary Margaret Mason," David explained. "She was captured by the Indians when she was fifteen. The Masons moved heaven and earth and spent a fortune to get her back. She fought returning to her old world, having become more Indian than white. Now she lives on the edge of the Mason property. She dresses as an Indian, talks their language, and has little to do with anyone but the prairie settlers. Hers is the perfect place to hide until we can figure out what to do." David looked outside. "I'll get the sleigh and Kambur. You and Pearl wait at the tunnel exit. I'll come back for you shortly."

And he was gone.

Chapter 9

From Illinois to Kansas the prairie stretched miles without number, a gray wasteland filled with empty silence and boundless cold. A hard wind from the northwest pushed across the flatland, but in this deep fold of earth, it was calm. David pulled the sleigh to a halt in front of Yarrow Woman's cabin. He had heard many stories of this strange woman, but he tried not to believe them.

The slab door creaked open, and David hoped they weren't going to be looking down the barrel of a shotgun. Showing no signs of surprise, Yarrow Woman motioned them in. "Hurry, all of you."

David didn't need a second invitation. He helped the two women out of the sleigh, and they entered the dusky interior, a small room that served as Yarrow Woman's kitchen, parlor, and dispensary. Shelves lining the walls were filled with bottles and vials. A blend of aromas wafted from bunches of dried herbs hung from the rafters. In the kitchen area a small cooking stove occupied the corner next to the copper sink, which had an indoor water pump. Kerosene lamps on the windowsills and the round oak table gave off a yellow glow. Yarrow Woman sat Pearl and David at the table and Lucinda in a willow rocker near the fireplace. Two gray cats on the hearthstones stirred and coolly examined Lucinda with their green eyes.

Yarrow Woman also studied Lucinda. "You arrived at the Tillotsons' in time."

Lucinda managed a wan smile. "I did, and as you predicted, I served a very short time."

David wondered how much Yarrow Woman had already guessed but told her the whole story, anyway.

"I've been waiting for you." She smiled. "The hens are laying well. I will whip us up an omelet." Without waiting for a response, she busied herself at the kitchen counter.

"We apologize for placing you in such danger, but we had nowhere else to turn," David explained.

She brought them steaming mugs of coffee. "I have been thinking of what we can do. I have spent far too many years baking scones and listening to the troubles of settlers. My bones tell me it is time to go home." The room grew silent. "Come, Lucinda, you must eat. I doubt they fed you at the Tillotsons'."

David bounded to his feet and helped her to the table. His heart ached when he looked at her. She was pale, and dark circles ringed her eyes.

Yarrow Woman came carrying a silver serving tray. After the blessing, they feasted on the omelet and generous slices of bread.

"Lucinda, you are almost asleep," Yarrow Woman said when they finished the meal. "Let me tuck you into bed while we pack the sleigh." She guided the exhausted girl to

CHRISTMAS ON THE PRAIRIE

the bed in the adjoining bedroom.

While Yarrow Woman filled boxes with food and bottles with water, she directed Pearl in filling several gunny sacks with herbs. David laid fresh straw over the bed of the sleigh and stacked up bales of hay for the horses. The food and water he padded with quilts and pillows. Finished, they sat down for a last cup of coffee and some elk jerky.

A mighty crash thundered against the door.

They leaped out of their chairs.

The door exploded open.

David stared into cruelty: A middle-aged man with a red beard on a skeletal face glared at them from behind a Remington shotgun. A white scar zigzagged down his cheek, pulling his mouth into a perpetual sneer. Nothing in his expression suggested goodness or mercy. Cold, black eyes raked the room.

David, his insides knotted, forced himself to stay calm. "Who?"

"Don't try to stall me. I ain't stupid. Where is the new maid that tried to kill the judge's wife? The judge wants her real bad."

"I don't know about a new maid trying to kill anyone."

"Word's spread over the county. New maid hired yesterday disappeared from the Tillotson place sometime after midnight. Old judge is paying a thousand dollars silver for her return alive, no questions asked."

David couldn't believe the judge would post a reward. He knew Lucinda was his daughter and would want her safe. Tillotson servants must have seen easy money in the return of Lucinda, David guessed, and exploited the situation. "Do you have a wanted poster or anything to prove your story?" David stepped toward the antsy gunman.

He shifted the weathered shotgun and pointed it directly at David's midsection. "Word I got is straight from someone at the mansion. Countryside's crawlin' with bounty hunters. Nobody's thought to look here yet."

This fellow probably wasn't a bounty hunter. Under the brim of his greasy hat, sweat beaded on his forehead, and his hand holding the gun twitched nervously. His desperation and lack of experience, however, made him more dangerous.

His ugly bearded face took on a sly look. "I says to myself, I says, I'll just have a look around the squaw's place." He brandished the gun at Yarrow Woman, but she didn't move a muscle. "And look what I find. A sleigh at the front door and three innocent-looking people with nothin' in common, getting' ready to leave." He pointed his gun at the boxes and sacks stacked in the corner. His laugh was low and coarse. "Wonder where the fourth one is?" Keeping the gun trained on them, he began a thorough search of the room, including looking through all the drawers and cupboards and tapping the walls and floors for signs of hidden closets or trapdoors.

David spoke up. "As you can see, there are no hiding places here."

The ruffian looked toward the bedroom. "That must mean you got her stowed away in the other room." His heavy boots thumped on the floor as he walked to the door.

David's heart turned over. There was no place in that room to hide. *Think, David, think. You have to do something.* He turned toward the fireplace and the poker resting there. The man whirled and leveled the gun. "See the notches on the butt?" David could. "You wanna be another one?"

He would be no good to anyone if he were dead. David

froze, but his heart raced.

The old hunter unlatched the door and eased it open with the toe of his boot. Silently the door swung open to reveal a single bed spread with a tan Indian blanket in the corner of the small room. On the opposite wall stood an ornate mahogany armoire with a large mirror beside it. A small table next to the bed and a single willow chair completed the furnishings. The floor was bare pine slabs; a large rag rug lay rolled up in front of the armoire. The thug pulled open the muslin curtains covering the single window and looked out over the snowy yard.

Oh, dear God in heaven, don't let him look down, David prayed. A small scrap of blue fabric hung from a nail on the side of the window. *Lucinda! She has more courage than anyone I know. But where is she hiding out there in the wind? She'll freeze.*

Apparently convinced Lucinda was still in the house, the ugly man looked under the bed and poked the mattress with the gun barrel. Nothing. He turned his attention to the armoire. After checking every drawer, he then gave the rug a solid kick with the side of his boot, thumped it with the butt of his gun, shrugged, and went about tapping walls and floor for hollow sounds. He found nothing. He rested his foot on the rug and snarled, "I know ya got her stashed somewheres." He bent down and started to unroll the rug.

David clenched his fists and wished he hadn't packed his pistol away in the wagon. Pearl turned her back and clamped her hand over her mouth. Yarrow Woman's face remained stoic, but her black eyes sparked rage.

The rug flopped open. Nothing. He swore his disappointment. "Well, folks, she cain't stay hidden ferever. I'll just wait it out."

David stormed through the doorway, his hands working, his breath coming hard and fast. "Your search is over. Get out!"

The man thrust the gun in David's face. "Lucky fer you I'm feelin' generous, or you'd be dead. But shoot you I will. It'll give me pleasure to let you stew not knowin' when." His look included them all. "I'll be watchin'."

He tromped outside, waved his fist in the air, and yelled obscenities at David, who stood in the doorway with Yarrow Woman's gun trained on the man. The old scoundrel mounted his horse and rode out of range. He stopped and hung his leg around the saddle horn, making it plain he was prepared to wait out their departure.

They rushed to the window and threw open the sash. "Lucinda," David called softly. Her face appeared around the corner of the house. "Come, we'll help you in." She grasped the rope David lowered and hung on tight while he hoisted her up and into the room. "Lucinda, oh, Lucinda, are you all right?"

She looked up into his eyes, and he caressed her face and hair. "How brave you are. That's a long drop to the ground. Are you hurt?"

"I don't think so. Just terribly cold."

Yarrow Woman pushed David out of the way. "I'll tend to Lucinda. You finish with the sleigh."

David tied Kambur to the rear of the buckboard sleigh and checked the traces of Yarrow Woman's gray Percheron. Satisfied that all was well, he took off his oilskin and climbed into the sleigh. Yarrow Woman appeared, and they quickly stretched a canvas top over a frame to keep out the worst of the storm and block the view of the front door.

"Pearl, you get in. We'll get Lucinda."

They wrapped her in the rug. David picked up one end and Yarrow Woman the other. Gently they carried her to the wagon. Pearl guided the burden inside until it rested on the straw.

"Can you breathe all right?" David asked. He was thankful to hear a muffled yes. He leaned the front door in place and climbed up on the seat beside Yarrow Woman. A mewing caught his attention. Beside her on the floorboard was a basket containing her two cats. *She's such a softy under that rough exterior.*

"I'm glad you know the way," he said to Yarrow Woman.

She nodded and slapped the reins, and they were off. When they reached the prairie, David looked back. A solitary horseman followed close enough to be seen.

Minutes later, David looked back again. *He's still there and drawing closer. He's going to do exactly as he said. We're all going to be dead before nightfall except Lucinda.* He couldn't even think about what would happen to her.

By mid-afternoon, David realized the man was not going away. Up the road, another snow squall stalled and waited for them to drive into a whiteout.

They were almost out of time, but David still had no idea what to do. After they drove into the whiteout, he had Yarrow Woman stop. He crawled into the back and got his gun. He untied Kambur and mounted up. "Go on. I'll catch up," he shouted over the wind.

He rode to the edge of the whiteout and waited. It wasn't long until the hunter rode by, his head bent against the blizzard. He had let down his guard. David waited until he passed, then followed him. The wind carried away all sound. David rode up beside him. He cocked his pistol and pointed it at the man's head.

"Hands in the air!" he shouted. David reached over and lifted the shotgun out of the old man's raised hands. He pitched it far out into the whiteness. Searching through the man's pockets, he found a pair of handcuffs. David cuffed his hands, turned the horse around, and with a solid boot to the rump, sent the horse galloping back the way it had come.

David felt no remorse as he turned around and again faced the wall of white. The bounty hunter wouldn't die, and he couldn't hurt Lucinda anymore. David sat very still, with no idea of which way to go. Letting the reins go slack and with a prayer on his lips, he allowed Kambur to move forward on his own.

The storm had stopped by the time David spotted Yarrow Woman's sleigh before a sod house with an attached stable. Another sleigh stood in the yard. David leaped down from Kambur and made his way to the door, realizing that this must be the "inn" Yarrow Woman had referred to earlier. Tacked there was a sign: DIPHTHERIA. His heart sank.

"Hey, there," a voice called from near the stable. "Praise be to God! We're having a baby. Your friends are inside the stable helping my wife."

David turned and recognized Andy Henderson, the Tillotsons' former head groomsman.

Chapter 10

T he stable was quiet. Lying on beds of fresh straw and wrapped in buffalo robes, the weary travelers encircled the makeshift fire pit. Andy kept watch over Gigi and baby Gabriel asleep in her arms. The animals rested in stalls beyond the flickering firelight.

Unable to sleep, Lucinda sat up and stared into the fire. "This is the most amazing Christmas I've ever had, but I feel as though something more will happen," she said to no one in particular.

"It has been a sacred experience," Pearl agreed and rolled to a sitting position.

David roused up and looked puzzled. "It does seem incomplete, somehow. I, too, feel like I'm waiting for something more."

"Maybe that's why I don't want the night to end." Lucinda felt David's loving eyes on her, and they smiled across the fire.

Soft drumbeats sounded from a dark stall at the back of the room. With great dignity, Yarrow Woman in her white buckskin dress with its heavy beaded designs, her dark hair in two thick braids down her back, came to the fire. She pulled up a log stump and sat. "Before we sleep this night, we must give thanks for this lowly stable as refuge from the storm and protection from the disease in the cabin beyond. Please bow your heads."

Lucinda closed her eyes and listened intently to the prayer. Yarrow Woman expressed all that was in Lucinda's heart and warmed her with peace and gratitude. When Yarrow Woman pronounced the amen, Lucinda and the others echoed it.

Again Yarrow Woman softly beat the little drum. "It is now Christmas Day. Would you like to hear the legend based on the birth of our Savior as told by my people?"

Lucinda's breath caught. Was this what they had been waiting for? "Yes. Oh yes." Her voice chimed in unison with the others.

"In the country north of us," Yarrow Woman began in her firm but soft voice, "there is the *he sapa*, a range of pine-covered mountains so green that from a distance they look black. At the foot of the *he sapa* are the mysterious *mako sica*, or Badlands, a mass of buttes and spires that stretch as far as the eye can see. The Badlands end at the sweeping prairie, long and wide and rolling. To the Northern Plains tribes who live there, all of creation—animals, birds, insects, plants, and humanity—are part of the sacred hoop. The Lakota express this as *mitakuye oyasin*.

"A very long time ago, the people who had been full of goodwill and generosity of spirit began to lose those virtues. The wise men were much concerned and fasted and prayed diligently to the Great Spirit for help. He heard their prayers and told the grandfathers to bring the people together on the longest night in the month of the moon.

"Out of curiosity, they came, hard of heart, selfish and arrogant, to wait and watch. They were not disappointed, for as the light darkened, they saw an eagle. It soared in high, wide circles above the Black Hills and out over the mysterious Badlands until the setting sun struck fire upon its wings. This was the signal, the grandfathers said. For what, they refused to say.

"The night settled like black velvet, and the people lit a huge bonfire. They encircled the fire and sat, watching the sparks rise among the stars. The air, cold and crisp, was scented with the sweet smoke. The night sky was radiant, the silence vast, peaceful, expectant.

"When the hush became so deep the titmouse could be heard, the representatives for *mitakuye oyasin* began to arrive— Those Who Fly and the Four-Leggeds—and take their place in the circle. They sat together around the glowing coals until all their heartbeats were as one.

"Then the snow goose stepped forward. 'The people have gone astray from the cycles of their journey and are lost. I will teach them the patterns of the seasons.'

"The chipmunk came to the fire. 'The Two-Leggeds wander, hungry and without purpose. I will teach them to gather and store the harvest. I will share my store of nuts.'

"The great buffalo lumbered up and stood with lowered head. 'The people waste what they take and share nothing. I will give my flesh to feed them and, to warm them, my coat. I will give myself away.'

"The eagle flew up and landed in the forming circle. 'The Two-Leggeds are blind. They do not see the aftermath

166

of their actions. Perhaps if I give them my eyes, they will see beyond the present.'

"Each representative moved to the circle to tell of a gift, the most precious portion of themselves, that they wished to share until all had spoken and the night was silent again.

"When the very air quivered with anticipation, from inside the night came the deep, sad voice of the Creator. 'Those Who Fly and Four-Leggeds, you waste yourselves. They will accept your gifts and take the credit unto themselves.' There was heavy silence. 'It is I who must give myself. I will come, innocent and small.'

" 'How is that possible?' asked the relations. 'A Babe will be born, the Son of the Great Spirit. He will be born among the Four-Leggeds and Those Who Fly. He will give hope where there is hopelessness. He will bring love where there is hate. His name will be great among the people of the world.'

"And the people's hearts grew soft and loving. They looked at themselves and asked what they could give to the Small One. They were told they were free to give anything, anything at all, as long as the gift required the giver to make a great sacrifice.

"So the people went in search of perfect gifts to lay at the feet of the Small One. Some found their gifts at once; others searched longer; but many searched most of their lives before they found gifts perfect enough. Some never found a gift, because once more they strayed far from the virtuous life, the Red Road. The Small One was sad about that.

"On the longest night in the month of the moon, each gift was honored and the giver given a blessing and a promise. And for a little while, the people were once again full of goodwill and generosity of spirit.

"And so it is in our time, on the longest night in the month of the moon, we bring a perfect gift to somebody and give it in the name of the Small One. Tonight I give my gift—this drum given to me by the grandfathers, that I have cherished for many years—to Baby Henderson, in the name of the Small One, our Savior and Lord, Jesus Christ."

A holy silence filled the stable and was disturbed only by an occasional snap of an ember.

Lucinda remembered all the lavish Christmas celebrations and presents of her past. Nothing had stirred her heart like the message of this simple story. She fingered her necklace and thought how she had counted on it for her strength. It had become an idol to her! This knowledge came with a shock. *Do I have the faith to give it away?* It was a perfect gift and would help the young couple. She herself could never sell it for money. Giving it was truly a sacrifice.

She looked at David and found him studying her, his eyes filled with a love she had never known. As though he read her mind, he smiled and nodded.

Slowly, Lucinda returned the nod and sent her love to him. She understood. *I must trust God to take care of me and not depend on things.* With a prayer for strength to release the necklace and the past it represented, she slid from beneath the robe and knelt before Gigi. "In the name of the Small One, I give this necklace, cherished by generations of the House of North. It is the last tangible object from my past. It will become the foundation of the future for the House of Henderson." And she fastened the necklace around Gigi's neck.

Lucinda entered into the silence that once again settled over the stable as the gift was honored and the spirit of the season entered each heart.

Then David rose from his bed and walked to Kambur's stall. He returned with the bridle and saddle blanket, knelt, and laid them at Andy's feet. "Lucinda and I will be traveling west by train. We'll go as far as Nebraska, where I have something I must settle with my brother. After witnessing all that Lucinda has been through, all that she has suffered, I realize I have some fences I must mend. I need to find work and let Lucinda get to know me and my family."

"I would like that," she said quietly.

A broad smile lit his face, and he turned back to Andy. "You have a gift with horses, so I know you will treasure Kambur and take good care of him. If you choose to breed him, the charge for his services will support your family well. Kambur is a choice animal, and I give him to you in the name of the Innocent One who left His heavenly home to come to earth and sacrifice Himself for us." He moved to sit beside Lucinda, cradling her in his arms.

Again the silence descended and deepened. Lucinda, safe now, felt the very air change. God's presence seemed to come into the stable to watch with approval. Soft tears streamed down her face, and her heart burned with joy.

The fire burned low. David stirred the coals and added a log. The smoke carried sparks up through the smoke hole in the roof and left the scent of apple wood inside the stable. He returned to his place beside Lucinda, and she leaned her head on his shoulder. He again put his arms around her and held her close. "You realize that all we have in this world is eighty dollars."

She smiled and dug into her coat pocket. "I have twenty-five cents. We are rich. Very rich."

They both looked over at Yarrow Woman. David then

looked back at Lucinda and framed her face with his hands, kissing her gently, tenderly. "We are indeed rich beyond our grandest fantasies."

The straw rustled as Pearl pushed back her robe and stood. All eyes focused on her. "I have been praying to know what I should do. I have raised Lucinda from babyhood, and she is like my own. But she is grown now and has found a wonderful man to love and who loves her. I need to let you go and make your own way."

Lucinda felt stricken. It had never occurred to her that Pearl would not want to be with her and David. "You're not leaving us for good, are you?"

"Never that." She smiled, kissed Lucinda, and crossed to where Gabriel lay. Dropping to her knees in front of the baby, she said, "I have no worldly possessions to bring, but I can give myself in service to the Lord by serving Gabriel and his family. Will you accept my gift?"

Andy and Gigi gaped at Pearl, and disbelief filled their eyes. Gigi finally found her voice. *"Oui, oui."*

"Then I shall see David and Lucinda safely to their destination in Nebraska and return to you by the time you are ready to travel."

Andy wiped away a tear and nodded. "We will love you, and you will have a home with us all the days of your life." He turned to David and Lucinda. "Earlier we discussed this. Gigi and I would like you to be godparents to our firstborn."

David and Lucinda nodded, unable to speak. Pearl hugged them and then moved her bed next to the baby.

Yarrow Woman stood and raised her arms. "The circle is complete. We recognize that the true meaning of Christmas is Christ's sacrificial birth, life, death, and resurrection for us. These gifts are our poor attempts to remind us of His great sacrifice and to show our gratitude for it. May the Spirit of the Lord abide with us this day and every day during the coming year. Amen."

Easy Fruit Cobbler

½ cup butter
1 cup flour
1 cup sugar
1½ teaspoons
   baking powder

¾ cup milk
2 cups fruit
1 cup sugar

Preheat oven to 350 degrees. Melt butter in oven in 9 x 9-inch pan. In bowl, mix flour, 1 cup sugar, baking powder, and milk. Blend well. Pour batter into pan with melted butter; don't stir. Pour fruit over the top and sprinkle with remaining 1 cup sugar. Bake 25 minutes. Serve hot with vanilla ice cream.

MARYN LANGER

Maryn descends from a long line of storytellers. She combines the history of the West with the romance of the heart. She gave her life to the Lord at an early age. He has shepherded her beside still waters and green pastures and through the valleys of temptation. Her prayer is that those who read her books will be entertained and reassured that there is a loving God who loves us and answers our prayers.

Epilogue

by Pamela Griffin and Maryn Langer

D avid helped Lucinda off the wagon and nodded to the driver. "I can't thank you enough."

A gap-toothed smile split the face of the elderly man, who'd introduced himself as Jebediah Meyers. "Well, now, I sure couldn't let you and your purty little bride sit at the train station when your chaperone left on the return train. Since I wuz headin' home anyway, it wasn't a problem."

David didn't bother to correct the man on his assumption that he and Lucinda were married. He hoped by spring they would be, and David greatly looked forward to that day. However, at this moment his stomach twisted in knots as if he'd overindulged in a six-course dinner. His brother was a stubborn man, not known for granting forgiveness once a wall had been built, and David had certainly built a thick one. Could he climb over it? Had he made a mistake in coming to this place?

Any courage he'd shown during their escape days ago felt just out of reach now.

Lucinda slipped her hand into his. "It will be all right. Yarrow Woman told us that God directs His people on which paths to take. I believe we have chosen the right course."

David nodded, though he heard the underlying tightness

174

in her voice. Her palm felt moist, and he gently squeezed her hand.

"The people you're lookin' for live in that purty white timbered house over yonder," Jebediah said. "Cain't miss it." He laughed at his own joke, then flicked the reins on the mules' backs while making a clicking sound with his tongue for them to proceed. "Have yourselves a prosperous New Year, folks."

Once the wagon rattled away, David eyed the scarce town of Leaning Tree with its total of seven modest buildings, most of them sod. Jebediah was correct. Finding the right house wouldn't be difficult. He guided Lucinda over the snowy ground and up the few steps to the porch. Before he lost his nerve, he knocked loudly on the front door.

Seconds later, an exotic-looking woman with flowing black hair and gold hoops in her ears answered. She held a baby against her colorful dress.

David's greeting froze on his lips. Had he misunderstood Jebediah and approached the wrong house? He glanced at the few buildings to his right but saw nothing that resembled "white" or "timbered" or even "purty."

"I'm looking for Winifred Morgan—er, Pettigrass," he said. The driver had told him Winnie was married.

The woman only stared, a slight smile on her lips. She shook her head, as if to show she did not understand.

"Juanita, who is it?"

The familiar voice met David's ears. His breathing instantly felt constrained, and he struggled to retain his composure.

Winifred came into view, plumper and prettier than he remembered. Her blue eyes widened when she saw him, and she lifted her palms to her rosy cheeks. "Dai? Is that you?"

David hadn't heard his Welsh name in so long, he wasn't prepared for the emotion it evoked. He'd adopted the English version of the name Dai seven years ago when he turned his back on his older brother and went to Illinois intent on building his own life. Until this moment, he had not realized how horribly he missed his family. He felt Winifred's arms encircle him but seemed powerless to lift his.

"Come you inside. It is freezing." Quickly Winifred ushered them into the house in time to hear what sounded like a plate crash to the floor. Running footsteps thudded against the wooden planks.

"Dai? My Dai's come back to me?" His mother rushed from the rear of the house.

Emotion cut off any possible words at the sight of her beloved wrinkled face. Sobbing, she approached and embraced him, and David was finally able to lift his arms. He held her and Winnie a long time. The women's tears soon mixed with gentle laughs and choppy phrases.

Suddenly David was aware of a stylishly dressed woman and a tall man walking down the corridor toward them. So engrossed were they in conversation that they didn't notice the reunion taking place in the entryway.

"Boston, I don't mind you buying things for our house, not one bit," the man said in amusement. "But don't you think you should wait 'til I build it first?"

The lovely woman's face flushed pink. "I can't help myself, Craig. The prospect of having our own home is so exciting. I had no idea that fifty dollars could go so far—beyond even what I bought for my family." She stopped suddenly, catching sight of David. "Oh, hello," she said curiously.

Winnie and his mother pulled back, blotting their faces with their fingers and laughing self-consciously. Their gazes went beyond David and remained fixed. Suddenly, he realized why. With what he hoped was a look of contrition for forgetting her even for a moment, he held out a hand to his love. Lucinda moved forward, looking at David with understanding in her eyes before she turned them toward his family.

"Mother, Winnie, this is Lucinda. My fiancée."

His mother's eyes widened, and Winnie gulped in a nervous laugh. David tensed as his mother eyed Lucinda a long moment, paying particular attention to her ill-fitting coat and yellow-and-blue-striped cap. Then she smiled and moved forward to embrace her. "Welcome. Come, sit. I will fix us something hot to drink to warm you both up."

They made their way into the living room. The man stepped forward and held out his hand. "I'm Craig Watson, and this is my fiancée, Ivy. Welcome to Leaning Tree."

David shook his hand, but before he could introduce himself, Winifred blurted out, "This is Dai!"

"So, you're my stepfather's brother," Ivy murmured as she stood beside Craig and smiled. "It's a pleasure to meet you both," she said.

"Stepfather?" David asked.

"Mairwen passed on to glory three years ago," Winifred explained. "Our brother has remarried."

The brisk cold touched the back of David's neck as the door opened again. He turned. A fair-haired older child stood on the threshold next to a smaller girl with the same features.

"Ah, here are Gwen and Crystin," Winifred said. "Come then, girls. This is your uncle Dai."

Gwen's face immediately brightened. "Uncle Dai?" She rushed forward and hugged him hard around his middle, surprising David.

Crystin was less demonstrative, though she did smile. "Hello."

David swallowed over the lump in his throat. "Hello. You were only a baby when I last saw you. And your sister, here, had just turned six."

Suddenly a shadow from the doorway blocked the outside light. David looked up and tensed when he saw Gavin.

Gavin stood motionless. A woman came up beside him, looking like an older version of Ivy. Her dark brows drawn in apparent confusion, she looked at Gavin, then at the gathering.

"Gavin," Winifred finally said, nervousness evident in her tone. "Look who's come back to us. Our Dai has come home."

"Is this true now?" Gavin asked, his voice gravelly and deep. "Have you come home?"

David shared a look with Lucinda. Her green eyes encouraged him.

"For a short time, yes. I have the prospects of work in San Francisco. Lucinda and I plan to build our life there. I wanted to see everyone again. So we took the train. We found it imperative to leave Illinois." His lawyer's brain calculated recent facts, but the information seemed slow in reaching his mouth, and his words came out choppy.

Gavin nodded once. David tensed as his brother approached, then held out his work-worn hand. "You are welcome," Gavin said. "It is good to see you."

David felt rooted in shock, unable to shake his brother's hand. "It is?"

"Yes. I had much time to think, and perhaps I was wrong to expect you to follow my dream." Gavin looked toward their mother, then again at David. "You must follow your own dream."

David rapidly blinked back tears and tried to maintain control. When he was younger, he'd looked up to his older brother. He may not always have understood him, but he always loved him. And then that day on the dock. . .

"I said some horrible things," David croaked, feeling nineteen again. "I never should have struck you."

For the first time, Gavin smiled, and David saw the old familiar light of teasing in his eyes. "Perhaps I should not have struck back. Yes? Though your fresh mouth did deserve it."

Knowing that this was his brother's way of saying all was forgiven, David grinned and took Gavin's hand. They shook hands until Gavin pulled David into a fierce hug. Tears rolled down the faces of both men.

"Praise be to God!" David heard his mother exclaim. "At last, my prayers have been answered."

Colder Than Ice

by Jill Stengl

Dedication

With love to my daughter and toughest writing critic,
Anne Elisabeth Stengl, and to my sister, Paula Ciccotti,
who introduced me to prairie life in Iowa.

Chapter 1

Coon's Hollow, Iowa—1885

"Hello! Sir, hello!"

As Frank Nelson jogged his horse past the Coon's Hollow train station, he noticed a strange woman waving a handkerchief from the sunbaked platform. At first he thought she must be beckoning to someone else, but a quick glance around ended that hope. "Ma'am?" He reined Powder in and halted near the steps.

Clad in black from her bonnet to her boots, the woman twisted the handkerchief between her gloved hands. A large trunk waited beside the empty depot office, and two carpet-bags sat on the bench. "I'm sorry to disturb you, sir, but can you deliver a message for me?"

"Deliver it where?" After a sleepless night, he was in no mood to serve as messenger boy. He squinted, thinking she looked vaguely familiar. "Who are you?"

She drew herself up and stared at him down her long, narrow nose. Hot, gusty wind sent her bonnet flapping around her gaunt cheeks and ballooned her ruffled skirts. Soot streaked her forehead, and dust grayed her garments. "If you would ask someone from the hotel to collect my luggage, I shall be grateful."

That incisive voice rang a bell. "Have we met?"

"Never."

Squinting against the wind, he studied her face. Shadowed eyes, sharp chin, and prominent cheekbones. "Are you related to Paul Truman?" Certainty filled him. "You must be his sister from Wisconsin. What are you doing here?"

"I cannot see that it is your business," she began, then informed him, "I have been offered employment in the area."

"That was months ago."

"And how would you know?" Queen Victoria herself could be no more imperious.

"I'm Frank Nelson, the pastor. I offered you the job, Miss Truman. I hope you at least informed Paul and Susan that you were coming."

"*You* are the minister?" Chin tucked, she looked him up and down. Her shoulders squared. "Has the position been filled?"

"No."

He was tempted to tell her he no longer needed a secretary. Let the harpy go back to the big city and terrorize small children there. Coon's Hollow held its quota of odd characters. And he definitely didn't need another eccentric spinster in his life.

"Why don't you come with me to the parsonage, cool off in the shade, and have some lemonade, and I'll send someone to Trumans' with a message from you. It's only going to get hotter on that platform." His shepherd calling wouldn't allow him to leave even an ornery ewe to the mercy of the elements. She would be in no danger from wolves, that was certain.

She blinked. "Very well."

Frank dismounted, leaped up the steps, and grabbed her carpetbags. "They're planning a new depot with a covered waiting area, but it won't happen this year. Have you been here long?" *She must have arrived on the morning train.*

"What about my trunk?"

"It'll be safe here until Paul comes for it. The parsonage is just around the corner." He hopped down and swung the two bags up onto Powder's saddle. When he turned around, Miss Truman had descended the steps. She was tall, he noticed. And thin. Truly spindly.

"Miss Truman?" He extended his arm. She curled her gloved fingers around his forearm and fell into step along the dusty street. Powder followed behind, led by one loose rein. Now that Frank had offered lemonade, he remembered drinking the last of it yesterday afternoon.

He tried to recall details about Miss Truman. Upon hearing of their mother's death, Paul had offered his only sister a home with his family, adding the further incentive of a job as the minister's secretary. "Taking her into my home is the Christian thing to do," Paul had said with the air of a martyr. "And she could be a great help to you if she doesn't drive you to an early grave."

Frank gave the woman a side glance. She appeared more underfed and exhausted than dangerous. "Why did you decide to come to Iowa after all? When Paul had no reply from you, he assumed you weren't coming."

"My circumstances became. . .insupportable," she said in a flat voice. "If you no longer require my services, I shall find employment elsewhere."

"What did Paul tell you about me?" He felt awkward asking.

"He told me that you are attempting to write a book and need someone to transcribe it for you. Is your office in your home or at the church?"

"At the parsonage."

"I assume your wife will act as chaperone."

As if this woman would require one. "My housekeeper will chaperone; my wife died eight years ago."

"You have no family?"

"Not living with me. My daughter, Amy, is married and living in Des Moines. My son, David, recently bought a farm near your brother's and is fixing up the farmhouse. He is betrothed to your niece, Margie. They are to marry Christmas Eve, so you and I shall soon be related in a way."

"I see."

"Here we are." Frank wrapped Powder's rein around the post and pushed open the picket gate. Seeing Miss Truman examine his home, he scanned it himself. A riot of perennials overflowed the garden fence, invaded the weedy lawn, and sneaked across the walkway. Morning glories strangled the hitching posts and attempted to bind the picket gate shut.

A wide veranda wrapped around most of the house, offering shade and a breeze. Beyond the stable out back, cornfields stretched as far as the eye could see. A windmill squeaked out its rusty rhythm. Water trickled from its base into a huge tub. A swaybacked horse plunged its nose into the sparkling water and playfully dumped waves over the tub's far rim.

"The Harlan Coon family donated this house and the stable to the church twenty years ago. Those are Coon cornfields, but Bess there is mine. She's too old to work, but I keep her as company for Powder." A handy excuse for keeping an oversized pet. "The church is a good stretch of the legs up the road from here, but the walk gives me exercise."

The woman said nothing. These long silences seemed uncanny from a female. Perhaps she was tired. "Have a seat here, Miss Truman, and I'll find you something to drink. Mary should be around somewhere." It occurred to him that the simplest course of action would be to hitch up his own buggy and take the lady to Paul's house.

The screen door squealed, and Mary Bilge stumped onto the porch. An unlit cigar dangled from her lips. "Who's this?"

"Miss Truman, newly arrived from Wisconsin. Miss Truman, this is Miss Bilge, my housekeeper." He watched the two women eye each other and shake hands. "Miss Truman has agreed to assist me with preparing my manuscript for publication."

Mary's dark gaze pinned him. "How's the Dixons' baby?"

"Better, the doctor says."

"Humph. I'll bake them a raisin loaf."

He would believe that when he saw it. "Uh, do we have any of that lemonade left, Mary?"

"You oughta know, seein' as how you drank the last of it." She disappeared back into the house, letting the screen door slam.

Frank avoided Miss Truman's gaze. "I'm sorry."

"May I enter your kitchen?"

"Certainly." He opened the screen door and beckoned her inside. She peeled off her gloves, surveying the room, the largest in his house. To his surprise, she opened the firebox and added two sticks of wood, picked up the kettle, and nodded. "I can make tea, if you have any."

"Help yourself. I don't know what I have. People give me food sometimes. Like the lemonade Mrs. Wilkins brought over."

Miss Truman searched through cupboards, canisters, and the icebox, producing a tin of tea, a sack of white sugar, and a small pitcher of cream. Frank watched her brew tea in an old china teapot. Whenever she glanced his way, he found himself standing straight and holding in his gut.

"You may summon Miss Bilge." The lady located cookies in the jar and laid them on a plate, loaded the waiting tray, and carried it out to the porch before Frank could stop her.

"Come and have tea on the veranda with us, Mary," he called, uncertain where she might be. "Then I need to hitch up Powder and take Miss Truman home."

He heard Mary thumping and muttering on the cellar stairs. What had she been doing down there? He didn't dare ask.

"Tea on a day like this? La-de-da! Give me coffee."

"But Miss Truman brewed tea."

"Coffee's good enough for me. Got some left from breakfast."

Frank grimaced at the idea, but Mary poured herself a cup and shuffled outside. In hot or cold weather, she always wore the same man's overcoat over a sacklike gown, heavy boots, and a broad-brimmed hat. She seemed about as wide as she was tall. Slumped into a rocking chair, she seared Miss Truman with her stare.

Serenely composed, Miss Truman perched in another

chair, prepared to pour the tea. "Cream and sugar, Reverend Nelson?"

"Thank you." After pulling up a third rocking chair, he watched her prepare his tea and accepted the cup. Her remote gaze caught his once more. "Reverend Nelson, when do you wish me to begin work?"

He sipped the tea. Sweet, creamy—better than he had expected. "How about Monday? That should give you time to settle in at Paul and Susan's. I warn you, my papers are a disaster."

"Huh," Mary said, cradling her grimy coffee cup against her chest.

Frank started to grin but stopped when his lips quivered. He took a handful of cookies.

Silence lengthened. Frank wondered if the women could hear him chewing. No telling how long those cookies had been in the jar. Since spring maybe.

A large black cat strolled across the veranda, gave Mary wide berth, oozed between Frank's boots, and sat in front of Miss Truman. The lady moved her teacup to one side, and the cat flowed into her lap, curled up, and disappeared against the shiny black fabric.

"Dirty critter," Mary muttered.

Miss Truman stroked the cat, and Frank heard a rumbling purr. Again he met Miss Truman's gaze and, for the first time, saw in her pale eyes a fleeting emotion. "I like cats," she said.

Frank gulped down the last of his tea. "We have several roaming about the place. Belle is the queen cat and the best mouser. We used to have a dog, but he died a few years back of old age."

Miss Truman watched the cat as she petted it, and Frank

watched her long hands caress its glossy fur. Abruptly she took a sip of tea. The cup rattled in the saucer when she replaced it, and Frank suddenly noticed the slump of her shoulders. The poor woman must be exhausted almost beyond bearing, yet he'd kept her drinking tea on his veranda and talking business. He hopped up, leaving his chair rocking wildly. "We'd best be off, Miss Truman. If you'd like to rest awhile longer, I'll take the buckboard to the station for your trunk first and return for you."

She nodded. "Thank you, Reverend Nelson." Rising, she gathered up the tea things and carried them inside. The screen door closed quietly behind her.

"You're gonna hire that woman? She's gonna be here every day?" Mary glowered.

"I'm hiring her as secretary, not replacement house-keeper. Your place is secure."

Scowl lines deepened between Mary's brushy brows. With another grunt, she set her empty coffee cup on the floor and rose. Nose high, she stumped down the porch steps and headed toward her little house across the road.

When Frank drove through town with Estelle Truman at his side, he encountered curious glances from towns-people. She shaded her face with a black silk parasol and sat erect on the bench seat. Polished boot toes emerged from beneath her gown's dusty ruffles. For the first time, he noticed the worn seams on her sleeves and a rip in the skirt, repaired with tiny stitches.

"We'll have you home in no time," he promised as they left the schoolhouse and one last barking dog behind. "So, Miss Truman, you have lived in Madison all your life until now?"

"I have. Reverend Nelson, I do not wish to confide my life story in you during this drive to my brother's farmhouse. I'm sure you will understand."

He deflated. "Of course."

"I overheard your conversation with Miss Bilge today— something about the illness of a baby?" She spoke quietly.

"Ben and Althea Dixon's first child. Only nine months old. He took ill last week. The doctor thought he would die, but he rallied during the night and seemed almost back to normal. I was on my way home from their house when I met you at the station."

"Were you with the family all night?"

"Yes. They asked me to come and pray, and this time God chose to restore little Benjamin's health. We lose a lot of children here. Paul and Susan's daughter, Jessamine, died of typhoid a year ago, and they nearly lost Joe, too."

"Paul never wrote of their daughter's death."

"Jessamine was sixteen. I believe the sorrow and strain have drained Susan's strength, yet her spirit is stronger than ever."

Miss Truman's chin tipped up. "I shall not increase Susan's burden. She will find me useful around the house."

"I pray you'll also find time to assist me in preparing my book for publication. I often fear I should abandon the project and turn my mind to more practical pursuits, but then I feel as if God is pressing this work upon my heart and I must keep writing it." He looked down at her marble profile and wondered if she could make any difference.

"I shall assist you to the best of my ability, Reverend Nelson, commensurate with my pay."

Rather than respond to that baffling remark, he pointed.

"Ahead is Paul's farm. All this corn around us is his. He also raises hogs. He's a good man. Good farmer. Good friend. I'm honored to have my son marry his daughter." He turned in at the Trumans' drive, wondering how the family would react to this maiden aunt's arrival.

The barn and the white farmhouse looked insignificant in the vast expanse of surrounding prairie. One large tree shaded the house. Chickens ran clucking from the buckboard as it rolled up the drive, and a cow bawled. Frank glanced at Miss Truman. Her expression revealed nothing.

"Hello, Frank. Who's that with—" The question cut off sharply. Paul jogged across the farmyard, his eyes locked with his sister's. "Estelle!"

"Hello, Paul. I came."

He stopped beside the buckboard, still staring. "I can't believe it."

"If you have changed your mind, I can take a room in town."

He seemed to start back to reality. "No, no. Here, let me help you down." He offered her a hand, and while she climbed to the ground, he turned his head to shout over one shoulder. "Josh. Alvin. Joe. Get out here *now*!

"I just can't believe it. You haven't changed much, Stell." Paul gave her a quick hug.

Frank saw her lips quiver before she stepped back to straighten her bonnet. "Twenty years, Paulie."

One after another, Paul's three sons appeared from barn and fields. Frank saw little Flora poke her head out the kitchen door, then duck back inside, probably to inform her mother about their visitors. Eliza, the farm dog, came running, tail wagging as she sniffed around Miss Truman's shoes. To Frank's surprise, the woman held out one hand to the dog and gave her a pat.

While Paul introduced his sister to the boys, Frank unloaded her trunk and bags from his wagon. She spoke to the boys politely and shook their hands. Frank caught an exchange of uncertain glances between Al and Joe. Josh unobtrusively punched the younger boy when he made a comment behind one hand.

Susan and her daughters emerged from the house, and Frank felt himself relax. A welcoming smile wreathed Susan's face, and her daughters were beaming. "Estelle! This is a wonderful surprise. My dear, please come inside out of this heat. The men will bring your things in. You can share Margie's room until she marries." Amid a spate of further instructions and welcomes, Susan took Miss Truman's hand in hers and led her toward the house. The three boys picked up the luggage and followed.

Paul met Frank's gaze. "I can't believe it," he repeated. "What are we going to do?"

"You invited her here," Frank said. "She came. Susan doesn't seem to mind. Why should you? She's *your* sister."

Paul still looked dazed. "How did you meet her?"

Frank related the scene at the depot. Paul kept shaking his head until Frank wanted to shake him. Miss Truman might be haughty and reserved, but she was no monster. "She agreed to start working for me on Monday, so she won't be around your house all day. I assume you thought of transportation."

"She can use the dogcart."

"She told me she won't be a burden to Susan."

Paul let out a huff. "Don't look at me like that, Frank.

You don't understand. Stell and I were good buddies as children. But she changed during the war. When I came home. . .trust me: That woman has a block of ice in place of a heart. I won't let her destroy my home like an encroaching glacier."

"Do you want me to stay around this evening?" Frank offered. "Just for a while?"

"No, thanks. We'll manage." Paul gave Frank a sidelong glance. "But I'd surely appreciate your prayers."

Chapter 2

Without looking in their direction, Frank knew when the Truman family neared his position at the open double doors. He patted an elderly parishioner's hand, gazed into her eyes, and thanked her for her compliments on his sermon. "God's Word is my source, Mrs. Coon. A preacher cannot go far wrong if he sticks to his source. Bless you, ma'am." The widow of the town's founding citizen always had something kind to say.

For two days Frank had been wondering how Miss Truman was adapting to her new surroundings and how her family was adjusting to her. He both dreaded and anticipated introducing her to his dilapidated manuscript on the morrow.

Paul gripped his hand hard. "Good message. Supper with us this evening? David's already coming."

"Lately it seems the only way I get to see my son is to meet him at your house. Can't imagine why," Frank said, grinning. "Thank you. I'll be there." Anything beat Mary Bilge's Sunday stew. And the fellowship at Paul's house was always excellent.

"Pastor Nelson, thank you for that wonderful sermon." Susan's smile radiated inner beauty. "I always leave this church inspired to live another week in the Lord's presence."

Miss Truman stood nearby, hearing every word. Frank lowered his gaze, cleared his throat, and said, "It's the Holy Ghost, not me."

"I know, but you're His instrument. Come by at five o'clock tonight."

Susan moved on. Margie, Joe, and Flora each shook his hand in turn. Josh and Alvin had passed through the line earlier. Flora asked him, "You met Auntie Stell, didn't you? She likes cats."

He looked into the child's pale blue eyes, then up at her aunt's, noting the resemblance. "I know she does. She met Belle at my house the other day."

"And she is going to make me a blue gown for Margie's wedding."

"Indeed?"

"Today we're going to make pies from the blackberries Joe and I picked yesterday. I get to roll the crust, Auntie Stell says. Margie never lets me. You get to have pie after supper tonight."

"I can hardly wait."

Flora returned his smile and walked on, head high, shoulders back, without her usual bounce. Frank suspected imitation of her aunt, and the realization surprised him.

He turned to face Miss Truman. "I trust you are adjusting to your new home? Flora is evidently smitten with you."

"She is a sweet child." Yet no hint of a smile curved the woman's tight lips. "Thank you for your inquiry, Reverend." After barely touching his hand, she moved on.

Frank shook hands with the last few people, then walked around, straightening hymnals and picking up rubbish. Two calls to make that afternoon, then supper at the Trumans'. These next few weeks should prove interesting in many ways. Perhaps after all these years, he would begin to make headway on his manuscript.

"How are things going with your aunt?" Frank asked Alvin that afternoon as he stabled his gelding in the Trumans' barn.

"Not bad."

Hardly the informative answer Frank desired. "She gets along with your ma?"

"Yep. She's a good cook."

"And your pa doesn't fight with her?" Frank bent to pat Eliza, letting the dog lick his hand.

"Nope. She don't talk much."

A family trait, apparently. "See you at supper."

"Yessir."

Paul greeted him at the front door.

"How are things going?" Frank asked, hanging his hat on the hall tree. He ran his fingers through his damp hair and hoped he didn't stink of sweat and horses.

"Surprisingly well. My sister jumped right into the chores, cooking and cleaning. Even washed and ironed the family's laundry along with her own and started in on the mending. I didn't know she had it in her. Guess she's learned how to work since our childhood days."

Paul led him to the kitchen. "Pastor's here."

Miss Truman and Flora worked over at the counter. Neither one looked up.

"Hello, Dad." David sat at the kitchen table, conversing with Margie while she helped prepare the meal. "Good sermon this morning."

Frank reached across the table to shake his son's hand. "Thank you. How are things going?"

"Very well. If you have time this week, I could use help replacing the windows in the parlor. The frames are rotted, and two of the panes are cracked. I decided to replace them entirely. It's slow work, but I expect to have the house ready by December." David smiled at Margie, who gazed adoringly into his eyes.

"What about the harvest?"

"Mr. Gallagher put only three fields into corn and beans this year before I bought the place. Harvest should be quick. Got five hogs ready for market by next week. It's a great farm." Enthusiasm burned in David's eyes. Frank recognized himself at that age. So zealous for life, with a promising future and a lovely bride.

When David's attention returned to Margie, Frank allowed himself a look at Miss Truman. Wearing a calico apron over her black mourning gown, she laid a circle of pastry atop a mounded heap of blackberries, all the while chatting with Flora. Her sleeves were rolled up, revealing white arms. Silver laced the waves of dark hair around her forehead.

"Hello, Pastor Nelson." Susan's greeting from the pantry doorway jolted him back to reality. Holding up two jars, she said, "Estelle, I have pickled beets and dilled cucumbers. Which do you think?"

"With chicken pie, I would serve the cucumbers, but this is your home, Susan."

"Nonsense, sister," Susan said. "It's your home now, too.

And it's your chicken pie."

"Hello, Susan. I didn't see you there," Frank said. "Can I do anything to help?"

She gave him an odd look. "You needn't shout, Pastor. My hearing is excellent."

Frank felt his face burn. Anxiety sometimes increased his volume.

"If you truly wish to help, you may carry the chicken pie to the table once it's baked." Susan moved toward the work counter.

Frank tried to make himself small to let her pass, but she stepped on his boot. "Excuse me, Pastor."

"Sorry." He shuffled back, colliding with Miss Truman. "Pardon."

Giving an exasperated huff, Miss Truman planted one hand between his shoulder blades and pushed away. He turned to see her brushing flour from her skirts and staring downward. Following her gaze, he beheld his scuffed, cracked brown boot toes emerging beneath striped gray trousers. Did his feet look as large to her as they felt to him?

Without a word, she returned to her pie, and Frank felt himself scorned. "I'd best remove myself from the kitchen before I break something." He laughed and saw Estelle wince. Another loud-mouthed gaffe.

Before he could escape, Flora slid in close and caught his sleeve. "Auntie Stell made an extra pie from my berries for the Dixons 'cause their baby was sick. She made a chicken pie for them, too. Josh took supper to them, but he'll be back before our supper is cooked."

"How thoughtful," Frank said quietly. "I'm certain Althea and Ben will appreciate your kindness."

Flora beamed. Miss Truman did not even glance in his direction. Frank patted Flora's shoulder and tried to smile. He longed to slink away and lick his wounds.

At supper, the men discussed the town baseball team's latest game while Margie chatted about wedding plans with the ladies. Alvin, Joe, and Flora remained politely silent. Needing no urging, Frank accepted a second helping of chicken pie. Its crust flaked over creamy gravy and tender strips of chicken. He wanted to compliment the cook, but her expression discouraged light conversation.

Susan voiced Frank's thoughts. "Estelle, this pie is delicious."

"Where did you learn to cook like this?" Paul asked. "Not at the office of Blackstone and Hicks, I'm certain."

"Our great-aunt Bridget taught me to cook while she lived with us."

Paul chuckled. "Aunt Bridget! I haven't thought about her for decades. Remember the time we brought the litter of raccoons into the parlor while she and Mother were having tea?"

Joe and Alvin stared in silent disbelief.

"We truly did." Paul nodded. "Back in those days, we were a pair of rascals. Most of our pranks were Stell's idea. I was the trusting little brother."

Miss Truman's lips tightened. "Nonsense."

"Aunt Bridget, the ornery old buzzard." Paul leaned back in his chair and reminisced. "We called her 'the witch' when our parents weren't around. She always wore black, and she always looked disapproving. Aunt Bridget taught you more than cooking, Stell."

"She also taught me piano."

"That's not what I meant. You're just like her. I hadn't

realized until you mentioned her name; then the resemblance struck me."

Frank heard several sharp gasps around the table. His chest felt tight, but not one beneficial word came to mind.

Miss Truman pushed back her chair and rose. "I must check the pie."

Paul glanced at Susan and wilted. Making a visible effort to amend the situation, he said, "You should hear Estelle play piano. She used to play the pipe organ at our church in Madison, too."

"Might she be willing to play piano for our church?" Susan asked, turning to watch Estelle remove the berry pie from the oven. "Estelle, would you? We've had no pianist for years. The old piano just gathers dust."

"She could give music lessons, too," Margie suggested. "Flora has always wanted to play piano."

Flora nodded vigorously, her eyes glowing.

"If Miss Truman wishes to play piano for the church, we would all be grateful. We have plenty of hymnals." Frank watched her work at the counter, keeping her back to the table. "Not that I wish to impose, Miss Truman."

"I shall be pleased to play the pianoforte for Sunday meetings." She laid down a knife and squared her shoulders. "This pie needs to cool for a time before I slice it."

"Let's go sit on the porch and enjoy the evening," Susan suggested.

Dishes clinked and flatware clanked in the tin dishpans as Margie and Estelle hurried to use the last minutes of twilight. Two cats plumped on the kitchen windowsill, tails curled around their tucked feet, yellow eyes intent on the aerial dance of fireflies and bats above the lawn. Stars already twinkled in the pink and purple sky over the small orchard of fruit trees.

Although barnyard odors occasionally offended Estelle's nose, she savored the stillness of a country evening. Perhaps Iowa was a small corner of heaven, for her new life here held an almost magical charm. She found the big boys, Joshua and Alvin, somewhat boisterous and intimidating, though they spoke to her kindly and complimented her cooking. Gangly young Joe seemed aloof, but she suspected he was merely shy. Marjorie treated her like a bosom friend, and little Flora hung on her every word. Susan seemed grateful for her assistance with the housework.

Paul was the only fly in her ointment. *Aunt Bridget, indeed!*

"Tell me what you think of David, Auntie Stell," Margie said, rousing Estelle from her reverie. "Don't you think he's handsome?"

She contrived an honest compliment. "He has kind eyes."

"Doesn't he? Bluer than blue, with those thick yellow lashes. And I love his golden hair and his dimples. He sunburns easily, but in the winter his skin gets white like marble. I call him my Viking."

"I had the same thought." David's parson father required only a Wagnerian opera score to accompany his clumsy swagger.

"Did you?" Margie gave a delighted chuckle. "The pastor looks even more like a Viking with his bushy beard. I was afraid of him when I was little because he's so big and has such a loud laugh, but I soon figured out how kind he was."

Recalling the pastor's sympathetic expression and obvious

efforts to please, Estelle felt a twinge of guilt. There was more to the man than enormous feet and a forceful voice. His sermon that morning had been excellent.

Susan entered, carrying a lamp. "Why are you two working in the dark?"

"Our eyes had adjusted," Margie said. "It didn't seem dark until you brought in the lamp. But now I can see better to wipe off the table. We're almost finished, Mama. David had to leave, so I plan to spend the evening sewing."

"The rest of the family is in the parlor, absorbed in newspapers and checkers. Pastor Nelson said to tell you both good-bye, and he'll see you in the morning, Estelle."

"Isn't he nice, Auntie? I'm so glad you'll be helping him with his book. David says he had about given up on ever finishing it, so you're an answer to prayer. You should see the pastor's study—papers everywhere!"

"It will also be wonderful to have a pianist for our church," Susan said as she placed glasses in a cupboard. "We haven't had one since Kirsten Nelson passed away."

"Reverend Nelson's wife played the piano?" Estelle asked.

"The church piano was hers," Susan said. "You can set those plates back on the china dresser if you like, Estelle. I can never thank you enough for your work around the house. You're a godsend to all of us, and no mistake." She gave Estelle's shoulders a quick squeeze and returned to her task. "I can't recall the last time I felt so rested of an evening."

Estelle couldn't recall the last time anyone had thanked her, let alone hugged her.

"Mrs. Nelson was a nice lady," Margie continued, "cheery and friendly. I remember how she always played hymns so high that no one could sing them. And we sang the same five songs over and over. David says they were the only hymns she knew."

"Marjorie, that is unkind."

"I don't mean it to be unkind. I liked Mrs. Nelson. I sometimes wonder if Pastor should move in with David and me after we marry, to be certain he eats meals and gets his wash done. David says Mary Bilge causes more dirt and mess than she cleans up. She'd probably go back to drinking if Pastor fired her, so he keeps her on."

Estelle hung her apron on a hook and straightened her hair. "If you don't mind, I'll do some sewing tonight as well."

"Of course I don't mind! I want you to teach me how to make piping and those tiny ruffles." Margie caught her aunt by the hand and towed her upstairs.

Chapter 3

Frank shifted a stack of papers from one chair to another, then placed a second stack on top. No, that last pile needed to be separate. He moved it to the first chair and used a rock as a paperweight. When he slid a stack of books aside to search, it tipped. He grabbed at the sliding top book, but it eluded his grasp and landed open on his boot. Then the bottom half of the stack disintegrated and dropped to the floor with successive plops. He juggled two last books, caught one by its flyleaf, and watched the page rip out.

A morning breeze wafted the tattered window curtains, and notes fluttered about the room like moths. A horse whinnied outside. Hoofbeats passed the house. Frank ducked to peer outside. Estelle Truman, regal upon the seat of a dogcart, drove toward the barn.

Frank dropped the flyleaf and abandoned his study. Hearing the screen door slam, Miss Truman stopped her horse and looked over her shoulder. "Good morning, Reverend Nelson."

He took the veranda steps in two strides. "Good morning.

I'll unhitch your horse today. Since you'll be coming regularly, I'll hire a boy to care for him from now on."

"You are kind." A hint of surprise colored her voice as she accepted his assistance to climb down. "Paul says Pepper can be difficult to catch. It might be best to stable him." She reached back to lift a covered basket from the cart.

"On such a fine day, I'll put him in the paddock with Bessie. Don't worry. If he gives us trouble later, we'll bribe him with carrots." Frank grinned, wondering if anything could make her smile.

"If you say so. Shall I begin work in your study?"

"Uh, you might want to wait for me. How about. . .how about you make tea again?"

She lifted one brow. "Most men prefer coffee."

"I like both," he said, stroking Pepper's forehead. The pony began to rub its face against his belly. Miss Truman's eyes followed the motion and widened. She tucked her chin, turned, and walked away, her swishing skirts raising a cloud of dust.

Once his new secretary had entered the house, Frank looked down at his blue plaid shirt and found it coated with horse saliva and white hair. "Thank you, Pepper," he muttered.

Freed of his harness, the pony bucked about the paddock, sniffed noses with the swaybacked mare, then collapsed to roll in the dust. Frank stowed the dogcart in his barn, hung up the harness, and rushed toward the house. Miss Truman must not see his study until he had a chance to pick up that last avalanche.

He stopped inside the kitchen door. The tea tray waited on the kitchen table. A basket of blackberry muffins and a bowl of canned peaches sat beside his filled teacup. Miss Truman poured hot water from the kettle into the dishpan, whipping up suds with her hand. The black cat rubbed against her skirts, purring.

"I brought muffins from home. Flora thought you might enjoy them. I found the peaches in your cellar. While you drink your tea, I'll wash up these dishes. Is Miss Bilge off duty today?"

"She usually shows up late. You don't have to do that." He waved at the dishpan.

"I cannot concentrate in an untidy environment. Tomorrow I shall come earlier to prepare your tea. The morning is already half gone. At the office in Madison, I began work at seven each day."

"And how late did you work?" Frank sat at the table, bowed his head to give silent but fervent thanks, and picked up a muffin.

"Until seven at night. I shall be unable to work that late here, however, for I must help with chores at home." She scrubbed dishes as she spoke. "My mother became accustomed to dining late."

"You prepared supper for your mother after working twelve-hour days?" He polished off his second muffin and took a sip of tea.

"When Aunt Bridget was alive, she cooked. After her death. . ." Her shoulders lifted and fell. "We lived simply." She wiped down the countertops, the stovetop, and the worktable. Sinews appeared in her forearms as she wrung out the dishcloth. Hefting the dishpan, she carried it outside. He heard water splash into the garden.

Only then did she take another cup and saucer from

the cupboard and pour herself a cup of tea. "May I carry this into the study?"

He nodded and stood up. "I'll carry the tray." He didn't want to leave those muffins behind. But then, picturing the study as he had last seen it, he realized there would be no place to set a teacup, let alone a tray. "Wait."

When she gave him an inquisitive look, her eyes were almost pretty.

"Let me go in first and pick up. I. . .had trouble this morning."

"You hired me to make order from chaos, Reverend Nelson. Please direct me to the study and trust me to earn my pay, which, by the way, has not yet been discussed."

"Down the hall and to the right." To the left of the hall lay the parlor, which completed the house's main floor plan. Upstairs were two small bedrooms, and below the kitchen lurked the earth-walled cellar, where she had found the peaches. Not much in this tiny parsonage to interest a cultured woman.

Estelle took a sip of her tea and set the cup and saucer on the table. With a lift of her chin, she swept past him into the hall, her skirts brushing his legs. Belle trotted after her, trilling a feline love song. The study door creaked open. Frank sat down, crossed his forearms on the table, and dropped his head to rest upon them. A silent plea moved his lips.

The screen door slammed, and his heart gave a jolt. Tea sloshed on the table from the two cups, and a muffin fell from the basket. Halfway to his feet, he gaped at Mary Bilge.

"You sick, Preacher?" Her dark eyes scanned the tidy kitchen, the teapot, and the muffins—and narrowed. "Eating sweets at this hour musta soured your stomach. What you need is strong coffee." She filled the coffeepot from the pump, poured in a quantity of grounds from the canister, and clanged the pot on the stovetop. "Reckon I'll put on beans to soak for supper before I start the laundry."

Frank nodded. Beans again. He took another muffin. "No coffee, thanks. I've got calls to make."

"She gonna be here all day?" Mary jerked her head toward the study. Beans rattled into a cast-iron pot. She dropped the empty gunnysack, placed the pot in the sink, and pumped until water gushed to cover the beans.

"Yes. Let me lift that, Mary. You want it on the stovetop?" Frank couldn't sit by and watch a woman heft such a load.

"Yup." Mary grinned at him. "I'll keep an eye out to make sure that woman don't cheat you."

Frank hoisted the pot to the stove. "Want this over the heat?"

"No, it's just gotta soak a few hours. You go on, Preacher. I ain't no city lady with skinny arms and a frozen heart. You can rely on me. I'll do your wash today."

Frank smoothed his hair as he approached the study. Still in the hall, he heard Estelle give a little cough, then the shuffle of papers. "Miss Truman, I have calls to make. I'll be back after midday. Can you cope alone until then?" He closed his eyes while waiting for her answer, feeling like a coward.

"Yes, Reverend Nelson. Remember to wear a clean shirt."

He glanced down at himself and brushed at the imbedded hair. "Of course." *If I can find one.*

Minutes later, he cantered Powder through the stable yard and out the gate. August sun baked his shoulders and wind whipped his cheeks, but for a few blessed hours he was free from controlling women.

First he visited the Dixons and their recovering baby. He prayed over the tiny boy, rejoiced in his increasing strength, and promised to return soon. Althea Dixon gave him a hug and a jar of tomatoes before he left. She reminded him of his own daughter, Amy.

While riding to his next call, he wondered about Estelle. Upon his return, would she resign her position and inform him that his scribblings could never form a book? Would her cool blue eyes mock his pretensions? A confusing blend of fears troubled his heart.

In a sunlit sitting room at the rambling Coon homestead, old Beatrice Coon talked with him at length about family concerns, particularly one great-grandson. "Jubal's boy, Abel, is shiftless and sly. I pray for him every day, as I do for all my loved ones, but I do believe the boy is deaf to the Lord's call. His great-grandfather surely turned in his grave when Abel left college." She dabbed tears from her wrinkled cheeks.

Frank sympathized, well aware that Abel had been expelled from the university. The young man was rapidly becoming a bane to the community as well as a sorrow to the honorable Coon family.

When Frank made noises about heading out, Beatrice protested. "Why so restless today, Pastor Frank? You can't be leaving without reading to me from the Good Book."

Although Mrs. Coon lived with her grandson Sheldon's large and literate family, any member of which could have read to her throughout the day, Frank couldn't deny her request. She rocked in her chair and knitted while he read, and when he did finally say good-bye, she handed him a blue stocking cap with a tassel. "Soon the snows will be upon us, and you'll find it useful to warm places your pretty yellow hair doesn't cover anymore."

His hand lifted to the thinning patch on top of his head, and he returned her grin. "Thanks, Mrs. Coon."

"I made it to match your eyes," she said with a feminine titter. "Can you blame an old woman for keeping a handsome man near using any means she has?"

Freedom from controlling women was a pipe dream. He chuckled, squeezed her gnarled hands, and prayed with her before he left. Being near the feisty octogenarian made him feel young and spry, a rare sensation since the passing of his fiftieth birthday last spring.

As he entered town and approached the parsonage, he noticed the rundown condition of Mary Bilge's house across the way. Mary's personal habits seemed unaffected by her profession of faith. True, she no longer inhabited the saloons, a mark in her favor. But her slovenly attire, cigar smoking, and lack of ambition persisted. Hiring her as housekeeper had been his daughter Amy's idea, a kindhearted attempt to build up Mary's dignity. Instead of dignity, Mary seemed to have developed expectations Frank would rather not think about.

Pepper whinnied a greeting from the paddock. Young Harmon Coon, another of Beatrice's great-grandsons, should arrive soon to hitch up the old pony. Frank trusted the boy to keep his end of the bargain. Those Coons were principled people. A founding family to be proud of, despite their one black sheep.

Frank's laundry waved from the line behind the house, neatly pinned. Shirts, trousers, combinations, nightshirt, all looked. . .clean. Kitchen towels and dishcloths gleamed white under the summer sun.

As he mounted the veranda steps, a pleasant aroma made him stop and sniff. Had Mary baked bread? Maybe the perceived competition from Miss Truman had prodded her into action. Brows lifted, Frank pursed his lips in a soundless whistle and let the screen door slam shut.

He placed the jar of tomatoes on the kitchen counter. "Hello?" Belle, curled on a kitchen chair, lifted her head to blink at him sleepily. Two towel-draped mounds on the countertop drew his attention. He peeked under the towel and nearly drooled at the sight and smell of warm, crusty loaves. Something bubbled on the stove. He lifted the lid of a saucepan to find not beans but a simmering vegetable soup.

Mary Bilge could not create such artistry if her life depended on it. Had she and Estelle fought for control of the house? How would two women fight? Flat irons at ten paces? Rolling pins to the death? The mental image of Belle the cat battling a mangy upstart to maintain her queenly status made him smile. No wonder the cat had bonded with her human counterpart. However—his smile faded—Mary had been here first.

The only way to find out for certain what had occurred was to ask. "Miss Truman?" He pushed open the study door and actually saw carpeting instead of books and papers. His gaze lifted to discover shelves full of books, papers stacked on the desk, and his flighty notes weighted by the rock. The file cabinet stood open, and Miss Truman appeared to be labeling files.

She had removed her jacket. A tailored shirtwaist

emphasized her slim figure. No longer did she look scrawny to Frank. He knew her as a creative powerhouse. How had the woman accomplished so much in one day? And she still managed to look unruffled.

She glanced up. "Reverend Nelson, I require your assistance. I believe it would be helpful to create an individual file for each topic or chapter of your book. As I look over your outline, I see distinct categories which will simplify this task."

His heart thundered in his ears. "You do?"

"Yes. We should also file your published periodical articles along with their research material in case you decide to reuse any of them in your books. My suggestion would be to create a file for each doctrinal issue—eschatology, predestination, divine attributes, and so forth. You may discover a need for further breakdown of these categories, but this will give us a start."

"A start," he echoed. While she continued to describe her system, he moved closer and looked over her shoulder at the miraculous way his stacks of paper fit neatly into her files. She smelled of fresh bread and soap. Although her skin betrayed her advancing age, sagging slightly beneath her pointed chin and crinkling around her eyes and mouth, it looked soft to touch. She must be near fifty, since she was Paul's elder sister. Just the right age.

Her eyes were like diamonds with blue edges, keen and cool, focused on his face. He suddenly realized that she had asked him a question. "Pardon?"

"I asked if you were planning to work on your manuscript tonight. If you prepare a few pages, I'll transcribe them for you tomorrow. I do request that you attempt to write more clearly. Some of your letters are illegible."

"Can you. . .can you write from dictation?"

"Yes, although I find that few people organize their thoughts well enough to dictate good literature." She tucked one last sheaf of paper into the file, slid the drawer shut, and leaned her back against it. Her expression as she surveyed the room revealed gratification. "A promising beginning to our work, Reverend. Tomorrow I shall clean this room before we begin."

The thought of her returning in the morning warmed him clear through. "I noticed the bread and soup in the kitchen. Mary had planned beans for tonight. I don't see her around anywhere. What happened?"

Her long fingers rubbed the corner of the file cabinet, and her gaze lowered. Pink tinged her cheekbones. "I smelled the beans burning and went to stir them. Reverend, she did not rinse the beans, and they had not soaked long enough to soften before she set them to boil. You would have had crunchy beans for supper tonight, along with rocks and sticks."

It wouldn't have been the first time. "And the laundry?"

Her lips tightened into a straight line. "She was washing your clothes without soap and draping them over the line dripping wet."

"So what did you do?"

"I advised her to use soap. She dropped your. . .uh, garment in the dirt, called me some unrepeatable names, and walked away. I have not seen her since."

"So you washed my laundry, baked bread, cooked my dinner, and filed my papers, all while I was away for a few hours. Miss Truman, you will exhaust yourself at this pace."

Her gaze snapped back to his. "Nonsense. I enjoyed myself." Suddenly her color deepened. With a quick lift of her chin, she slipped around him and headed for the entryway. "I had better leave, since my chaperone is missing."

He followed her. "You won't stay for soup?"

Tying her bonnet strings, she glanced up at him then away. "They will expect me at home. The soup should be ready for you to eat. I made it with canned vegetables from your cellar and a bit of bacon."

She opened the front door. Pepper, harnessed to the dogcart, waited at the hitching rail out front. Afternoon light dotted the lawn beneath the trees, and sunflowers bobbed in a breeze. "Good day, Reverend Nelson. I shall return in the morning."

"You'll make tea?" He wanted her to look at him.

"Yes, but you need to purchase more." When she gazed into the distance, her eyes reflected the sky. "You need to bring in your laundry. It should be dry."

"I'll do that. Thank you, Miss Truman."

"It was my pleasure. I'll iron tomorrow." She hurried down the walkway and climbed into the cart. Frank watched her drive away. Almost as soon as she disappeared from view, he set out down the street toward the general store to stock up on tea.

❈

Later, after piling his clean laundry into a basket, he sliced bread and buttered it, then ladled out soup into a truly clean bowl. He spooned a bite into his mouth. Slightly spicy, rich, and hot. Perfect with the tender bread. He ate his fill, then put the rest away for lunch tomorrow. Remembering Estelle at his sink, sleeves rolled up as she scrubbed, he rinsed his supper dishes and stacked them in the dishpan. In a happy daze, he sat and rocked on his veranda until evening shadows fell.

How could this be? A man his age couldn't be fool enough to fall in love with a woman for her cooking. He scarcely knew Estelle Truman, yet his heart sang like a mockingbird every time she entered his thoughts.

"Lord, what do I do now? I don't even know if she's a believer, though she spoke about doctrine with familiarity. She is so serious and. . .and cold." His brows lowered as he remembered Paul's analogy.

Although his memories were fading, he still recalled Kirsten's round, rosy face with its almost perpetual smile. Plump, blond, and talkative, she had been Estelle's exact opposite. No, not exact. Kirsten had been a good cook and housekeeper, too.

"And she loved me," he murmured. "I wonder if Estelle could love me."

Warmth brushed his leg, and a cat hopped into his lap. Belle, of course, purring and almost maudlin in her demand for affection. He rubbed her cheeks and chin, assured her of her surpassing beauty, and stroked her silken body while she nuzzled his beard and trilled. Of course, if he had picked her up uninvited, she would have cut him dead with one glance, growled, and struggled to be free.

"Is Estelle like my cat, Lord? Maybe she'll respond to undemanding affection. How does a man go about courting a woman who's forgotten how to love?" He sighed. "Why do I have the feeling I'm going to get scratched if I try?"

Chapter 4

Cold seeped through the study windows as a late October wind moaned around the parsonage. Frank lifted the new calico curtain to reveal a gray early morning, then settled back in his desk chair with a contented smile. Soon Estelle would come and turn the cold, empty house into a home.

Since she had arrived in August, his life had exchanged confusion for comfort. Organization had never assumed a more appealing form. Even Mary now accomplished work around the house—sweeping, dusting, beating rugs, and laundering. Frank suspected the woman hadn't known how to keep house until Estelle trained her.

And music had returned to the church. From his seat on the platform, Frank could watch Estelle's profile as she played piano for the morning service each week. Since her arrival, people had started requesting a longer song service, Lionel Coon had led the singing with renewed enthusiasm, and attendance had increased until there would soon be need for two Sunday services unless the church could afford to enlarge the sanctuary. Whatever the board decided was fine with Frank. More people heard God's Word each week—that was the important thing.

He occasionally finagled a supper invitation out of Paul and had opportunity to observe Estelle in her brother's household. Frank sought evidence of thawing around her heart, but she seemed as detached and cool as ever. Flora obviously adored her maiden aunt. Did Estelle care at all for the child? Margie raved about her aunt's needlework; Estelle had helped design the wedding gown and the gowns for the attendants. Yet did she derive any pleasure from her accomplishments? Thanks to Estelle's help around the house, Susan had regained much of her strength. Although Susan rained affection and appreciation upon her, Estelle appeared to endure rather than enjoy her sister-in-law's attention.

Only once had Frank witnessed affection from Estelle Truman. Its recipient had been, of all things, Belle the cat. Returning early from a call, he had stopped at the post office, then entered his house quietly, examining his mail. Hearing talk in the study, he had approached and stopped outside the door, amazed to recognize the cooing voice as Estelle's. Loud purring plus an occasional trilling meow identified her companion. Another step revealed the tableau to his astonished gaze. Estelle cradled the fawning creature in her arms and rubbed her face against Belle's glossy fur, wearing a tender expression that stole Frank's breath away.

The floor had creaked, revealing his presence. Two startled faces had looked up at him. Belle leaped to the floor and scooted past his feet. Estelle brushed cat hair from her gown and turned away, but not before he witnessed her deep blush. He could not recall what had been said in those awkward moments.

Would Estelle ever look at him with warmth in her eyes? After all these weeks, he still felt uncertain in her presence. While she no longer openly scorned him, neither did he receive affectionate glances from her. They frequently shared pleasant companionship, sipping tea while discussing the arrangement of paragraphs or catching up on community news. She pampered him with delicious meals and fresh-baked bread. Yet she maintained an emotional distance that discouraged thoughts of romance.

He entertained such thoughts anyway. Kirsten had often accused him of being a hopeless romantic; perhaps it was true. A more hopeless romance than this he could scarcely imagine.

Returning to the present, he flipped through notes for the final chapter of his book. The last chapter. How had it all happened so quickly? Estelle insisted the book had been complete before her arrival; she had simply put his notes in coherent order. He knew better. The book never would have been written without her. How had he survived before she entered his life? He never wanted to return to the colorless, disordered existence he had endured since Kirsten's death.

If he could convince Estelle to marry him, his problems would be over. Well, some of his problems. Actually, marriage often presented a new set of problems. Despite his prayers for God's leading, he hesitated when it came to proposing. Maybe God had been trying to show him that such a union would never work. Or maybe he feared rejection. Estelle might fix her keen gaze on him and question his sanity. His touch might fill her with loathing. With a groan, he crossed his arms and laid his head on his desk.

Oh, to be a cat.

"Reverend Nelson?" He lifted his head and turned, blinking at the embodiment of his dream. "I saw the lamp-light. Did you spend the night here?" Estelle's gaze flickered across his manuscript.

He rubbed his stiff neck and rolled his head and shoulders. "No, I rose early to work. I never heard you drive up."

"It's windy today. Paul says a storm may be coming." When she approached to open the curtains and let in morning light, her full skirts brushed his left arm. "It's cold in here. I built up the fire in the stove. You'd better come into the kitchen until the house warms up. I'll make pancakes if you like, or oatmeal."

"Pancakes, please. And tea, as long as you drink it with me." He followed her to the kitchen. Belle greeted him, winding around his feet. He pulled a chair near the stove, let Belle hop into his lap, and watched Estelle work. Her every movement seemed to him graceful and efficient. Like poetry or music.

While whipping eggs for pancake batter, Estelle glanced at him. "You're quiet this morning. Did you accomplish much work?"

"No. I was thinking about you."

For an instant, her spoon froze in place; then slowly, she began to stir again. After greasing the griddle, she poured four small circles of batter. "Since the book is nearly complete, I imagine my employment here will soon end."

"I don't know what I'd do without you."

She swallowed hard. Once she opened her mouth to speak, then closed it. "I don't understand."

He wanted to stand up, turn her to face him, and

declare his love—but he knew better. Like Belle, she would struggle and growl and resent his advances.

"You have become part of my life. Part of me. I can't imagine a future without you here in my home every day." He rubbed the back of his neck again. "If I have your consent, I want to ask your brother for permission to court you."

She looked like a marble statue: *Woman with Spatula*.

"The pancakes are burning."

Breath burst from her, and she flipped the cakes. "But why?"

He almost made a quip about things burning when they cook too long but thought better of it. "I think you're a wonderful woman, Estelle."

She sucked in a breath and closed her eyes.

Encouraged, he elaborated. "You are accomplished and creative and thoughtful. Out of the kindness of your heart, you have made my house back into a home, so much so that I hate to leave whenever you're here. You've trained Mary Bilge into a decent housekeeper, a miracle in itself. Your list of piano students lengthens daily. Without a word of complaint, you took a disastrous mass of scribbling and turned it into an organized manuscript, possibly worthy of publication."

She snapped back into motion, rescued the pancakes, and poured a new batch, scraping out the bowl. Quickly she buttered the cakes and sprinkled them with brown sugar. "Eat them while they're hot."

"Thank you." He bowed his head, adding a plea for wisdom.

When he opened his eyes and began to eat, she was staring at the griddle. "You don't really know me."

He finished chewing a bite and swallowed. "I want to

know you better. Everything I see, I like. Is there hope for me, Estelle?"

She turned the pancakes. "I need time to think."

"Do you want to take the rest of today off?"

After a pause, she nodded. "I'll clean the kitchen first."

"When you're ready, I'll hitch Pepper."

Frank attempted to work on his manuscript, but concentration was impossible. He needed to be with Estelle, needed to know her thoughts. At last he gave up, saddled Powder, and rode to the Trumans' farm. Susan greeted him at the door, and Paul came from the barn. "What brings you out this blustery day, Frank?" he asked, wiping axle grease from his hands with a rag.

"Come inside out of the cold," Susan said.

Frank stepped into the entry. "I'm looking for Estelle."

Susan closed the door behind Paul and took Frank's hat and scarf. "She came home for a short time and left again. I thought she must have forgotten something; she never said a word."

"Did she take anything with her?" Fear shortened Frank's breath.

"I'll go look," Susan offered, then hurried upstairs.

"You might as well tell us what happened. I can guess, but it's easier to ask." Paul led him toward the kitchen, where Eliza left her warm bed by the stove and came wagging to greet him.

After patting the dog, Frank slumped into a kitchen chair and accepted a cup of coffee. "This morning I told her I planned to ask your permission to court her. She said she needed time to think, so I gave her the rest of the day off."

Paul set his own cup down and sat across from Frank. "You don't want to marry her, Frank. Trust me on this one."

Susan bustled in. "No, no, don't bother getting up; I'll join you in a moment. Estelle's trunk is open, and it looks as if she took something from inside, but her clothing and bags are all here. What happened, Frank? Did you propose to her? I know you're in love with her. I think everyone in town knows."

Heat flowed up his neck in a wave.

"Estelle is a good enough person, I guess," Paul said, "but she would make a poor choice of wife. She closed her heart to love twenty years ago."

"What happened then?" Frank asked.

Paul sipped his coffee and grimaced. "She was engaged to a ministerial student by the name of John Forster. A sober fellow with social aspirations. When the war started, he joined up as chaplain. Made it through the war unscathed, then died of a fever before he could return home. Estelle was furious with God."

Frank bowed his head. "Understandable."

"Yes, but she never got over it. She turned bitter and heartless. When I brought my wife home to meet the family, my only sister rejected her simply because she had worked as a maid."

Susan shook her head. "Now that's not entirely true, Paul. Estelle stood with her parents in public, but before we left, she secretly gave me that heirloom pin of your grandmother's. I think she felt bad about the way your parents behaved, but who could stand up against your father? He terrified me. I can't blame her for bowing to his will."

Paul huffed. "You're too forgiving."

"Can anyone be too forgiving?" Frank asked, turning his cup between his hands.

"Paul, tell about when you wrote to your parents," Susan said.

He sighed deeply. "Around two years ago, you preached a series of sermons on forgiveness, Frank. I wrote to my parents, trying to restore the relationship. Estelle wrote back to tell me that our father had died soon after Susan and I moved away, leaving them penniless. Estelle had been working at a law office all those years to support our mother and, for a time, our great-aunt. Mother never answered my letter."

"And you didn't contact Estelle again until she wrote to inform you of your mother's death," Susan said.

"Which was when Paul came to me," Frank finished the tale, "and asked if I would hire her as secretary. She's had a lonely, disappointing life from the sound of it."

"True, but she didn't have to freeze into herself the way she did," Paul said. "Many people endure heartbreak and disappointment without becoming icebergs. As a child, Estelle was lively, full of mischief, loving toward me. She wept when I went off to war, and she wrote to me faithfully. I told her about my new wife in my letters, and she seemed excited. And then to have her reject us so coldly. . ." Paul shook his head. "She's worse now than ever."

"I think she is afraid to love," Susan said.

"I think she's angry at God," Paul insisted.

"I think I need to find out the truth from her," Frank decided. "Thanks for the coffee. I'll hunt for her around town. I have an idea where she is."

Chapter 5

F rank let Powder gallop toward the church. Gray clouds scudded across the vast sky. With the fields harvested, a man could see for miles. A raucous flock of crows passed overhead and faded into the distance. Wind tugged at Frank's hat, trying to rip it from his head.

The church's white steeple beckoned as if promising refuge. As Frank expected, Pepper dozed in the shed out back, still hitched to the dogcart. When the wind shifted, tempestuous music filled the air.

Frank opened the church doors and slipped inside. The music increased in volume again when he opened the sanctuary door. Estelle sat at the piano, her sheet music lit by tapers in the instrument's folding candle racks. Her strong hands flew over the keys. Frank thought he recognized Beethoven, a violent piece. Its intensity covered his footsteps until he could slide into a seat four rows behind her. When the song ended, she turned a few pages and played a yearning sonata, then moved on to several complex and stirring works of art. After a pause, she performed a hauntingly romantic piece. The music flowing from her fingers brought tears to Frank's eyes.

As the last notes faded away, she clenched her fists beneath her chin and hunched over.

"I've never heard anything more beautiful," Frank said.

Estelle hit the keyboard with both palms as if to catch herself. Instantly she jerked her hands up to end the discordant jangle and glanced at Frank over her shoulder. "I didn't hear you enter." She checked the watch pinned to her shirtwaist, exclaimed softly, closed her book, and slid the felt keyboard cover into place. "How long have you been here?"

Frank rose and approached the piano. "Not long enough. Whatever you were playing there was powerful. Music for the soul."

Estelle avoided his gaze. "Thank you."

"I felt, while listening, that at last I was seeing and hearing the real Estelle."

"Your wife played. Does it bother you to hear me play her piano?"

He rubbed one hand across the piano's top, then brushed dust from his fingers. "Kirsten never played like you do. Her music was cheery and uncomplicated, a reflection of her personality. Your music is rich and passionate, a reflection of your soul."

With shaking hands, Estelle began to gather up her music. "That was Schubert, not me."

He lowered his voice. "Paul and Susan told me about John Forster's untimely death. Paul believes you're angry with God. Susan believes you're afraid to love. I wonder if both are correct."

She paused. "If they are, my feelings are justified."

"Tell me."

Her oblique gaze pierced him. "Why should I?"

"As I said this morning, I want to know you. And I think you need to talk. Anything you say is confidential; I will tell no one."

She breathed hard for a few moments, staring at the keyboard. "John didn't die in the war," she said with quiet intensity. "God took him from me. Then my parents rejected Susan, so Paul went away hating me. Then my father died of a heart attack, leaving behind debts that consumed his entire fortune. For twenty years, I slaved in an office to support my mother and my great-aunt, who spent the remainder of their lives complaining about my insufficient provision and warning me never to trust a man."

Frank could easily picture them, having encountered human leeches before. "Did your mother never work? I remember when Paul learned of your financial ruin—long after the event, I'm sorry to say. He told me how socially ambitious and dependent your mother was and wondered how you managed her."

"Mother took to her bed years ago, though she was not truly ill until last winter. Doubtless you will think me a monster, but I have shed no tears since her passing. Her death came as a blessed release, as did Aunt Bridget's demise ten years earlier. The last person I mourned was my father, the model husband and father, who betrayed us all by keeping a second family on the far side of town. The other woman made her claim after his death."

Frank's jaw dropped.

"I did not want to believe her assertions, but once she proved my father's infidelity, I did right by my five half brothers and sisters. They are all grown men and women by now; at the time, they were helpless children."

"Does Paul know any of this?"

"No. When it occurred, I was unaware of his location. He contacted us a few years ago. Mother refused to acknowledge him, so I wrote to him secretly."

"He told me what happened when he brought Susan home with him after the war."

"She had been a housemaid. Far too good for any of us Trumans, actually." Estelle closed her eyes. "At the time, I thought it my duty to uphold my parents' decision, but Paul will never forgive me. Oh, life is unpredictable and cruel!" Her voice broke.

"The people who should have loved and protected you failed you, Estelle." Frank spoke softly. "I understand your anger and your bitterness. I've had a share of heartbreak in my life, but unlike you, I've also had people who loved me faithfully."

"The only people who might have loved me, God took away."

"That's not entirely true."

She glared at him. "Now I'm to hear the sermon about God's faithful love."

Frowning to conceal his hurt, he rubbed his beard. "I didn't know I annoyed you so much."

He heard her sigh. "I apologize. That accusation was unkind and unfair. Your Sunday sermons challenge my mind, as does your book, yet often when you preach, I hear only riddles and contradictions. 'God's plan of salvation is simple,' you say, yet as I work on your manuscript, I am overwhelmed by the complexity of the Christian creed."

"I thought you understood."

Shaking her head, she watched her fingers fold pleats in her skirt. "Aunt Bridget told me that my salvation lay in religion and duty. I have done my best, but sometimes the loneliness is too much to bear."

"Good works cannot regenerate your sinful spirit or mine. Our righteousness is as filthy rags in God's sight. He must transform us from the inside out."

"But what if He doesn't?" The pain in Estelle's expression tore at his heart. "I do believe that Jesus is God's Son, sent to earth to die in my place, but my belief seems to make no difference. What if I'm not one of His chosen ones?"

Frank prayed for the right words. "Belief involves more than an intellectual acceptance of fact. It involves acknowledgment of your unworthy condition, surrender of the will, dying to self. If you come to Him, He will certainly not cast you out."

Emotions flickered across her face—longing, defiance, resolve. "You say God is love and God is all-powerful. If He is both, how can there be sin, deceit, murder, and ugliness in this world? Why do innocent people suffer? Why doesn't God allow everyone into heaven if He loves us all so much?"

"We're all sinners. One evidence of God's love is that He doesn't simply give us what we deserve—eternal damnation. Instead, He offers everyone the opportunity to love and serve Him or to reject His gift of salvation."

She nodded slowly.

Encouraged, he continued, "Each day of your life you choose between good and evil, as do the murderers and liars and adulterers of this world. Our choices affect the people around us, and the more those people love us, the more deeply they are affected. You have chosen a life of isolation rather than to risk the vulnerability that comes with love." As soon as the words left his lips, he knew he'd made a mistake.

Shaking visibly, she leaped to her feet and poked her forefinger into his chest. "You have no right to judge me!"

He bowed his head. "It's true. I have no right to judge; only God has that right. For a man who makes his living with words, I'm bad at expressing my feelings. Because I care, I want you to share the abundant life God gives, but the choice is yours to make."

She folded her arms across her chest and stared at the floor. "You ask me to risk everything by loving a God who has never yet shown Himself worthy of my faith."

"The request for your faith comes from God, not from me. He said a Savior would come to earth, and He did; we celebrate that kept promise at Christmas. He said He would die for us, and He did; we commemorate that sacrifice on Good Friday. He said He would conquer death and rise again, and He did; we rejoice in that triumphant victory at Easter. You can trust Him to keep His promises, Estelle. He desires your love and trust enough to die for you."

Estelle's head jerked back. "I need to go home."

Frank swallowed hasty words and bowed his head. "Yes, it grows late. I'll follow you home."

Outside, the wind knifed them with the chill of winter. Estelle clutched her shawl around herself and gasped. Frank closed the church doors. "You need more than a shawl in this wind. We can stop at the parsonage for blankets and coats. I think we might get snow overnight."

He took Estelle's hand and led her back to the shed where the horses waited. Without protest, she let him tie

Powder up behind the dogcart, climb in beside her, and drive through the dark churchyard to the main road. Wind whipped trees and scattered leaves across the road.

"Hang on to me, if you want," he offered, raising his voice above the wind. She immediately gripped his arm and buried her face against his shoulder. He grinned into the gale.

When Pepper stopped in front of the parsonage, Frank heard Estelle's teeth chattering. "Come in for hot tea before I take you home." He rubbed her unresisting fingers. "Your hands are like ice."

"But it's nearly dark," she protested.

"Just for a moment." He helped her from the cart. Within minutes, he was stoking the fire in the oven and filling the kettle. Seeing Estelle shiver, he hurried to find blankets.

When he returned, she was pouring tea. Lamplight turned her eyes to fire as she glanced up. "I hope Susan doesn't worry."

"I told her I would find you. She won't worry." He accepted his teacup and pulled two chairs close to the stove. "Wrap this blanket around your shoulders and soak up that warmth. We can't stay long, you're right, but I want to feel heat in your hands before we head home."

She nodded and obeyed, huddled beside him beneath a quilt. "I shall consider what we discussed at the church," she said. "I plan to read the Bible while looking for the principles you laid out in your book. Until tonight I thought them mere dogma, intellectual pursuits, and I privately mocked your insistence upon applying scripture to everyday life."

He sipped his tea to conceal his reaction to the affront.

"I shall pray for insight as I read." She laid her hand on his arm and peered up into his face. "Reverend Nelson, I must thank you for taking time to hear my tale and offer your sage advice. I understand why your parishioners seek your counsel. You are a man of many gifts that were not immediately evident to me."

He swallowed the last of his tea and stood up. "We must be off. Wrap up in that quilt, and I'll bring another for your feet." She had met and exceeded his one criterion—warm hands. The imprint of her hand would burn on his arm for hours to come.

"Thanks for bringing Estelle home, Frank," Paul said while Susan poured hot coffee. The four sat near the glowing oven in Susan's kitchen. "You can sleep on the sofa tonight. I already told Josh to stable your horse. It's no night to be on the road."

"I appreciate the shelter." Frank studied Estelle in concern while speaking to Paul. "That wind held an awful bite. Wouldn't be surprised to see snow on the ground come morning." Would she take ill from exposure? He had tried to protect her from the wind, but she still looked pale.

Paul frowned. "Estelle won't be returning to the parsonage. You can bring work here for her. From all I've heard, the book is nearly ready to submit to a publisher."

Estelle's head snapped around. "I most certainly will be working at the parsonage. I need access to the files. Why should Reverend Nelson have to bring my work here?"

"Because your situation has changed. Frank is courting you; therefore, it is no longer appropriate for you to work in his house. A minister must observe proprieties, perhaps even more carefully than most people do."

Frank barely concealed his surprise and dismay. He had interpreted Paul's earlier discouraging comments as a refusal of his courtship request. When had the story changed?

Estelle met Frank's gaze across the table. "But what will you eat?" As soon as the words left her lips, she flushed and looked away.

"Eat?" Paul said, glowering at Frank. "Is my sister a secretary or a cook? I don't like the sound of this."

"Now, Paul, I'm certain they have behaved properly," Susan inserted gently as she handed out steaming cups of coffee. "Don't jump to conclusions."

Embarrassment and frustration built in Frank's chest. "Thank you, Susan. You can rest assured that nothing untoward occurred while Miss Truman worked at the parsonage, but I respect Paul's decision. I don't mind bringing work here until the book is complete. I can drop by each morning before I make calls, and we can discuss progress and objectives then. I'll still pay her to complete the job."

Later that night, Frank wedged his frame into the confines of the hard horsehair sofa. Between the effect of strong coffee and the discomfort of a chilly parlor, he knew sleep would be long in coming, so he prayed. *Lord, I know now why I had no peace about proposing to Estelle. I was wrong to blurt out my feelings today, but at least we had our first meaningful discussion of You, and I know where she stands. I can't say I'm happy with the situation, but knowing is better than living in the dark.*

He rolled to his side, pulled a quilt over his shoulders, and felt a draft on his feet. *Much though I would like to, I can't blame my present dilemma on Paul. Today I, a minister of the gospel, declared my love to an unbeliever, and now we are officially courting. Calling myself all kinds of a fool also leaves the problem unsolved. What can I do? If I withdraw my offer of love, I'll be one more person letting her down. If I don't, she'll be expecting me to court her. . . .*

Chapter 6

Weeks passed, and Estelle's life again settled into a routine. Frank stopped by the Truman farm each day before beginning his round of calls or planning his sermons. He behaved like a pastor and friend; no hint of the ardent lover reappeared. Estelle began to wonder if he had changed his mind about courting her. Not that she intended to marry the man, of course. But as revisions on the book neared completion, she realized how much she would miss seeing Frank each day when he no longer had a reason to call.

Thanksgiving Day arrived. David joined the Truman family, but Frank traveled to Des Moines to visit his daughter, Amy, and her husband. Estelle helped prepare the Truman feast and took part in the family celebration, struggling to conceal her loneliness. When had Frank's presence become essential to her contentment? This need for him alarmed her. She needed to make a complete break if she was to maintain emotional independence.

One morning in mid-December, Frank dropped by as usual. Shaking snow from his overcoat, he let Estelle take his hat. "I brought out the cutter this morning. Winter is here to stay. Which reminds me, will you join me for the Christmas sleigh ride this year?"

Estelle hung his hat over his scarf. "Christmas sleigh ride?"

"You haven't heard about it? The sleigh ride is a Coon's Hollow tradition—when we have enough snow, that is. It's an unofficial event; people ride up and down the main streets and out into the countryside. Some of the young fellows have races, but us older folks prefer a decorous pace. My little cutter carries two in close comfort. I'll bundle you up with robes and hot bricks, and we'll put Powder through his paces." He looked into her eyes and smiled.

Despite the pastor's flushed face and disheveled hair, Estelle found him appealing. For the moment, her emotional independence diminished in value. "I shall be honored to join you."

His dimples deepened, and his eyes sparkled. He caught her hand and squeezed gently. "Soon we need to have another serious talk, Estelle." He glanced around, and Estelle became aware of Joe and Flora chatting in the kitchen. "Privacy is scarce these days."

Tightness built in Estelle's chest. Desperate to escape its demands, she pulled her hand from Frank's warm grasp and focused on the portfolio beneath his arm. "Did you make revisions on the final chapter?"

He blinked, and the sparkle faded. "I did. This next week

I plan to read through the entire thing, and if no major flaws turn up, I'll mail it off to Chicago. My brother, who pastors a large church there, spoke with an editor who happens to attend his church. It seems this editor is eager to see the manuscript. I didn't seek these connections, but apparently God has been making them for me."

Hours later, Estelle lifted her pen and stared at the final page, revised as Frank had requested. After just over three months of work, the book was complete. She laid the paper atop her stack, selected a clean sheet, and dipped her pen again. The concluding chapter contained a scripture passage and application she wanted to keep for her own study. Reading Frank's words was the next best thing to hearing his sermons, and writing them down fixed them into her memory. Lately his explanations of Bible passages seemed clearer, though she still often found herself perplexed.

Eliza, lying across Estelle's feet beneath the table, moaned in her sleep and twitched as if chasing a dream rabbit. Estelle rubbed the dog's white belly with the toe of her shoe.

She paused to flex her fingers and stare through the kitchen window. Where green lawn had once met her gaze, blindingly white snow now drifted in gentle waves. She imagined skimming over the snow in a cutter, snuggled close to Frank beneath warm robes, and a smile teased her lips. Often lately she sensed a hazy, tantalizing possibility, as if someone offered a future of beauty and hope but kept it always slightly out of her view.

Rapid footsteps entered the kitchen. "Would you care for a cup of tea, Auntie Stell?" Margie offered. "How is the book coming?"

"Thank you, yes," Estelle said. "My fingers need a rest.

Have you finished sewing on the seed pearls?"

"Almost. They are perfect on the headpiece. I still can't believe you gave them to me."

"I removed them from your great-grandmother's wedding gown years ago after moths spoiled it." Estelle gave her niece a fond look. "I can imagine no better use for them."

"A few weeks ago I despaired of finishing my gown in time, but now I believe we'll make it. Only two weeks until my wedding!"

"Fifteen days until Christmas. Flora's gown is ready, and mine needs only the buttonholes."

Margie left the teapot to give her aunt a hug. "You were wonderful to sew Flora's gown, and I can't express how excited I am that you will come out of mourning for my wedding."

Estelle patted Margie's hand on her shoulder. "It has been more than six months since my mother's death."

"Yes, but—" Margie stopped and returned to preparing the tea.

"You've heard that I've worn mourning since my fiancé's death twenty years ago?"

The girl nodded hesitantly.

Estelle pursed her lips and flexed her fingers. "I no longer believe it necessary." Abruptly she picked up her pen and began to write again.

"Here's your tea, Auntie."

Estelle accepted the cup and saucer, meeting her niece's worried gaze. "Thank you, Marjorie."

"You're welcome. Why are you frowning? Did I offend you?" Margie sat across from Estelle and stirred her tea. "I'm sorry if I did."

"No, child. I was preoccupied."

"Thinking about Pastor Nelson?" Margie clinked her teacup into its saucer and leaned forward, resting her chin on her palm and her elbow on the table. "So are you going to marry him? David told me about his courting you. Pa doesn't seem to think you ought to marry him, but I think it would be wonderful! You'd be my mother-in-law, sort of. David says he's been afraid Pastor would let Mary Bilge bully him into marrying her, so he would be thrilled to have you as a stepmother instead."

"Mary Bilge?" Estelle nearly choked. "I hardly think so."

Margie covered her mouth. Her hazel eyes twinkled above the napkin.

"She must be several years his senior." The idea turned Estelle's stomach. "Do you think he might marry her if I turn him down?"

"I hope not! But David says she has turned into a decent cook and bought herself some new clothes. He suspects she's hunting for a husband, and her sights are set on Pastor. Have you seen her at church recently?"

"No. I am usually at the piano before and after services."

"She comes late and leaves early. But no matter how well she cooks or how much better she looks, she's not the woman for Pastor. I think she scares him."

Recalling how he had overlooked Mary's shoddy work, Estelle was inclined to agree. "I taught her to clean and cook," she said, staring blankly at the table. "I felt sorry for her. She resented me, but I had no idea. . ."

"You had no idea he would fall in love with you," Margie said.

Estelle knew her cheeks were flushing. "Nonsense."

Margie chuckled. "And I think you're in love with him, too, though you don't know it yet. How sweet!"

Estelle gathered up her papers and stacked them. "With your wedding date approaching, you are in a romantic state of mind. Reverend Nelson considers remarriage for purely practical reasons."

Smirking, Margie picked up the empty teacups and carried them to the sink.

Falling snow sparkled in the light of Frank's lantern as he hiked home from church one evening humming a Christmas carol. Snug beneath its white blanket, the parsonage welcomed him with a warm glow. He climbed over the buried gate and slogged to the front door. The path would require shoveling come morning, but not even that prospect could dim his joy.

Ever since Estelle had agreed to join him for the sleigh ride, his hopes had been high. Although he seldom spoke with her in private, her questions about his manuscript told him she was seeking God's truth. He needed only to be patient.

Smiling, he burst into song as he stepped into the entryway. "Glory to the newborn King. Peace on earth and—"

"Take off your boots. You're messing up my clean floor." Mary appeared in the kitchen doorway, wiping both hands on her apron.

"Oh, you're still here?" He stated the obvious.

"I baked you a chicken, and it ain't done yet," Mary said and pointed at his feet. "The boots."

After hanging up his coat and hat, he obediently used the bootjack, but his mind rebelled. It was time, past time, to put Mary back in her proper place. Lately she had taken to spending entire days in the parsonage, rearranging and. . .

He didn't know what else she did all day, but he knew it wasn't cleaning. The woman behaved as if she regarded his house as her domain.

He set his jaw and padded into the kitchen. Mary was removing a pan from the oven. As she straightened, he observed pleats across the expansive waist of her white apron. Navy skirts swept the floor, and iron-gray fluff surrounded her head. "What happened to your coat?"

Lines deepened around her mouth. "Got myself two new gowns and warshed my hair nigh on a month ago, and you just now noticed?" Her dark eyes skewered him with a glance.

He floundered for a proper response. "You look cleaner. Quite unobjectionable."

She grunted, sliced meat from the chicken, and slapped it on his plate. "Want preserves on your bread?"

"Please."

She jerked her head toward the cellar door. "Down cellar."

He blinked, then picked up a lamp, lifted the latch on the door, and descended into the clammy hole. Canned fruits and vegetables, gifts from parishioners, lined the wooden shelves protruding from the frozen sod walls. He found a jar of peach preserves and climbed back upstairs. After placing the jar on the table, he folded his arms. "Mary Bilge, it's past time you and I had a talk."

A wave of feminine emotion flitted across her face. She reached up to pat her hair into place. "Yes, Preacher?"

The quick changes in her attitude and expression confused Frank. One moment she was a bad-tempered harridan;

the next moment she became an amiable woman.

"I pay you to fix my meals and clean my house, not to tell me what to do. I don't expect a slave, but I do require respect. If my future wife decides to retain your services around the house, you will need to give her the same measure of respect."

Only her trembling jowls revealed life.

"Mary, I don't want to seem ungrateful. . . ."

She turned around, picked up the pan holding the roast chicken, and dumped it upside down into the sink. Brandishing a wooden spoon, she approached Frank. He looked down into eyes like sparking flints.

"Next time I see that skinny icicle woman, I'll break her in half." With a loud crack, she snapped the spoon in two over her knee.

Stunned, Frank watched as Mary Bilge hauled on her tattered coat, hat, and overshoes and stumped outside through the kitchen door, leaving a rush of icy air in her wake.

Satin gowns in varied shades of blue were draped over armchairs around the parlor. Margie's gown enveloped the sofa, shimmering in snowy splendor. Susan stepped back and reviewed the finery once more. "We'll curl our hair before we leave home and hope the curl lasts until the ceremony. Estelle, I truly don't know how we would have managed without you."

Estelle rested in a rocking chair near the fireplace. "These months since I arrived in Iowa have been the best of my life. I'm grateful to be part of this family."

"My gown is glorious," Margie said, clasping her hands

at her breast and closing her eyes. "I can scarcely wait until David sees me in it tomorrow!"

"And I can scarcely wait to see Auntie Stell in her new gown," Flora added. "We'll be twins." The girl wrapped one arm around Estelle's neck and leaned close. "And we'll be ever so beautiful."

Estelle kissed the child's soft cheek. "Beautiful we shall be, my dear. And humble, too."

Flora giggled. Tapping all ten fingers on a side table, she pretended to play the piano. "Wish I could play the wedding march tomorrow. I can play it really good. Can't I, Auntie Stell?"

"Indeed you do play well," Estelle said. "Your progress has been remarkable."

Susan smiled. "I imagine someday you'll play piano for many weddings, but not this one. Now off to bed, Flora. Tomorrow will be a busy day."

"And the next day is Christmas!" Flora exclaimed. "I hope it snows more and more. Joshua promised I could ride with him for the Christmas sleigh ride this year."

"Oh, did he?" Susan accepted her daughter's good-night kiss.

"He says this year I'm his best girl, and I'm light, so he'll win all the races."

"Ah, the truth comes out." Margie laughed. "Josh is determined to beat Abel Coon this year."

Flora skipped into the hall and thumped upstairs.

Paul entered through the front door in a gust of frigid wind, brushing fresh snow from his shoulders. His ladies shooed him away from the satin.

"I hope it doesn't storm tomorrow," Margie said, her face

clouding. "Any other year I would be thrilled at the prospect of snow for Christmas Eve, but not now. People might not be able to come to my wedding if the weather is bad."

"All you really need is a minister and a groom."

"Papa!" Margie protested.

Paul chuckled. "Last night at home for our girl." He hugged Margie, blinked hard, and cleared his throat. "Best get some sleep, all of you. I'm heading up to bed."

"You're right, Papa. Good night, Mama. Good night, Auntie Stell." Margie followed her sister and her father upstairs.

Susan took Margie's empty chair. "It seems like a dream. My little girl will be married tomorrow."

"She'll make a good wife for David. She took me to see her house last week. Such a lovely home it will be." Estelle gazed into the fire.

"You needn't envy her, Estelle. You'll make the parsonage into a lovely home, I imagine."

Estelle fanned her face. She had never been one to blush, but everything seemed different since her arrival in Iowa. "I never intended to marry."

"I believe Frank never intended to remarry, but then he met you. And tasted your cooking."

Estelle met Susan's twinkling gaze. "You believe he wishes to marry me for practical reasons."

Susan laughed aloud. "Not for a moment. He loves you, Estelle."

"I understand practical. I don't understand love."

Susan stared into the fire and spoke in dreamy tones. "Does anyone understand love? Why do I love Paul? Sometimes he annoys me; often I irritate him. Yet we are devoted to each other. God calls Christians to demonstrate love to one another whether we wish to or not. The amazing thing is that feelings often follow actions. I was afraid to love you when you first arrived here, Estelle. Yet I resolved to demonstrate God's love to you, and to my surprise, I grew to love you dearly."

Estelle listened in silent amazement.

"Love is perilous," Susan continued. "God knows this better than anyone, for He loves most. At Christmas we celebrate His greatest risk of all. When I think of God the Almighty lying in a manger as a helpless baby, the chance He took for the sake of love quite steals my breath away."

"Chance? God?"

"Yes, chance. For love of you, Estelle, He was mocked, beaten, and brutally killed. Then He conquered death and sin and returned to heaven to prepare a beautiful home for you. He could force you to love Him in return; He has enough power to make you do anything He wants you to do. But He doesn't desire the love of a puppet, so He simply woos you as a lover and longs for you to return His love."

Susan's words burned into Estelle's soul like a hot iron. The pain finally propelled her out of the chair and upstairs, where she lay in bed and shivered for hours.

Chapter 7

Estelle smoothed a calico apron over the skirts of her blue satin gown and glanced around at the other women working to decorate the hotel dining room. Frank's parishioners had leaped at the chance to help prepare the wedding reception for their minister's son. Of course, many of these women had known Margie since her birth. Estelle found the townsfolk's loyalty appealing.

Of particular interest to Estelle was the plump, golden-haired young woman helping Susan arrange table centerpieces—Amy Nelson Syverson. Amy had greeted Estelle earlier with a twinkle in her blue eyes. She must know about her father's intent to remarry, and apparently she approved. The knowledge boosted Estelle's spirits.

Entering the kitchen to see if she could be useful, she discovered several ladies in a huddle. Their concerned expressions roused her curiosity. "Is anything wrong?"

"Nothing serious," Mrs. Isobel Coon said. "We need a few more jars of fruit for an after-dinner sweet, but I suppose we can stretch what we have here to feed fifty people.

If only Loretta hadn't broken—"

"Plenty of fruit in the parsonage cellar."

Estelle recognized that gruff voice. Mary Bilge stood at the huge cast-iron stove, stirring a pot, the old slouch hat pulled down over her eyes. Her change in clothing style had been short-lived.

Mrs. Coon nodded. "Pastor Nelson is probably at the church already, but I'm sure he'd be willing to donate fruit for his son's wedding reception. And the parsonage is just down the street. Where is Amy? Someone ask her to fetch us a few jars of peaches or pears."

Mrs. Fallbrook shook her head. "I saw her and Susan leave. Mary Bilge, would you—"

"No." Mary turned her broad back.

The other ladies blinked at each other, obviously trying to remain pleasant. "Well then, I suppose we must do without." They bustled off to finish their preparations.

Estelle approached Mary. "I can stir that soup while you get the fruit. It'd be a shame to run short of food at David and Margie's wedding reception."

"La-de-da. If you want it, you get it."

Her lips tightening, Estelle nodded. "Very well. I shall. Tell the others where I've gone." She hung her apron on a hook and located her cloak and overshoes. She would have to hurry. Josh had promised to stop by and pick her up on his way to the church.

Estelle left the hotel by the side door closest to the parsonage. A light snow frosted her woolen cloak, but she was able to keep her skirts hoisted above the drifts lining the street. If her new gown became soiled before the wedding, she would never forgive Mary Bilge. The selfish woman!

What had gotten into her lately? She seemed like the old Mary again, even smelling of cigar smoke.

Frank must have shoveled his walk that morning. The front steps were icy but clear. It seemed strange to enter the parsonage uninvited. Belle greeted her in the hallway. "So you are lady of the house today?" Estelle stooped to stroke the cat. A mildew odor from the rug told her that Mary's housekeeping enthusiasm had waned along with her personal cleanliness. Poor Frank.

The kitchen was warm and smelled of something burnt. Restraining her urge to tidy up, Estelle peeled off her gloves and lit a candle at the oven's banked coals. She lifted the wooden latch on the cellar door and stared down into darkness. Stale, frigid air wafted up the steps. "You stay up here, Belle. I don't want to accidentally shut you in. I'll be only a moment."

Her shoes clopped on the wooden risers as she descended into the hole, keeping her skirts from brushing the whitewashed earth wall. Shivering, she scanned the shelves and located two jars of spiced peaches and one of pears. To carry three quart jars and a candle while safeguarding her gown would be impractical, so she hunted for a tote basket. Candle lifted high, she spotted a dusty one on the end of a top shelf.

Just as she reached for it, something banged up in the kitchen and Belle let out a yowl. Dust sifted through between the boards overhead. At that moment, the cellar door shut and the candle extinguished. Estelle spun about and heard the thunk of the latch dropping into place.

"Oh, no!"

Above, the floorboards creaked, and Belle meowed.

Maybe the cat had bumped the door, causing it to close. Feeling her way in the darkness, Estelle hefted her skirts and climbed the wooden steps. She pushed at the unyielding door, then felt for the latchstring. It was missing. A cat would not have pulled it through to the other side.

Someone had shut her in the cellar. Mary Bilge was the only person who knew she had come for the fruit. Mary must have done it. But why? What could she hope to gain by such a petty, senseless act?

Rubbing her upper arms, Estelle sat on the second step down. At least she still wore her woolen cloak. Her gloves lay on the kitchen table, and her overshoes were near the front door. Frank would surely find her soon.

Something furry touched her hand, and she yelped. A mouse? The something scrabbled at the door and gave a soft meow.

Estelle relaxed. "Belle?" She felt along the crack beneath the door and found a paw. The cat was reaching for her. "You scared me." Estelle slid her fingers through the opening and touched a warm, vibrating body, a shadow against the dim slit of light visible beneath the door. *At least I'm not entirely alone. Someone will come after me before the wedding starts. They need me to play the piano.*

She tucked her feet in close and huddled beneath her cloak, resting her cheek against the solid door. "It's cold down here, but I'm sure Frank will find me before I freeze to death, and you're here to keep my fingers warm, Belle. Why would Mary lock me in the cellar? The person she hurts most by doing this is poor Marjorie, who will have no music for her wedding if they don't find me soon." Her voice sounded thin.

Long minutes passed. Aside from Belle's occasional mew and rumbling purr, Estelle heard only her own thoughts. She considered calling for help, but who would hear? The cellar had no windows.

She tried to estimate the amount of time passing. The gray slit beneath the door finally vanished. Would they go ahead with the wedding? She pictured Margie in her gown, gazing up into David's adoring eyes. How lovely the bride would be, and how handsome her young groom!

Trying to ignore the cold, she hummed the wedding march. Outside, snow would sparkle in the lantern light, turning Coon's Hollow into a Christmas wonderland. At the wedding there would be laughter and rejoicing, yet for Estelle the night was silent.

"Why did You allow me to miss Margie's wedding, God?" Despite her disappointment, she couldn't rouse herself to anger. Her recent studies of God's ways and His nature assured her that He allowed nothing to happen without reason. Oddly enough, her soul felt peaceful as her thoughts drifted back over last night's chat with Susan.

"Lately it does seem that every conversation, every argument circles back to the subject of love. Your love for me and my lack of love for others." She spoke just above a whisper. "I arrived here in the heat and light of summer, yet my heart was colder than ice. Now I sit in frozen darkness and feel the warmth of Your love. Your presence, not my circumstances, makes the difference."

Music wafted through her thoughts, and she began to hum, then sing quietly. "Silent night, holy night. Son of God, Love's pure light." She hummed again, pondering the words. "All these years I have denied Your love. I struggled alone in despair when I might have rejoiced daily in the knowledge of You. Because my parents failed me, Paul left, and John died, I quit believing. You offered to share my burdens and ease my load, but I refused You."

Tears welled up in Estelle's eyes, overflowed, and burned her cheeks. "It's not too late for me, is it, Lord? I acknowledge my hopeless condition; without You I am nothing—a selfish, cold, meaningless woman. Love is painful—You know that better than anyone—but I want to live and love and hurt along with You. Forgive my anger and my unbelief, and truly be Lord of my life."

The walls of ice split apart and crashed into the sea of God's love. The floodgates of Estelle's soul opened wide, sweeping away every icicle of bitterness and anger and filling her with living water. For the first time in more than twenty years, she wept cleansing tears of joy.

She must have slept, for the next thing Estelle knew, the door swung away and Frank lifted her into his arms. Still groggy, she felt his brushy beard against her cheek. He trembled as if he were cold, yet his embrace enveloped her in warmth. She rested her face on his waistcoat and patted his shoulder. "Dear Frank, is the wedding over?"

"How on earth did you get shut in there?" he asked, his voice breaking. "We've been looking everywhere for you! I knew something must be wrong when you didn't show up for the wedding, but I waited until after the ceremony to panic. How did you end up in my cellar?" He sat on a kitchen chair and settled her on his lap, rocking her like a child. His big hands pressed her to his chest, stroked her face, tucked her cloak around her, then hugged her again as if he could never bring her close enough.

Light from the lamp on the table glowed in Belle's golden eyes. A moment later the cat leaped into Estelle's lap to join the embrace. "Belle kept me company and warmed my fingers." Estelle tucked a fold of her cloak around the purring cat.

Worry still vibrated in Frank's voice. "I've got to let Paul know you're safe. First tell me what happened. Josh feels terrible; he was supposed to pick you up at the hotel, but when he arrived there, you were already gone."

Estelle told her short tale. "Mary Bilge is the only one who knew where I went. I suspect she shut me in the cellar, but, Frank, please don't confront her about it."

"Why ever not?" His eyes blazed in the lamplight. "You might have frozen to death down there!" He smoothed hair from her temple, and she felt his fingers shaking.

"Nonsense. It isn't that cold, and I'm sure Mary expected you to find me today. Her conduct was spiteful and childish, not vicious," Estelle said. "But poor Margie! Did she walk down the aisle in silence?"

To her surprise, Frank chuckled. "No. Your prize piano student played the wedding march with more animation than accuracy."

"Flora?" Estelle sat up straight.

"Yes, Flora. The child performed well, and Margie seemed as happy as any new bride despite the lack of refinement in her accompaniment."

Estelle laughed aloud. "I would almost suspect Flora of shutting me into the cellar, if she'd had any opportunity. The little sprite undoubtedly enjoyed her chance to shine."

Frank stared.

Estelle touched her face, wondering if she had smeared

dirt on her cheek or nose. "What is wrong?"

"I've never heard you laugh before."

Suddenly conscious of her position on his lap, Estelle pulled away and rose. Belle squawked in complaint and jumped to the floor. "Would you like a cup of tea? I need something warm to drink."

"No, thank you."

She moved the kettle over the heat. "I must tell you something, Frank. You deserve to know."

He looked wary. "I'm listening."

Estelle busied her hands with setting out a teacup. "Although I'm sorry I missed the wedding, I believe the Lord wanted time alone with me."

When she looked up, surprise lit Frank's features. She glanced away, still trying to control her emotions, yet her voice trembled. "I finally understand about love."

"You do?"

A smile broke free and spread across her face. "Oh, Frank, how much I have missed all these years! You tried to explain, but only God could reveal the wonder of His love. I know I can never make up for the years I've wasted, but all the life I have left belongs to the Lord."

He covered his face with both hands. Emotion clogged his deep voice. "I'm so glad, Estelle. So glad." He pulled a handkerchief from his jacket pocket and mopped his eyes, avoiding her gaze.

Her hands formed fists. She hid them behind her back, sucked in a deep breath, and took the plunge. "I would gladly spend the rest of my life with you, Frank Nelson."

He pushed back his chair and arose but remained at the table. "No more anger?"

She shook her head.

"No more fear?"

"Actually, I'm terrified." Her legs would give out at any moment.

He sounded short of breath. "So am I. Dearest Estelle, are you certain you can endure living in this tiny old parsonage with a rustic boor of a minister? You're so genteel and elegant, and I feel like a buffalo around you sometimes. I know my loud voice annoys you, and I leave my clothes lying around and forget to change into a clean shirt or polish my boots. . ."

Estelle dared to look at his face. "Then you need me to remind you. I want to feel needed. The happiest days of my life were the days I spent caring for your home and preparing meals for you. I shall try to be gentle and meek instead of bossy and high-handed."

"And I shall endeavor to be considerate." He folded his arms across his great chest. "Often you remind me of Belle, the way she demands affection only on her terms."

Estelle translated his unspoken question. "You fear angering me with unwelcome attentions?"

He slowly nodded.

She lowered her gaze and pondered the matter. "I have never possessed a demonstrative nature, and adjusting to the demands of marriage may require time. If you can be patient, I shall accustom myself to fulfilling your needs." Her face grew hot.

"I promise the same to you. And now, much though I hate to end this moment, we must consider the needs of our family and friends and assure them all of your safety."

Estelle lost interest in tea. She moved the kettle off the

stovetop. "I have no idea what time it is. Are we too late for the wedding reception?"

"Not at all. The wedding ended less than an hour ago. The food should be hot and plentiful. Let's join the guests at the hotel and announce our own news." He paused, and his brows suddenly drew together. "We do have news, don't we? You will marry me?"

Estelle smiled. "I shall."

His face beamed like a summer sunrise. "I confess I jumped the gun and told Amy about my hopes. She seems to approve of my choice."

"I suspected as much; she was particularly friendly to me. A lovely young woman, Frank."

"I think so." He glowed with pride.

Estelle drew on her gloves. "I hope Paul approves. I know Susan will. Oh! We mustn't forget the three jars of fruit."

"I'll fetch them. You stay out of that cellar until I fit it with a modern doorknob that doesn't lock." Frank tapped her cheek with one finger. His eyes caught her gaze and held. "I love you, Estelle."

"Frank," she whispered, then found herself wrapped in a mighty hug. Her arms slid around him, and she pressed her cheek to his chest. His hand cupped her head, destroying her hairstyle, but she didn't care.

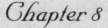

Chapter 8

Christmas morning dawned clear and bright. "No wind yet," Josh announced as the men came in from chores for breakfast, red-cheeked and stamping snow from their boots. "It's a perfect day for a sleigh ride."

Flora squealed and danced a little jig with Eliza frisking around her skirts. "Did you see what St. Nicholas put in my stocking, Josh? An orange, and horehound candy, a penny, and a little doll with a real china head!"

Estelle smiled as she set a dish of fried potatoes on the table. She had purchased the doll head at a shop in Madison many years earlier, unable to resist its sanguine smile. Together she and Susan had completed the doll for Flora and created its miniature wardrobe.

Joe played with his new gyroscope until Paul reminded him that the breakfast table was an improper place for toys. Joe hid it beneath the tablecloth. "Did this really belong to you when you were my age, Pa?"

"It did. Your aunt saved it all these years and brought it for you."

"Thank you, Auntie Stell."

"You're most welcome." Estelle basked in her nephew's approval and his first use of her pet name. She sat beside Susan and passed dishes of food to the other ravenous young men. Not even Margie's empty place at the table caused sadness this glorious Christmas morning. Estelle imagined the young bride preparing breakfast for her young husband at their new home and smiled with satisfaction.

She met her brother's gaze. Paul reached over and grasped her hand. That one gesture expressed his forgiveness and acceptance. Her voice held a sister's lifetime love. "Merry Christmas, Paulie."

"And a blessed Christmas to you, Stell. Having you in our home and full of joy is the best gift I could receive today, I think." After one last squeeze of her fingers, he returned his attention to his breakfast. Noting his heightened color, Estelle let the emotional moment end.

Josh advised Flora to hurry if she still wanted to accompany him on the sleigh ride. Glowing with excitement, the little girl raced through her chores and ran upstairs. Estelle wondered when Frank would arrive. As soon as the kitchen was tidy, she did some primping of her own.

Along with the blue satin gown for Margie's wedding, Estelle had found time to add two new shirtwaists to her wardrobe, one white and one of gray calico with pink sprigs. They would enliven her worn black skirts and jackets until she found time and means to sew more colorful garments.

Regarding her reflection in the small mirror above the dressing table in her dormer bedroom, Estelle coaxed the wisps of hair behind her ears into loose curls. The mere memory of Frank's expression when she removed her cloak at the hotel last night brought a smile to her face. He found her attractive, she knew, and the realization pleased her beyond measure.

At the reception, he had kept her at his side throughout the evening. The most disturbing moment for Estelle had come when she met Mary Bilge's flinty stare. *That poor woman! Something must be done to help her. But what?* She was no worse off than Estelle had been upon her arrival in Coon's Hollow. God could bring joy and love into Mary's life, too, if she would allow it. With a nod at the mirror, Estelle appointed herself to pray for Miss Mary Bilge.

The pin-tucked white shirtwaist Estelle wore contrasted nicely with her black jacket, and a red ribbon at her throat gave it a festive touch. Hearing sleigh bells, she ran to the window. Powder trotted up the drive, blowing twin plumes of steam.

Lest she keep Frank waiting, Estelle hurried downstairs, tying a long scarf over her bonnet and tucking it around her throat. With the addition of her cloak, mittens, and overshoes, she considered herself ready to brave the weather. "Frank is here," she called, patting Eliza's silky black head.

"Enjoy yourself, dear," Susan answered from the kitchen.

Paul leaned against the kitchen doorframe. "Be home before dark," he warned with a twinkle.

"Yes, sir." Estelle gave him a hasty kiss before bustling outside.

Frank tucked her beneath robes and furs, climbed in beside her, and clucked to his horse. "Can't keep Powder standing when he's warm." At first the horse kicked up a frozen spray, but once he settled into his stride, Estelle uncovered her face.

"How beautiful!" Sunlight glittered on rolling drifts of pristine white. Silvery bells jingled with Powder's steady trot. The cold tingled her cheeks and froze inside her nose.

Frank's eyes seemed to reflect the vivid sky as he returned her smile. "Yes, you are beautiful."

Estelle unburied her arm enough to link it with his, then leaned her face against his shoulder. "This is the happiest day of my life."

"So far," he said with a grin. "I passed Josh and Flora on my way."

"They're off to the races, no doubt. I think Flora will be the envy of every eligible young woman in the county. I wonder why Josh hasn't started courting a girl yet," Estelle said.

"I imagine he hasn't found the right one," Frank answered. "I'm glad I waited until you came along."

Estelle snuggled closer. "I approve of your hat. It matches your eyes."

"So I was told by the lady who knitted it for me."

"Lady?"

He chuckled. "Jealous? Beatrice Coon was the lady."

The cutter swept through town, around on a looping county road, then back toward the Truman farm. Estelle waved at each sleigh they passed, recognizing chapped and smiling faces. David and Margie waved a joyous greeting but didn't pause to chat. Josh and Flora stopped to visit. Their horses pranced in place, steaming with sweat but still raring to go.

"I'm guessing by your smiles that you whipped Abel Coon today," Frank called.

"We beat him by a mile!" Flora shouted back. "But Abel says Josh cheated because I'm his sister and can't be his best girl."

Josh grinned. "He thought up that rule too late to do him any good this year."

Frank laughed. "Are you on your way home?"

"Yup. Got to give Chester and Sandy a good rubdown and some hot mash. They earned it today. Merry Christmas, and congratulations, Pastor Nelson. My aunt will make you a great wife." Josh winked at Estelle and clucked to his fretting horses.

"Good-bye," Flora called, and Estelle blew her a kiss.

Frank jiggled his reins, and Powder trotted on. "Amy and Bradley chose to remain at the parsonage today," Frank said. "Their best gift to me this year was the news that I'm to become a grandfather next summer. I hope you don't mind marrying a grandfather."

Despite his teasing tone, Estelle detected a hint of anxiety underlying his question. "As long as I get to be a step-grandmother, I favor the idea. I love babies. Since I can never have a child of my own, I shall treasure the opportunity to love your children and grandchildren."

Powder slowed to a walk. Estelle studied their surroundings. "Where are we?"

"Nowhere. I've been thinking and planning, but for the life of me I can't think of a place we could go today to find some privacy." Leaving his horse to set a moderate pace, Frank turned on the seat, caught her mittened hands, and brought them to his chest.

Estelle's heart thundered in her ears. Frost glittered in his eyebrows and mustache, but his expression warmed her face. His voice wavered. "This is our first Christmas together, and I want you to remember it always with joy." For a long moment, his blue eyes studied her. She saw his lips twitch with emotion and suddenly understood.

"I shall." She was too bundled up to move, so she put one hand behind his head and gently pulled his face toward hers. His frosty mustache tickled, but his lips on hers were surprisingly warm.

He sat back with a pleased smile. "Thank you."

"I love you, Frank."

His smile widened. Giving a little whoop, he snapped the reins and started his stalled horse off at a brisk trot.

JILL STENGL

Jill lives with her husband, Dean, and their family in the Northwoods of Wisconsin. They have four children and a busy life—Tom is an Air Force Academy cadet, Anne is in college, Jim is in high school, and Peter is Jill's last home-school student. Jill loves to write books about exciting times, historic places, and unusual people—and animals somehow sneak their way into most of her stories. Her goal, one of these snowy winters, is to take a real sleigh ride!

Readers may contact Jill at jpopcorn@newnorth.net.

Take Me Home

by Tracey V. Bateman

Dedication

To my sister, Linda Devine.
I love you dearly.

Chapter 1

Coon's Hollow, Iowa—1887

Afrigid wind assaulted Kathleen Johnson the second she stepped off the train onto the boardwalk in front of the Coon's Hollow station. A shiver began at the base of her spine and worked its way to a full-bodied shudder. Apparently Pa's prediction of an unusually frigid winter was coming true. Here it was barely mid-October and the gray clouds overhead seemed suspiciously plump. She wouldn't be surprised if it snowed overnight. Gripping her valise tight with one hand, she pulled her scarf closer about her head with the other and braved the few feet of cold wind until she reached the depot.

The smell of sawdust hung in the air, tickling her nose and throat. She gave a little cough and glanced about, looking for someone who might be looking for her. The telegram from Reverend Nelson had promised that someone would be at the station to collect her upon her arrival. But though she received numerous curious glances, no one seemed inclined to offer her a ride.

With a sigh, she made her way to the ticket booth and placed a gloved hand on the tall counter. "Excuse me, please."

The man glanced up. His brow rose, and his face split into a leer at the sight of her. "Well, well. How can I help you, little lady?"

Barely containing her revulsion at the lecherous tone, she swallowed hard, wishing that Pa or one of her four brothers were here to put this man in his place. The fact that she was on her own now for the first time ever washed over her with startling clarity.

She forced the deepest frown she could muster and raised her chin. "I am looking for someone—"

"Look no farther, beautiful girl," he shot back, his eyes traveling over her face and neck. Kathleen had never been more grateful for her petite height, which in this instance kept everything below her shoulders hidden from his view.

"No, I'm not looking for someone like that." Her face burned, and she wished she could think of a crushing retort, thereby reducing his cocky exterior to a puddle of shame. But as usual, when faced with conflict, words failed her.

He leaned on the counter, his elbow supporting him. His hand shot out and covered hers before she could antic-ipate the move and pull back. "Don't break my heart, honey. I'm looking for someone just like you."

A gasp escaped her lips at his boldness, and she snatched her hand away. He was bordering on more than rudeness. Before she could conjure a thought, rescue came in the form of a puff of smoke and a declaration. "Abel Coon, I've half a mind to tell your pa what I just overheard.

Bet your ma'd beat the tar outta ya, iffen she was still kickin', God rest her soul."

"Mind your own business." The man scowled over Kathleen's shoulder.

Kathleen whipped around and nearly passed out at the sight of her savior. The woman—at least she guessed it was a woman—wore a man's overcoat that hung open, revealing an ill-fitting brown dress. A fat cigar hung from thin lips, and a wide-brimmed hat rested on her mop of gray hair. Her broad forehead and large nose made her look rather masculine, and sagging jowls reminded Kathleen of her family's bulldog, Toby.

Abel gave a loud, pointed cough. "No smoking in the depot, Mary."

"It'll take someone a lot tougher than you to stop me, you little pip-squeak."

Though Kathleen was a bit taken aback by Mary's habit as well, she couldn't help but be glad the woman didn't obey the despicable flirt behind the counter.

Mary snatched the cigar from her lips and held it between her fingers as she sized Kathleen up. "You the new teacher?"

"Yes, ma'am."

"Thought so." She gave a curt nod. "The reverend sent me to take you over to the school, though why I do favors for the likes of him. . ."

Relief coursed through Kathleen. "Oh, thank you, Mrs. . . ."

Without asking, the woman reached out and took Kathleen's valise. "*Miss* Bilge, for now."

"Oh, are you soon to be wed, Miss Bilge?"

Abel's laughter echoed through the station. "In a pig's eye."

Miss Bilge's manly face turned scarlet, and she scowled at the ill-mannered young man. "Shut up, Abel. I don't see no gals takin' you up on any offers lately."

He reddened, and Mary Bilge nodded her satisfaction as she turned her attention back to Kathleen. "I ain't engaged, formally. But that don't mean I ain't willin' if the right fella came along. That's why I said I'm a *miss* for now."

"I see." Bewildered, Kathleen left her response there. Fortunately, Miss Bilge seemed ready to move on. She glanced about the floor, then looked back to Kathleen. "This your only bag?"

"Yes, ma'am."

She gave a loud snort, adding to her already unladylike demeanor. "Must not be plannin' to stay very long."

Kathleen once again felt her cheeks grow warm. "Well, I was. . ." What could she say? The astute lady was pretty much right. Her presence in Coon's Hollow was a trial run. First time teaching. First time away from home. Biting her lip, she fought the approach of hot tears.

Thankfully, Miss Bilge nodded in understanding, making it unnecessary for Kathleen to elaborate. "Ya want to make sure a town like Coon's Hollow is where you want to hang your hat permanently before you bring anything more than can fit in this here bag? Can't say as I blame a young thing like you. The last gal barely stayed a month."

Well, that explained the need for a quick replacement. The head of the Rosewood school board happened to be brothers with a member of Coon's Hollow's school board. Coon's Hollow had need of a teacher to fill in for the rest of the term. Kathleen's father, who sat on the Rosewood school board, had approached her with the suggestion. Though she hated the thought, she'd agreed to take the teacher's exam and left the results in God's hands. Two weeks later, here she was, shaking from head to toe from nerves and cold, feeling for all she was worth as though she'd bitten off more than she could chew in a million years.

Kathleen swallowed hard as Miss Bilge tossed her valise into the back of a wagon and offered her a hand up.

"Thank you."

The woman walked around to the other side of the wagon and swung herself up, forcing Kathleen to avert her gaze at the flash of a hairy calf as the patched skirt hiked. "Oops." Mary sent her an embarrassed grin and quickly righted her skirt. Kathleen couldn't help but return the smile.

Slapping the reins, Miss Bilge nodded in approval. "You'll do just fine. Don't worry about that Abel Coon. He's all talk. I'm thinking his pa regrets ever teaching him to speak."

Gathering all the bravado she could muster, Kathleen sat up a little straighter. "He didn't bother me. I was just about to put him in his place when you walked up."

"Sure you were. But I'm right proud of you for trying to be brave." She waved to a passerby. "The last gal nearly fainted every time she saw a mouse."

"M—mouse?"

"You scared of those furry little critters, too?"

Kathleen cleared her throat. "I should say not." She should say *so!* "A—are there any in the teacherage?"

"Tons of 'em. They come in from the field out back of the building. But don't worry. They ain't gonna hurt you. Just trying to get out of the cold."

Kathleen shivered as the wind whipped up and shook the wagon. "Well, I certainly can't blame them for that. I wouldn't mind getting out of this cold myself. Are we almost there?"

"It's just at the edge of town."

Kathleen followed the point of Miss Bilge's cigar. Her heart sank as she observed the clapboard structure. She'd expected a whitewashed building with a bell and a porch, like the school in Rosewood. She was sorely disappointed. The roof was straight across over one portion of the building, then slanted downward as though in an afterthought another room had been added. She assumed the afterthought would be her quarters.

Another gust of wind shook the structure, and Kathleen felt her spirits plummet further. It must be freezing inside with walls so thin. How would she ever stay warm? And it was only October. The term ended in two months, so she'd be home for Christmas. She could be brave that long. She hoped.

"Looks like someone built a fire." Miss Bilge's gruff voice broke through Kathleen's thoughts.

"Huh?"

"There's smoke comin' from the chimney."

"Oh, that's a mercy. My fingers are nearly frozen off."

The woman chuckled as she halted the team and hopped down. After wrapping the reins around the hitching post, she grabbed Kathleen's bag from the back. Kathleen stared. "Need help getting down?" the woman asked.

Heat warmed her cheeks. "I–I can do it."

She climbed down, careful to keep her skirt covering her legs. She stumbled a little as she touched the ground. Kathleen gathered her composure and followed Miss Bilge, who was almost to the door.

Suddenly, she was very glad that she'd decided against bringing a trunk. She'd already made up her mind. Coon's Hollow wasn't the town for her. She most definitely would not be accepting a certificate for another term. Lecherous train station men, crazy women who looked and talked more like men, mice in the schoolhouse. She shuddered.

How she wished she'd never agreed to this venture. Mama had warned her that she'd regret it, and as usual, Mama was right. Why had she ever listened to Caleb? Her favorite brother had been wrong in this instance. "Kat," he'd said. "Don't make the same mistake I did. You might find that you don't want to stay in Rosewood forever." At her gasp, he'd hurried on. "Now, don't think I'm not happy with Deborah and my girls, because I am. But maybe I would have liked the chance to make a choice. You have that chance. Take it."

And against her better judgment, Kathleen had taken his advice. Now she missed her family so fiercely it was all she could do to keep herself from bursting into tears. Though they'd said good-bye only this morning, her stomach tightened at the thought of them. Ma would be starting to fix supper, and the two younger boys would be finishing up chores while the two older boys helped Pa in the family-owned livery stable.

"Ya comin', gal?"

Kathleen jerked her gaze from the frigid ground to find Miss Bilge filling the doorway, her cigar a mere stub between her lips.

"Yes, I'm coming."

"It ain't much to look at, but we can get it fixed up in no time."

Kathleen couldn't stifle a gasp at her first sight of the schoolhouse. Every desk, including hers, was overturned, and many were broken. Dirt and mice droppings layered the floor, along with scattered books and tablets.

"What on earth happened?"

"Ain't no tellin'. My guess is a pack of ornery young 'uns with too much time on their hands since there ain't been no school. You can straighten 'em out in no time."

A sigh pushed from Kathleen's lungs. She would need at least a week to ready this room for school, and how would she ever control a group of students who were rowdy enough to cause this sort of damage?

Miss Bilge clucked her tongue and snatched up her valise once more. "Come on, gal."

"Wh–where are we going?"

"Back to the train station. This town ain't for the likes of you."

Chapter 2

At his first sight of the new teacher, Josh Truman nearly dropped the armload of wood he carried. He gaped at the young woman who followed quickly behind Mary Bilge, taking two steps to every one of the older lady's.

The teacher reached forward and took hold of Mary's arm. "Miss Bilge, please wait. I haven't said I want to go back."

A puff of wind caught the teacher's scarf, pushing it back from her face. Josh caught a glimpse of a lovely rounded face and enormous blue eyes. He sucked in a breath and tried to remember where he was. She reminded him of one of those store-bought dolls that Auntie Stell had brought back for his little sister, Flora, when she and the preacher returned from their honeymoon last summer. Only this living, breathing doll was a lot prettier.

He blinked. They sure hadn't made teachers like that when he went to school. As a matter of fact, most of his instructors looked more like Miss Bilge. Except they were all men.

He smiled at his own joke, then frowned as he realized the two women were moving away from the school rather than toward it. Where did that crazy Mary think she was taking the new schoolteacher? "Hey, where are you going?"

Mary snatched her trademark cigar from her mouth and tossed it to the ground, crushing it beneath the toe of her clunky men's boot. "New record for shortest time a teacher stayed. Looks like Wayne Sharpton wins the bet. He said Miss Johnson here would take one look at the schoolroom and hightail it home."

"Bet?" The young teacher's voice squeaked, and she stopped dead in her tracks. "Everyone's gambling about me? But that's. . .that's sinful. Besides, I never said. . ."

Feeling like he'd been kicked in the gut by her distress, Josh hurried to reassure her. "No, miss. Not everyone. Only the most disreputable characters in town."

Mary drew herself up and pinned him with a scowl fierce enough to scare a mama bear away from her cub. "There ain't no call to be insultin'."

Warmth flooded Josh's cheeks. "Sorry, Miss Bilge."

With a disgruntled snort, she hefted the valise she carried to the back of the wagon. "Not as sorry as I am. I lost two bits to that Wayne Sharpton." She shook her head in obvious disgust. "I gotta give up gamblin' on these teachers 'fore I end up in the poorhouse. I figured this one would stay for sure. Just had me a feelin'."

Miss Johnson gathered her dignity and squared her shoulders. "Pardon me for being the cause of your debt, Miss Bilge."

The young woman's offense was lost on Mary. "Debt? Naw, this is cash on the barrel. No one can bet lessen they got the money right then."

"Oh. Well, anyway, I never said I wanted to leave."

Mary squinted. "Don't ya? I thought sure it was all over for ya the second ya saw that wrecked building."

The young teacher hesitated. "While I admit I was a bit taken aback, I am not so easily deterred. I promised my father and the school board that I would teach until the end of the term."

Josh's heart soared. "Bravo, Miss Johnson."

Her eyes widened, and a dimple flashed in her cheek, sending his heart racing faster than at a log-splitting contest. "Thank you," she said, her tone velvety soft.

By the time he found his voice, she touched him lightly on the arm, and he lost it again.

She focused those beautiful, ocean blue eyes on him, nodding toward the wood in his arms. "Are you the one who built the fire in the schoolhouse?"

Josh nodded. "I was just about to go inside and start cleaning up the mess. I'd be honored if you'd allow me to continue with my plan and help get the room ready for classes." He hesitated. "Unless, of course, you've decided not to stay in Coon's Hollow."

"That's very kind of you." She turned to Mary and smiled. "Miss Bilge, I despise gambling as the devil's sport; however, you may just win that bet after all."

❈

Soapy water sloshed onto the plank floor as Kathleen pushed the bucket forward, then crawled after it to the next filthy spot in the room. Mary Bilge lit another cigar—her second in an hour—and stared at Kathleen, her lined face scrunching together as she appeared to be pondering.

Kathleen's face flooded with warmth. She knew the woman suspected that her quick turnabout was in response to Josh's presence. But that wasn't true. The least she could do was stay after the generous man had given of his time to chop firewood and offer to clean. Besides, it wasn't her idea to go back home in the first place, and she had been trying to tell Miss Bilge that very thing when Josh showed up.

Her reason for staying had nothing whatsoever to do with Mr. Josh Truman or his lovely brown eyes that reminded her so much of the dark trunk of the maple tree in her backyard. After all, she had no interest in courting a young man from another county. Mama would just about die if she even considered it. All five of the Johnson children knew they were expected to stay in or around Rosewood when they married, and of the two that were married already, they had, without fail, obeyed. Pa joked that Mama's expectation was similar to God instructing the children of Israel—absolutely no foreign marriages. Mama's word was law in their household.

Another puff of smoke wafted into the air, pulling Kathleen from her thoughts.

"Miss Bilge, things might go much faster if you'd consider lending your assistance." Kathleen hated to be rude, but the woman was making her nervous as she watched and smoked and made silent assumptions.

"Well, la-de-da, missy. I ain't here to work; I'm here to chaperone. If I get myself too wrapped up in cleanin', I might miss something between you two young people."

Kathleen's cheeks warmed. "I assure you, Miss Bilge, you

have no need to concern yourself about that. I've no intention of allowing anything between Mr. Truman and myself."

"That so?" The skepticism in her tone grated on Kathleen.

"Yes, it most certainly is."

"Then how come your voice changed when you spoke to young Josh? And how come you flashed those dimples when you smiled at him? And how come—"

"Why, I did no such thing." Only outrage could have caused her to rudely interrupt her elder, but Kathleen refused to stand by and be falsely accused of. . .flirting.

"Did too." Mary's cigar hung from her mouth as she folded her arms across her chest, stubbornly making a stand for what she believed.

"Okay, fine. Have it your way. But you're mistaken."

"We'll see. . . ."

Kathleen was about to argue further, but the blast of cold air blowing through the door silenced her. Josh stomped into the room, carrying a box of tools.

"Here we go," he said breathlessly. "I'll get started repairing the desks."

"That's very thoughtful of you," Kathleen said, making a conscious effort to keep her voice normal. Instead, it had a ring to it that sounded downright fake.

That Mary Bilge had the audacity to chuckle. Kathleen's ire rose. She sent the woman a glare that served only to make her laugh out loud.

"What's so funny, Mary?" Josh asked, shrugging out of his coat. He held his hands over the stove to warm them.

Kathleen sent Mary a silent plea not to further humiliate her.

CHRISTMAS ON THE PRAIRIE

"I reckon that's my own business," Mary said with a grunt.

Releasing a slow breath, Kathleen gave a grateful smile. Surprise flickered in Mary's eyes, and the hard lines of her face seemed to smooth a bit. She stomped to the door and tossed out her cigar stub, then turned back around. "Well, what are ya standing around gawking for? This here school ain't going to clean itself."

Affection surged through Kathleen. *The old softy.*

Josh brushed his hands together and stood, stretching his back. "That'll have to do for now," he said. He surveyed his handiwork with a sense of satisfaction. He'd repaired four of the damaged desks. The rest were beyond repair and would require rebuilding from the ground up. But he didn't mind. Not if it gave him a few more days to get to know the new teacher.

She smiled at him through a dirt-smudged face. "What a wonderful carpenter you are!"

Pleased embarrassment swept through him. "Thank you. Let's just hope they're sturdy enough."

"I'm sure they are." And to prove her point, she sat in each one and bounced. She grinned up at him. "See?"

Josh laughed out loud. Mary harrumphed. The woman had long since given up trying to help and now sat in the corner, her sharp eyes taking in every move he made. Why she had set herself up as Miss Johnson's watchdog, Josh wasn't sure. But it was apparent the two women held an instant affection for each other.

"Looks to be about suppertime," he mused.

"Oh, I'm sorry I kept you so long, Mr. Truman." Miss Johnson stepped forward and offered her dainty hand. He clasped it gladly, enjoying the smooth warmth of her slender fingers. "Thank you for your assistance. I don't know what I'd have done without you."

Miss Bilge snorted.

Miss Johnson glanced over her shoulder. "I don't know what I'd have done without either of you. You were both sent by God, and I'm truly grateful."

Miss Bilge stood to her full height. "The Almighty would not be sendin' the likes of me to someone such as yourself."

"Of course He would, and He did," the teacher retorted. She grinned and met Miss Bilge across the room. She slipped her arm around the woman's thick shoulders and gave a squeeze. "You're my very first friend here in Coon's Hollow and just like an angel unawares."

For the first time since Josh had known her, Mary Bilge blushed. It wasn't a pretty sight. Rather, she looked like a rabid dog. Her face screwed up, and Josh could have sworn she was about to cry. Instead, she scowled and shook off Miss Johnson's arm. "Angel, my foot." She pinned Josh with her stare. "You takin' her home for supper?"

"Yes, ma'am. If she'll accept the invitation."

"I wouldn't want to impose."

"Mama's expecting you," he assured the girl. "You'd be more than welcome as well, Miss Bilge."

"Thankee kindly, but I got plans. You comin' tomorrow to work some more?"

Josh nodded. "I planned to."

"Fine. I'll be here by nine. Don't come any earlier. Ain't no sense in compromising the girl."

Miss Johnson gasped.

Heat crept up the back of his neck. "Yes, ma'am."

"Well, get on outside and wait in the wagon whilst Miss Johnson cleans up."

Josh couldn't resist a glance at Miss Johnson. Her face was scarlet, and she didn't quite meet his gaze.

"I'll be waiting," he said softly, trying to put her more at ease. "Take all the time you need."

She nodded, and he exited the schoolroom. He whistled a lively tune as he headed toward the livery to pick up the team. He certainly anticipated the drive home. It would be nice to chat with Miss Johnson without the constant glaring from Miss Bilge.

As the wagon jostled up the pocked lane leading to Josh's house, Kathleen surveyed the white two-story home. A large oak tree stood next to the house, its branches encircling one side of the roof as though they were arms of protection.

"Home, sweet home," Josh said, breaking the silence.

"It's lovely." And it reminded her of her own house back in Rosewood. Loneliness clutched her heart.

Josh reined in the horses and hopped down. He walked to her side of the wagon and reached up to her. "May I?"

She nodded. Her stomach lifted with butterflies when Josh's warm hand closed around hers. He kept a firm grasp as she carefully climbed down. When her feet touched the ground, she looked at him, expecting him to release her hand. But he didn't. Instead, he caught her gaze and smiled. "You have the most beautiful eyes I've ever seen, Miss Johnson."

"I—I don't know what to say."

He placed his finger beneath her chin, the slight pressure encouraging her to return his gaze. "I didn't mean to embarrass you."

They were so close, she could feel his warmth. She'd never stood so close to any man other than family members, and her heart began to race. He smelled of wood smoke and fresh air, and she longed to lean closer. Feelings she didn't understand churned inside her. A wish that he would keep hold of her hand, that he would speak to her in that rich voice, that he would keep looking at her as though he never wanted to look away.

Too soon the moment ended as the door flew open. Kathleen jumped, snatching her hand away.

"Josh! You're finally home!" A little girl hopped off the porch, her brown braids flying behind her as she ran toward them. "Mama was just about to send Pa looking for you."

"Well, we're here. Time got a little away from us."

"I'll say." She turned to look at Kathleen. "I'm Flora Truman. Josh is my brother. You the new teacher?"

Kathleen smiled and held out her hand. "Yes, I am. Pleased to meet you, Flora. I'm Miss Johnson."

"I hope you like it here, Miss Johnson." She heaved a sigh. "Most teachers don't."

"All right," Josh said, taking the little girl by the shoulders and gently turning her toward the house. "Let's go inside."

He offered Kathleen his arm. "Don't let her discourage you. Coon's Hollow isn't so bad once you get used to it."

Unable to resist his boyish grin, she slipped her hand through the crook of his arm and smiled. "I can't help but wonder why your teachers seem to leave. It's not unusual for women to fall in love and marry, thus leaving their positions to be wives, but for someone to just leave for no reason, especially in the middle of the term. . ." She shrugged. "I don't know. It seems a little odd to me."

"It's not unusual for women to fall in love with a local man, eh?" He waggled his eyebrows. "Maybe you'll be a one-term teacher, too."

Kathleen's eyes widened, and she gaped as he opened the door and nudged her inside ahead of him.

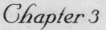

Chapter 3

Flopping onto her stomach, Kathleen tried desperately to find a comfortable spot on the straw tick mattress. She grabbed her feather pillow and hugged it into a ball beneath her head. Only the ping of ice balls hitting her window and the occasional *scritch-scratch* coming from the mouse population inside the building penetrated the vast silence.

After a lovely evening at the Trumans', she had enjoyed her ride home with Josh and Flora. But as they approached her teacherage, dread had clenched her stomach. They'd said a hasty good-bye so that Josh could get Flora home and out of the cold. Then the loneliness had set in, and there seemed to be nothing better to do than go to bed.

But sleep never came. Tears rolled down Kathleen's cheeks, soaking her pillow. She'd never spent the night alone before. Silence permeated the darkness. How she longed for the sound of her brothers' snoring from their respective rooms. The solitude was almost more than she could bear. Mama's words of warning rang in her ears: "Without family around you, Kathleen, you're going to be one miserable young woman. Mark my words."

"Oh, Mama," Kathleen whispered, "you were so right. I should have stayed home where I belong. How will I ever make it here until Christmas break?"

The two months loomed ahead of her as though they were two years. Gentle tears gave way to choking sobs, and finally, just before dawn, only shuddering breaths remained of her sorrowful night.

Despite the gentle light seeping through the cracks in the walls, she was just dozing off when a knock at her door startled her fully awake. Shivering in the cold of the poorly built room, she stepped onto the icy floor and grabbed her dressing gown. She opened the door just a crack.

Miss Bilge stood outside, her arms loaded down with a crate as wide as she was. "Thought you might need some supplies."

Kathleen pulled her wrapper close and peeked at her through the sliver of an opening she'd made when she opened the door. "Good morning, Miss Bilge."

"Well? Ya going to ask me in? Or didn't your ma teach you any manners?"

If it hadn't been so frigid, Kathleen's face would have been hot with embarrassment.

"Yes, ma'am. Come in, please."

Mary shivered and stomped inside. She set the crate on the table and looked about with a scowl Kathleen was beginning to get used to. "Ain't much warmer in here than it is outside. Don't you know how to make a fire?"

"Well, yes, but I haven't had a chance to yet. I just got up."

The woman's gaze swept over Kathleen's attire, and she

nodded. "Never been much of a late sleeper myself. Always get up before the chickens."

Defenses raised, Kathleen could just imagine the whole town thinking their new teacher was a stay-a-bed. "I always get up early, too. I just didn't sleep very well last night."

"Why not?"

"I'm just not used to being alone in a new place."

"Well, go on and make yourself decent while I build up the fire," she commanded, waving Kathleen toward the sleeping part of the room. Kathleen ducked behind the curtain. She dressed quickly and made up her bed. By the time she emerged, Mary's fire was already beginning to warm the room, and the table was set with fresh bread, a jar of milk, and a jar of preserves. Mary had pulled out a skillet and stood over slices of ham sizzling on the stove. She turned when Kathleen emerged.

"That's more like it."

Kathleen's curiosity got the better of her, and she peeked inside the box on the table. Flour, sugar, yeast, a crock of butter, fresh eggs, a slab of salt pork, and a pail of lard were packed together. Also, she'd included some apple butter. "Thank you for the provisions, Miss Bilge. Mrs. Truman was kind enough to fill a crate as well, so between the two of you, I'm all fixed up for a while."

"Weren't me, missy. That Mrs. Nelson sent it over."

"The reverend's wife? How kind. I look forward to meeting her on Sunday."

Mary harrumphed. "Not much to look forward to iffen ya ask me."

Picking up on the fact that she'd struck a raw nerve, Kathleen pushed the issue to the back of her mind to discuss with Josh later and broached another topic.

"How long do you suppose it will take before the schoolhouse is ready for the children?"

Mary forked a slice of ham and lifted it to a plate. She shrugged and reached for the second. "Near as I can tell, you oughtta be havin' school by Tuesday or Wednesday of next week. There's holes in the wall that needs to be patched up. Window's got a crack in it and has to be replaced. I reckon someone'll drive into Taneyville and pick one up. Ain't got no ready-made windows 'round here." She glanced at Kathleen. "I reckon young Josh'll be comin' every day to help out."

Kathleen's stomach jumped at the sound of his name. "He's very kind. But I don't want to impose."

"From the looks of it, you'd have to be rude to get rid of him. It's a funny thing. He's never been smitten before, leastways not that I can recall."

"Smitten? Oh, Mary, really. We've only just met."

Mary cracked an egg into the skillet and nodded back at her. "Well, I've known him since he was born, and I say he took a shine to you from the second he laid eyes on ya. And I don't think he's the only one who's sportin' a shine." Setting a plate in front of Kathleen, she cast a sidelong glance.

"I'm sure I don't know what you mean, Mary."

"Ha! I'm sure ya do."

Kathleen was just about to argue further when Mary silenced her with an upraised hand. "No sense denying it to me. I spent the day watchin' ya yesterday. I wouldn't be a bit surprised if he doesn't come courtin' and the two of you end up at the altar before the school term ends. Guess we'll be losin' another teacher after all."

The delicious picture Mary's words conjured up made Kathleen pause and dream—but only for a minute, as the memory of her lonely, sleepless night returned with aching clarity.

Mary's sharp gaze scrutinized her. Kathleen squared her shoulders and forced a firm tone. "You are mistaken. I do not intend to become entangled with anyone in Coon's Hollow. I am going back home in two months. And I'm never leaving home again."

Chapter 4

S unday morning dawned with warmer temperatures, a brilliant sun, and a return to more fall-like conditions. Kathleen woke much too early from a fitful night's sleep and was ready and waiting a full two hours before Josh arrived to escort her to the worship service. She could feel the stares searing her back as she followed him down the center aisle of the church. The whispers gave way to something akin to a buzzing hive of bees by the time the pair made it to the third row of pews where Josh's family sat.

A man with graying hair and blue eyes, whom Kathleen recognized as Josh's pa, stood and offered his hand. "Nice to have you here, Miss Johnson."

"Thank you." The sight of the large family packed into the pew pinched Kathleen's lonely heart, making her all the more forlorn. Her lip trembled as she smiled at Mrs. Truman. The tiny woman had a kind face, and her returning smile seemed tinged with sympathy. "Are you all settled in, Kathleen?"

"Yes, ma'am. The curtains you gave me last night at

dinner spruced the place right up. Thank you."

"I'm so glad." Warmth exuded from her, and Kathleen began to relax. Mrs. Truman turned to the younger boys sitting on the pew. "Alvin, you and Joe move back a row so Josh and Miss Johnson can sit with us."

Kathleen placed her hand on the woman's arm. "Oh, no. I can sit somewhere else. I don't want to put anyone out."

"Nonsense. They don't mind moving." Mrs. Truman waved toward the boys, who were already vacating the pew. "And you two best behave yourselves, or else."

"Yes, Mama," they replied in unison.

Mrs. Truman sat and moved her legs aside so Kathleen and Josh could slide into the seat. Flora sat next to her mother, and Kathleen took the spot next to the little girl. Josh squeezed in on the other side of Kathleen. His warm shoulder pressed against hers, causing her stomach to jump and her pulse to quicken. She pressed her hands together on her lap, reminding herself that Josh could not be the man for her.

Relief washed over her as Reverend Nelson walked to the wooden podium and greeted the congregation.

Kathleen's face grew warm when he singled her out and introduced her as the new teacher. The townsfolk shifted and murmured but didn't seem all that impressed. She had to wonder what was wrong with being the teacher in this town that they couldn't keep one for a full term.

She didn't ponder the question long, however, as the pastor invited a man to the front to lead the congregation in song. Mrs. Nelson's accompaniment on the piano was as beautiful as any music Kathleen had ever heard. The tinny chords seemed to flow outward from her very soul. Indeed, when the preacher's wife played "Blessed Assurance," tears choked Kathleen's throat, and she couldn't sing along.

Reverend Nelson preached a heartfelt message on the subject of contentment, and even with the distraction of Josh's warm shoulder pressed against hers, Kathleen bowed for the closing prayer more moved spiritually than she'd been in a long time.

Though guilt pricked her at her disloyalty to her own pastor, she had to admit Reverend Nelson's gentle delivery and transparent love for God were more inspiring than Rosewood's eighty-four-year-old pulpit-pounding preacher, Obadiah Strong.

After the benediction and subsequent dismissal, Mr. Truman turned to Kathleen. "I hope you'll come to the farm for Sunday dinner, Miss Johnson. My sister, Estelle, and the pastor will be joining us as well."

Relief washed over her. Her greatest dread had been what she would do with herself for an entire Sunday afternoon alone. She felt a gentle squeeze on her elbow and turned to meet Josh's gaze. He smiled. "Please join us. It would be my honor to escort you home this evening."

"Well, of course she's coming." Mrs. Nelson seemed to have appeared out of nowhere. "If we hadn't accepted Susan's invitation to dinner, I would have insisted the new teacher come have dinner with us. So, Miss Johnson," she said firmly but with a smile, "you must say yes."

"Then yes it is. And thank you for your kind invitation, Mr. and Mrs. Truman." She turned to the preacher's wife and grinned. "And Mrs. Nelson."

As had been the case the previous two nights, dinner at the Truman farm proved to be a noisy, fun affair. Only Josh's younger brother Alvin ate in silence while the rest of the family spoke above one another, laughing and reaching until Kathleen couldn't help but feel right at home.

When the last bite had been eaten, Flora hopped up and tugged at Kathleen's sleeve. "Eliza had puppies. They're so cute. Do you want to see them, Miss Johnson?"

"I suppose so, if it's all right with your ma and pa."

"Not so fast, little girl," Mr. Truman spoke up, placing a restraining hand on the child's arm. "First you have to help your ma clean up."

"I'll help, too," Kathleen offered, seeing the little girl's expression plummet. "Then maybe we can go see the puppies afterward."

Mrs. Truman stood and picked up the empty platter that had been laden with fluffy biscuits an hour earlier. "You'll do nothing of the kind," she said firmly. "As a guest in this house, you are not allowed to lift a finger to help. Josh, please escort Kathleen to the barn and show her the new puppies. Flora, honey, grab a towel and get ready to dry the dishes."

Flora scowled but looked down quickly before her mother noticed. "Yes, ma'am," she mumbled.

Kathleen's heart went out to her, and when Flora ventured a glance, she couldn't resist a wink at the child. Flora's expression brightened considerably, and she scurried off toward the kitchen.

Josh stood. "Shall we go and see the wiggly bunch of mongrels in the barn?"

Mindful of the vast interest coming from the family members still seated around the table, Kathleen felt her cheeks warm. "You don't really have to show me the puppies," she said.

His smile fled. "You don't want to see them? Or you'd prefer to wait for Flora?"

Was it her imagination, or did he seem deflated?

"Oh, no. I'd love to see them."

"With Flora?"

"Or you. I just didn't want you to feel obligated."

"It would be my pleasure to escort you to see the new puppies, Miss Johnson."

His adolescent brother, Joe, snickered. Josh's face tinged with pink, then deepened a shade when even tight-lipped Alvin joined the laughter. Soon, even the pastor couldn't hold back a smile.

Mr. Truman stood and slapped Josh on the back. "If you two don't head on out to the barn, those pups are bound to be weaned and having pups of their own by the time you finally get around to it."

"Yes, sir." His brown eyes seemed to entreat her to hurry and get him out of the humiliating situation.

With a nod, she rose and placed her napkin on the table. "Please excuse me," she murmured to the family without making eye contact with any of them.

She could feel Josh's relief match her own when they were outside, away from the amusement-filled room.

"Your family is quite nice," she said, if for no other reason than to break the heavy silence.

"Thanks. Sometimes they're a bit much. I'm sorry if they made you uncomfortable."

Kathleen laughed. "Being the only girl in a house with four brothers, I'm used to teasing. As a matter of fact, I miss it. So in a way, your family's ribbing helped ease my home-sickness a bit."

Josh reached out to lift the latch on the barn door. "Are you very homesick? You've only been here two nights."

"I've never been away from home before."

He nodded, stepping aside so that she could precede him into the barn. "I suppose I can understand that. Are you sorry you didn't take one look at the school and high-tail it home like Mary suggested? Please don't say you are. I'll be completely crushed if you do."

He grinned, and Kathleen nearly melted into a puddle. She chuckled at his crooked smile but answered honestly. "When I'm around people, I know I made the right decision. But it's difficult for me to be alone. The funny thing is that growing up I always longed for privacy. I often take a book and go down by the little creek that runs through our property and just sit for hours and hours reading and being alone with my thoughts. But now the solitude is almost painful."

As soon as the last sentence left her lips, Kathleen regretted it. She hadn't meant to be so transparent, but Josh's obvious concern combined with her need for conversation had brought the admission tumbling out. Before he could answer, she wandered away from his side and followed the sound of whimpering until she found a scruffy black-and-white mama dog surrounded by wiggling pups.

Approaching cautiously, Kathleen expected the dog to growl. Instead, the animal gave a welcoming whine. Kneeling on the hay, Kathleen reached out and stroked the mama dog's head while the blind puppies whined and nuzzled, trying to find a place to nurse.

"I don't believe it. Only Flora's been able to get anywhere near that dog since she had those pups day before yesterday."

"Well, she knows a friendly soul when she sees one. Don't you, sweet girl?" she crooned. "May I hold one of your babies?" Gingerly, she eased her hand under one of the milk-rounded bellies and lifted a shiny black pup. It trembled until she snuggled it close, speaking in soft, reassuring tones. "Oh, you're just so precious."

Kathleen could feel Josh watching her. She glanced up. Tenderness shone from those wonderful eyes, and his full mouth curved into a smile. "Sort of makes a fellow wish he was a puppy," he said, his voice husky and barely above a whisper.

She blinked. "I beg your pardon?"

"The way you're holding the puppy makes me wonder what it would be like to have your arms around me."

A gasp escaped her lips, and she set the dog down, then scrambled to her feet. Tossing out a look of utter disdain, she stomped past him toward the door.

"Wait, Miss Johnson." He caught up to her and took her firmly but gently by the arm, turning her to face him. "Kathleen, I'm sorry I offended you."

"I do not know what sort of woman you think I am, sir." Kathleen's lip trembled as it always did when she was angry.

"I think you're a fine young lady. And I can't help but admire you. Is that so wrong?"

"In so much that you are imagining my—my arms about you, it is quite wrong." Her voice cracked under the embarrassment. Her mind conjured the lecherous smile from the man at the train station, and her ire rose even higher. "I have never met such ill-mannered young men before in my life. And that's no affront to your ma's raising of you, either. I'm sure she did her best."

Rather than apologizing, Josh planted his feet, releasing her arm. A muscle twitched in his square jaw. "I don't know what sort of men court you back home, but if they don't admit to wondering what it would be like to hold you in their arms, they're just not being truthful."

"Wondering it and saying it are two different things, *Mister* Truman."

"Well, saying it and *doing* it are two different things as well."

He took a daring step closer. Kathleen's pulse sped up like a runaway train. Her thoughts jumbled together. Was he going to try to kiss her? Surely she couldn't allow such a thing. She moistened her lips. Josh's hand slid around her waist, and he pulled her close. A warm woozy feeling enveloped her, rendering her unable to think straight. She barely registered his head descending. Oh, Ma would be mortified. But how could Kathleen resist?

She was just about to close her eyes and surrender to her first kiss when the creaking of the barn door jolted her back to her senses. She leaped from his embrace as Flora skipped into the barn.

"Did you see the puppies? Aren't they adorable? Ma said I can keep only one. But I can't decide which one I like best. Which one do you like best, Miss Johnson?"

"I, um, I don't really know. I only held one." She tried to concentrate on the little girl's words, but Josh's nearness and the memory of what had almost occurred between them had her so rattled, she barely remembered her own name.

"Which?" Flora pressed.

"Um, a black one, I think."

"Oh, I like the black ones. There are two of those."

"Are there?" Why couldn't she take her gaze from Josh's? There was no triumph in his eyes, as one might expect from a young man who knew he'd almost been successful in his quest to steal a kiss. Rather, the look in his eyes nearly stole her breath away. His eyes spoke his respect for her, and only a quick glance to her lips and back to her eyes betrayed his regret that the kiss had been interrupted before it began.

Kathleen felt her own regrets at the moment. Later, however, after Josh, accompanied by Flora and Joe, had escorted her home and she sat alone drinking a cup of tea, she remembered Ma's edict. The Lord knew quite well where Kathleen lived. He was quite capable of sending the right young man to Rosewood. She didn't need to go off looking elsewhere.

Shame infused her. The guilty knowledge that she'd been on the verge of actually allowing a kiss made her squirm. She and her friends had a word for girls who teased the boys: *fast*. The only thing was that it didn't feel like she was being forward. It felt like a cozy fire on a cold day. Like the warm promise of spring as green grass pushed through thawed earth, the budding flowers after a dreary, colorless winter. That's what it had felt like when Josh held her close.

Kathleen shook herself from her thoughts. She had no intention of allowing herself to become infatuated with a boy living outside of Rosewood. How could she bear to be separated from her family permanently when two days away from them seemed like an eternity? She chewed her lip as she pondered the thought. Perhaps Josh would move to Rosewood. He could join Pa and the brothers at the livery.

Kathleen laughed into the empty room. She'd known

him for two measly days, and already she was planning his future for him.

That night, as she crawled into bed, she resolved to banish all romantic thoughts of Josh Truman. She had a job to do, and she would do it well. When her term was up, she'd return home and never, ever leave Rosewood again. If only she could convince herself of that fact. Instead, her traitorous brain insisted on replaying the scene in the barn over and over until finally she drifted into a dreamless sleep.

Chapter 5

K athleen rubbed her arms vigorously, trying to generate heat in the cold schoolroom while she waited for the newly built fire to warm the chill in the morning air. She glanced about with a satisfied nod.

It had taken her, Josh, and Mary Bilge the better part of a week—with the exception of the Lord's Day—to make the school presentable. Now the odor of fresh paint hung in the room, and the walls shone white without a smudge. The single window sparkled, and not a speck of dust could be seen on the desks or floor. And she'd already swept up this morning's traces of mouse droppings.

Kathleen knew pride was sinful, but as she surveyed their handiwork, she couldn't hold back a smile. They had taken a room filled with broken desks and scattered materials from messy to ready in such a short time. She glanced at the watch pinned to her dress and felt her heart pick up a few beats. The children would be arriving soon. Her palms dampened at the thought.

Despite her nervousness, she hoped to discover the reason

Coon's Hollow couldn't seem to keep a teacher for more than half a term. From her admittedly limited experience, the townsfolk didn't seem overly friendly, but neither were they rude—with the exception of the man in the train station upon her arrival. So she had to wonder why there was such a turnover of teachers that the seedier citizens had a running pool every time a new teacher arrived.

A wide yawn stretched her mouth. At least the nervousness served to keep her from dozing off. Sleep still eluded her at night. She had taken to heeding David's psalms. *In the night his song shall be with me, and my prayer unto the God of my life.*

What else was there to do but sing and pray to God when one was completely alone and wrestling insomnia? Sleeplessness was doing wonders for her spiritual life. Unfortunately, her physical body was running down.

Twenty minutes before school was set to begin, the door opened. Kathleen gave a startled glance up. Mary stomped in, her cigar hanging from her lips.

Kathleen scowled. "The cigar, Mary."

"What about it?"

"The children will soon begin arriving. I would rather they not be subjected to the sight of anyone smoking. It sends the wrong signal."

"Smoke signals? Ain't been no Injuns 'round these parts for quite some time. Leastways, none that'd be inclined to send up a signal." Mary cackled at her own joke.

Holding back a smile so as not to encourage her, Kathleen shook her head.

With a sigh, Mary straightened up. "Oh, okay. What sorta signal?"

Kathleen hesitated. She was loath to offend the woman, but neither could she take a chance on one of the children walking in to find Mary smoking in the school. She chose her words carefully. "I'm sure you understand that I can't allow it to appear as though I condone the practice. To children that would send a message that I believe it's all right for them to do the same. I am in charge of this classroom of students, and I must be morally upright."

"Well, la-de-da." Mary snorted but tossed her cigar out the door, then let it bang shut.

Somewhat surprised by the easy compliance, Kathleen gave her a thankful smile. "What can I do for you this morning, Mary?"

"Thought I'd come see how your first day's going."

A smile tipped Kathleen's lips. "Hmm, let me see. I got up, made my bed, and dressed. I ate a little bread for breakfast and wiped off my table. Then I came in here to build the fire. And that's about it so far."

Mary smirked, obviously appreciating Kathleen's humor. "Guess it is a bit early. I best get me on to the preacher's house. That missus of his wants me to scrub down the walls today." She shook her head in disgust. "I think she just does it to see me workin' hard. Like she's lording it over me just 'cause the reverend married her 'stead of me. Ya want to know why he picked her?"

"Why?"

" 'Cause I'm too much woman for him, that's why." She gave a decisive nod. "I just don't know what to say about a man that settles for a woman like that." With a heavy sigh, she clomped toward the door. "I best get on over there before she takes it as a reason to let me go. If they didn't pay so good. . ."

Kathleen stared in bewildered silence. Josh had told her that Mary worked for the preacher and his wife. And that the woman had once locked Mrs. Nelson in the cellar, but no one could prove it, and Mary wasn't confessing.

When she reached the door, Mary turned. "Now don't worry about anything today. If them rapscallions get out of hand, you give 'em a good smack. I'll be around at noon to check on ya and see how things are going."

Affection surged through Kathleen. Now she understood what had prompted Mary to stop by. She knew Kathleen would be a bundle of nerves at the anticipation of the children's arrival. "Thank you for the suggestion. Let's hope it doesn't come to anything more forceful than a stern word or at worst a few minutes in the corner."

"Harrumph. That last teacher didn't believe in corporal punishment, either. And look where she is now. Sometimes a good whack on the behind is the only thing a child understands. Spare the rod and spoil the child. And all that Bible stuff."

The word *Bible* reminded Kathleen of Mary's absence from church on Sunday. Though today was Wednesday, she'd forgotten to ask the woman about it. "Were you feeling poorly on Sunday, Mary?"

"Poorly? Me? No, ma'am, I'm as fit as a fiddle." She narrowed her bushy brows. "Why'd ya ask?"

"I missed you in church."

To Kathleen's surprise, Mary flushed, and pleasure lit the slightly yellowish countenance. "Go on, now. You didn't miss me."

"No, I really did. I don't have many friends in town, and I was looking for a familiar face."

301

"Well, I don't go in for religion much. I gave it a try about a year ago. But that was before. . ."

Before the preacher got married. Though Kathleen was aware of the woman's crush on the preacher, she would no more have humiliated Mary by letting her know than she would have admitted her own crush on the preacher's nephew-in-law Josh.

"It's a shame you stopped going. But it's never too late to return to the house of God."

"So you really missed me, did ya?"

"Yes."

"I might show up on Sunday. If I don't got nothin' better to do."

"That would be wonderful. I'll save you a seat."

A rare smile split the woman's face, showing a surprisingly healthy set of teeth. "You'd do that? Sit next to me and all?"

"Why, Mary, you have a beautiful smile. You should display it more often. And yes, I would be honored to sit beside you during the service."

Mary turned four shades of red, cleared her throat, and frowned. She slapped her man's hat onto her head. "Well, don't get your heart set on it. I said maybe." Without giving Kathleen another chance to speak, she opened the door and paused. "You look out for that Myles Carpenter, now. We think he's harmless enough. But you just never can tell with crazy people."

Before Kathleen could ask what she meant, Mary slipped through the door, slamming it shut behind her.

Kathleen didn't have much time to ponder Mary's warning, as two minutes later the first of a steady stream of students arrived. Boys and girls ranging in age from five to fifteen—a total of twenty-four in all.

Her legs trembled a bit as she called the school to order and the children took their seats, silently watching her. . .waiting for her to speak. She spotted Flora sitting in the second row of desks. Her glossy brown braids were tied with two blue ribbons that matched her eyes. Kathleen smiled, amazed at the difference a friendly face could make in such a nerve-racking situation.

Clearing her throat, she looked from left to right, including each child with her smile. "Good morning."

A scattered mumbling of "good mornings" came in reply. Not a very friendly group. But she'd warm them up in no time. She hoped.

"Let's begin the day by saying the Lord's Prayer. Please stand and remain next to your desks."

The sound of chairs scraping the floor followed as the children rose. Kathleen closed her eyes and took a deep breath as she started the prayer. When they'd finished with "for thine is the kingdom and the power and the glory forever, amen," she opened her eyes, ready to start her first day as a teacher.

By noon, she wished she'd gone back to Rosewood while the getting was good. Now it was too late, despite the unresponsive, disinterested children who barely knew the material. To make matters worse, they were unruly. Jonah Barker had yanked on Flora's braid hard, eliciting a howl from the girl and a retaliatory smack in the face. Kathleen had been forced to stand them both in the corner for thirty minutes. Snickers from the students during arithmetic had confused her until she realized Jonah was making faces at her. She'd

CHRISTMAS ON THE PRAIRIE

commanded him to stand in the back corner where she could keep an eye on him after that.

Now she sat alone eating her lunch of leftover ham between two thick slices of bread. She finished her sandwich all too quickly and stuffed her napkin inside the pail, then glanced at her watch. The children were allowed a full hour for lunch; forty-five minutes remained. She ventured to the window and smiled at the sight of her students playing base-ball in the schoolyard.

Wandering back to her seat, she yawned. Her eyes felt gritty from lack of sleep. The desktop looked so inviting that she folded her arms over the desk and rested her head. What could it hurt for just a few minutes? She closed her eyes and felt powerless as she slowly drifted to sleep.

Josh frowned as he heard the sound of children's laughter. He knew it was half past two because he'd just checked his watch a moment earlier. Why were the children outside?

He pulled into the schoolyard. Flora gave him an uncertain smile. He motioned her over.

"Hi, Josh. How come you're in town? It isn't time to pick me up yet, is it?"

"No. Ma sent me for some sugar at the dry goods store. Why are you outside playing instead of inside learning?"

Flora shrugged. "Miss Johnson never rang the bell after lunch, so David Kirk said we should just keep playing until she came out. Only she never did. I looked inside a little while ago, and her head is down on top of her desk. Sarah Thomas said she might be dead. I'm too scared to go find out." Flora's blue eyes implored him. "You don't think she's dead, do you?"

"Of course not, honey." Concern knotted his stomach. He wrapped the reins around the brake and hopped down from the wagon seat. "You stay outside while I go check on her, okay?"

Flora nodded. Josh recognized the look of worry in her eyes. He patted her shoulder. "Don't worry, sugar. I'm sure Miss Johnson is just fine."

He reached the door and slowly stepped inside. As Flora had said, Kathleen was at her desk with her head resting on her arms. With no attempt to keep his boots from making noise on the wood floor, he clomped up the aisle. His heart nearly stopped until he saw the rise and fall of her shoulders. Then it nearly melted. Tenderness such as he'd never before experienced washed over him. He reached out and caressed her silken cheek with the back of his hand. Still she didn't budge.

"Kathleen," he said, keeping his voice soft so as not to startle her. He squatted beside her. "Kathleen, honey, wake up."

With slow movements, she shifted, sighed, and nestled back into sleep.

Josh smiled and gave her shoulder a gentle shake. "Kathleen."

She moaned and shifted. Then her eyes became slits. In a beat, they opened fully. She gasped and sat up. "Josh!"

"Good morning, sleepyhead."

"Morning? What time is it?" Without waiting for an answer, she grabbed at her brooch watch. "Oh no! The children. Lunch was over an hour and a half ago. Where are they?"

"They're still outside playing baseball. They thought you were dead."

First her eyes widened in horror, but as she observed his

laughter, her own lips curved upward. She lifted her eyebrow. "Baseball, huh? My untimely demise must not have weighed too heavily on their little minds."

He chuckled. "Flora wanted to check on you, but she was too scared to take the chance, just in case you really were dead. You know how young 'uns are."

With a moan, she pressed the heels of her hands against her forehead. "How could I have fallen asleep like that? The school board will be sure to send me packing now."

"I don't think you have to worry about that. It's not as though they'll likely get yet another replacement this term."

A frown puckered her brow, adding to the lines still imprinted from her dress sleeves. "Josh, can I ask you something?"

When she gave him that beguiling, innocently confused look from beautiful blue eyes, she could ask him anything. He swallowed hard and tried to focus. "Sure."

"Why does Coon's Hollow have such a hard time keeping teachers? Pa said no teacher has ever stayed for a second term. And I know I'm taking over for the last one."

Josh stood and shrugged. "I guess a town like this isn't exactly too enticing for a young woman. Plus. . ." He hesitated.

"What?"

"Well, I take it Myles Carpenter didn't show up today?"

"Mary Bilge mentioned him as well, but I don't recall a child by that name."

"Myles isn't a child, except in his mind. He's about seventy."

"Then why would you ask if he showed up at school?"

"Sometimes he gets a little confused and thinks he's the teacher."

At her look of alarm, he hurried on. "He's a little strange but harmless. Unfortunately, he doesn't seem to value cleanliness, so he doesn't look or smell too great."

She wrinkled her nose and shook her head. "That's a shame, but what does it have to do with Coon's Hollow's inability to keep a teacher?"

He took a breath. "Apparently, Myles was once a schoolmaster. Then the War Between the States started, and he left to fight. When he came back, he wasn't the same. His wife welcomed him home, but they never had children. She died about ten years ago. The old-timers say Myles lost what was left of his mind when she passed on."

Pity clouded Kathleen's eyes. "How sad."

"Yes, and most of the teachers feel that same compassion until he orders them from his classroom three or four times." Josh smiled. "The board goes to him, and he promises to behave, but he always ends up back at the school. I've never thought him to be crazy, to be honest. Personally, I think he drinks too much."

"Oh, my. Does he frighten the children?"

"Naw. They're used to him."

"Well, I'll be on the lookout. Thank you for giving me advance warning."

"I suppose I should have told you sooner. But I was afraid you might not stay."

A smile curved her full lips. "I might not have."

He gazed speechless into her eyes, and it was all he could do not to finish the kiss he'd almost started a few days ago in the barn. Obviously, she realized his train of thought, because her eyes grew wide, and she shifted back. "Josh," she said, her voice faltering. "You need to know something."

"Yes?" He couldn't concentrate on anything when she looked at him that way.

"I'm not. . .free to become attached to anyone." Her eyelashes fluttered downward as she studied her hands in her lap.

Feeling like a bull had kicked him right in the gut, Josh winced. "I see. You're already spoken for by someone in your hometown?"

She glanced up quickly. "Oh no. Nothing like that."

Relief shattered the sick feeling of defeat. "Then you're free to be courted properly. You don't have to worry. I can restrain myself as long as we don't spend too much time alone. I won't try to steal any more kisses."

Her face turned several shades of pink. "It's. . .I mean I am free in that I'm not being courted by anyone." She gathered a long breath. "What I meant to say is that I cannot allow myself to become attached to a man who lives so far away from my family. I don't want to live apart from them."

That sick feeling stole over him again as he realized she was saying he had no chance. "I see."

"Do you?" Her beautiful blue eyes implored him to understand.

He was trying. Smiling, he pressed her hand. "Then we'll be good friends? Deal?"

Hesitation shone across her features, and Josh swallowed hard and hurried to add, "You don't want to go to the dance next month all by yourself."

"Dance?"

"Fall dance. We usually hold it earlier in October, but with the teacher leaving so suddenly and all, no one had the heart. It'll be the second Saturday of November."

"I see. Maybe I'll just stay home."

"A girl like you doesn't stay home from dances. Besides, it's held in the schoolhouse." He grinned.

Her lips twitched in amusement. "Maybe I'll go alone."

Josh knew they were playing a game, and he played along. "All right. But without an escort, all the fellows will buzz around and try to court you. You'll be doing an awful lot of explaining about how you're not to court anyone not from Rosewood."

She narrowed her gaze. "Are you teasing me or making fun?"

Tenderly, he knelt beside her and took her hand and pressed it to his heart. "I promise you, I will never make fun of you."

Tears sprang to her eyes, making them look like two clear pools. It was all Josh could do not to move in for a kiss. But she'd made her position clear. He had no intention of letting her go if there was any way to change her mind. But he'd let her get to know him. If he had to be her protector, her friend, until she realized he was the man for her, then so be it. He'd finally found the woman of his dreams, and he'd be a no-good disappointment to generations of Truman men if he didn't try his best to win her love.

Flora took that moment to burst into the schoolroom. "Josh! Come quick! Jonah's beating up Andrew Coon. We can't get them to stop."

Chapter 6

Kathleen fought tears as a paper wad zinged past her ear and smacked the wall behind her. She surveyed the unruly room—proof of her utter failure as a teacher—then allowed her gaze to settle on Flora. The girl stared back, her wide blue eyes clearly asking her why she was putting up with such shameful conduct from the boys.

The answer was that they were big. At fifteen, Andrew Coon was the size of a grown man. She was clearly at a disadvantage, and he knew it. Therefore, ever since the first humiliating day when she'd fallen asleep—had that really only been two weeks ago?—Andrew had essentially run the class. No one was learning, and she could barely hear herself think above the chatter and shouting.

A glance at her clock revealed a depressing one-thirty. Too early to dismiss.

Oh, Lord. What am I going to do?

Outside, the wind howled, shaking the place, and she found herself almost wishing for a blizzard to close the school down for a few days.

"Ow, Miss Johnson, help!"

The sound of Melissa Sharpton's pain-filled cry pulled Kathleen from her fog, and she leaped to her feet. "What is it, Melissa?"

Tears pooled in the eight-year-old's eyes.

Behind her, Andrew cleared his throat. . .loudly.

"Well, Melissa?" Kathleen asked.

"N–nothing."

Kathleen turned to Andrew. Triumph shone in his eyes. Indignation lit a fire inside Kathleen. Clearly the bully was terrorizing the smaller children.

"Andrew, I would like for you to stand in the corner."

"What for, teacher? I didn't do nothin'."

He had a point—she hadn't absolutely caught him. Still, she couldn't back down now. Not if she were ever to have a prayer of regaining control of her class. She planted one hand on her hip and pointed with the other. "In the corner. Now!"

The room became deathly silent. Andrew sneered. "I ain't doin' it."

Out-and-out defiance. Exactly what she'd been afraid of and the very reason she'd failed to confront Andrew thus far. Now what was she supposed to do? "You will obey me, or you will not return to my classroom. Is that clear?"

"Ain't nothin' you can do about it. I'm a Coon."

"I don't care if you're a squirrel. You'll do as I say."

The children snickered at her joke.

Andrew's face deepened to a dark red. "Shut up!" he bellowed. The room fell silent once more.

A gust of wind jolted them from the intensity of the moment. All eyes turned toward the open door. Kathleen gasped as a man—who could only be Myles Carpenter—

walked regally into the room. Though layered in filth and crowned with a thick head of uncombed gray hair, Mr. Carpenter owned the room from the moment he appeared.

"What can I do for you, sir?" Kathleen walked cautiously toward him.

"What can you do for me, young lady? You can control your students, that's what."

At least for the moment, he recognized that *she* was the teacher.

"What was that hollering I heard coming from in here?"

What did she have to lose? If she was going to be criticized by the town crazy man, how long was she going to have her job anyway?

She gathered a deep sigh. "I'm afraid that was Andrew Coon. He is disobedient, rude, and refuses to be disciplined."

The man's gaze narrowed. Then he turned to the classroom. "Which one of you, may I ask, is Andrew Coon?"

Every set of eyes in the room turned to stare at the culprit, but Andrew averted his gaze. Clearly his pride in his name had all but vanished.

But Mr. Carpenter got the hint. His odor trailed behind him as he sauntered across the room, his back straight as an English butler's.

Kathleen gathered the sides of her skirt into the balls of her fists to keep from pinching her nose.

"Stand up, young man," Mr. Carpenter ordered.

With a nervous laugh, Andrew turned his head and stared at the window as though he hadn't heard the man speak. In a flash, Myles's hand shot out. He grabbed Andrew by the scruff of his collar and lifted him to a standing position, knocking his chair back in the process.

"Hey! Turn me loose, old man! Wait 'til I tell my pa."

Despite Andrew's size, Mr. Carpenter had a good three inches of height on him. His strength seemed amazing as Andrew's attempts to free himself failed. "You have a deplorable lack of manners, boy." Keeping a firm grasp on Andrew's collar, Mr. Carpenter turned to Kathleen. "What would you have me do with the lad, miss?"

Kathleen blinked and fought to regain her voice. "I. . .in the corner, please."

"There are four of them; please specify."

Remembering the ridicule from Jonah the first day of school, she knew better than to stand Andrew in the corner behind her desk. She pointed to the back of the room. "Over there."

Mr. Carpenter nodded his filthy head, and Kathleen cringed at the layers of dirt encrusted on his neck. "Good choice," he said.

Laughter buzzed about the room as Myles walked Andrew on tiptoes to the corner. Kathleen looked about and shook her head for them to hush. They complied. Apparently no one wanted to be Mr. Carpenter's next target.

When he reached the corner of choice, Mr. Carpenter simply let Andrew go. "And stay there until your teacher says you may return to your seat. Is that clear?"

Obviously startled into submission, Andrew nodded without turning around. But Mr. Carpenter wasn't finished. "When school is dismissed, you will stay afterward and clean up the mess. It is disgraceful."

Perhaps his last comment was a bit like the pot calling the kettle black; still, Kathleen couldn't help but be grateful to the gentleman.

She expelled a pent-up breath, then wished she hadn't as she was forced to breathe in at the same time Mr. Carpenter returned to confront her. Fighting to contain her nausea, she offered a wobbly smile.

Her cheeks flooded with warmth at his look of utter contempt.

"You must show them who is in charge or you are wasting their time."

Their time?

Though he dwarfed her, she gathered herself to her full height, raised her chin, and looked him in the eye. "Thank you for your help, Mr. Carpenter. I'm sure I can take it from here."

His disparaging look told her more than she cared to know about his opinion of whether she could handle the situation. Nevertheless, he scowled and walked to the door, his shoulders squared. Such a show of dignity touched Kathleen's heart.

He turned when he reached the door. Though his face was caked with grime, his hazel eyes pierced her. "These children have precious few years to learn anything at all before their Neanderthal fathers stick them in the cornfields and squash the greater portion of all that wonderful knowledge from their heads. You must pack as much into their brains as possible, so that perchance they will retain what is most relevant."

He slipped through the door and was gone as quickly as he'd come.

Dread gnawed Kathleen's gut as she glanced toward the corner. At the very least, she expected Andrew to lean against the wall. But to her delight, he stayed put. Perhaps he was afraid Mr. Carpenter was watching from a window somewhere. Or perhaps the stench had rattled his brain. Whatever the case, after thirty minutes, she took pity and quietly suggested he return to his seat. He obeyed, sitting while the rest of the children took their turn at reciting their spelling words.

It was ten minutes after three before Kathleen realized they were over the time for school to be let out. "School is dismissed," she announced. In subdued silence, the children rose, gathered their belongings, and left in an orderly fashion.

She leaned her elbows on her desk, closed her eyes, and rested her forehead in the heels of her hands. Taking a few deep breaths, she willed herself to relax. When the door opened again a minute later, she looked up and gasped. Andrew stood, hands stuffed into his pockets.

She swallowed hard. Was he planning his revenge? Whatever the case, she couldn't show her fear. "Did you forget something, Andrew?"

"Yes." He sauntered up the aisle. He hesitated then scowled. "That crazy ol' Myles told me to clean the room after school."

She'd completely forgotten!

"Thank you for coming back, Andrew. The place is quite a mess."

"Yeah."

"How about if we clean it up together?"

He shrugged but remained silent as they spent the next fifteen minutes removing wads of paper, chalk, pencils, and even crusts of bread from the floor.

"I think that about does it," Kathleen announced.

"Fine. I'm leavin' then."

"All right. And Andrew?"

"Yeah."

"You know we're putting on a Christmas program the week before school gets out."

"What of it?"

"I was hoping you'd consider playing Joseph."

Interest sparked in his eyes, and Kathleen proceeded before she lost her nerve.

"Yes, Rebecca Dunn has already agreed to play Mary."

His face turned three shades of red. "Rebecca?"

A bit of guilt nipped her insides like a troublesome pup. She'd caught Andrew staring at an oblivious Rebecca more than once. She figured he might have a chance if he'd simmer down.

"Yes. I thought the two of you would make a handsome Mary and Joseph. What do you say?"

He kicked at the floor with his boot and shrugged. "Ain't got nothing better to do."

"I take it that's a yes?"

A sigh lifted his chest. "I guess."

"Wonderful. We start rehearsal Monday after school. Please tell your pa to come speak to me if he has any problems with you remaining after class."

"He ain't gonna care." He slipped through the door before Kathleen could press further.

Kathleen stared at the closed door for a few seconds. After one last look at her tidy schoolroom, she adjourned to her quarters for another lonely evening.

"Then he stayed in the corner until Miss Johnson told him he could sit down."

Josh listened to Flora's recounting of her afternoon with a combination of concern and amusement.

"And he didn't order her from her classroom?" Ma asked, setting a platter of ham on the table.

"No, ma'am. He didn't seem all that crazy to me. Just stank real bad."

"Flora! Don't be rude."

"Sorry, Ma. But he did. Bad." She grinned at Josh. "Miss Johnson looked like she might faint. Everyone said so."

Ma cleared her throat, a clear sign that Josh was not to encourage the child.

"Paul, perhaps we should speak to Frank about this. After all, he is the preacher. If anyone should talk to Myles, it should be him."

"How do you figure? Myles hasn't darkened the doorstep of our church in longer than I can remember—not since Frank asked him to kindly take a bath." He winked at Flora. "So that the ladies didn't faint at the smell of him."

Flora giggled, and Ma frowned at them both.

"I suppose you're right about Frank. All the same, someone should talk to him about not interrupting Miss Johnson's class. After all, the young woman is doing us a kindness by taking over at the last minute. How many more teachers are we going to let that man run off?"

"Miss Johnson didn't seem to mind him too much." Joe spoke with a mouthful of potatoes.

"Mercy, Joe," Ma admonished. "Swallow first."

He swallowed hard, then washed down the bite with a gulp of milk. He wiped his mouth with the back of his hand, forked another bite, and held it in front of his mouth. "Miss Johnson was a lot nicer to him than the other teachers ever were." He shoveled the bite inside.

Josh listened to this news with tenderness. Her kindness was only one reason he was falling for Kathleen Johnson.

Still, Ma didn't seem convinced. "Well, the girl's obviously been raised with better manners than some, but that doesn't mean she'll put up with constant interruptions, especially if he gets confused. Someone had better give him a good talking to before he runs her off like all the others." She gave Pa a pointed look, but Josh judged from Pa's scowl that he had no intention of butting into the situation.

Her gaze shifted to Josh.

He nodded. He only had a few weeks to prove to the girl of his dreams that he was the man for her, even if he did live fifty miles away from her family. There was no way he would let an outside influence like a crazy former schoolmaster send her running home even one day earlier than absolutely necessary.

Chapter 7

K athleen shot straight up, unsure why she'd awakened so suddenly. Outside, the wind howled and shook the thin boards. The fire had died down, and the air inside the room bit through her, chilling her to the bone. She pulled the quilt up to her neck and shivered in an attempt to warm herself. Finally, she pushed the covers aside and tiptoed across the icy floor to the stove.

Moments later, wood crackled as the glowing coals caught. Another gust of wind shook the little room.

She shuddered. The clock on a shelf over the stove clearly showed four o'clock. Too early to get up. Yawning, she headed back to her bed.

Thump, thump.

Footsteps? Cold fear swept through Kathleen as the sound in the schoolroom came closer. She eyed the door that separated the two rooms and was suddenly aware of the absence of a lock. She spun around, searching for anything with which to defend herself. Hesitating only a second, she snatched up a large kitchen knife and inched toward the door.

Crash!

Kathleen jumped, her heart nearly beating from her chest. Clutching the knife firmly with both hands, she listened for more sounds. Anything that might mean someone was about to burst through her door. Numbness crept into her feet as she remained barefoot on the icy floor.

Muscles knotted, stomach tight, she waited, and waited . . .and waited until, finally, the fire died again, and she was forced to hang on to the knife with one hand and add wood to the stove with the other. Muted light slowly expelled the darkness from the room, and when Kathleen dared to take her gaze from the door, she noted the clock read seven-thirty.

The children would be arriving for school in less than an hour. How could she cower in her room and allow any one of them to step into a possibly dangerous situation?

Lord, give me courage.

Reaching out with trembling fingers, she grabbed the latch, gathered a deep breath, and flung open the door. A split second seemed like an eternity as she waited for her attacker to strike. When all remained calm, she took a cautious step across the doorway.

A body lay atop the remains of one of the newly repaired desks. She couldn't make out a face, but the stench was unmistakable. Her heart beat a rain dance within her chest as she approached. She grimaced at the thought of having to touch his filthy chest to ascertain whether or not he was breathing. He moaned, and she jumped back.

Relief like a fresh summer breeze washed over her, and her wobbly legs refused to hold her another second. She made it to the last desk and sank into the seat, dropping the knife to the ground.

The clatter woke her intruder.

"What on earth is that racket?"

Kathleen blinked as he sat up, brushing away the splintered wood.

He was asking *her* about racket?

"Well? Speak up!"

"I–I dropped my knife."

"Why, pray tell, do you have a weapon inside the school? You are not fit to teach these children. I knew that from the first moment I saw you."

Tears pricked her eyes, and her throat clogged. What could she say? The man had a point.

She stood, offering him her hand. Ignoring the gesture, he averted his gaze. "Miss, I must insist you go at once and do not return until you are properly attired."

With a gasp, Kathleen realized she was in her nightgown. No dressing gown or house shoes—she'd been too afraid to remember either.

"Oh, my. I am so sorry. Of course. I'll just go and get dressed."

Not until she had changed into her gown and hooked her boots did she realize the irony of Mr. Carpenter scolding her about her appearance. She grinned as she headed back into the schoolroom.

Warmth met her from the fire Mr. Carpenter had built in the stove.

"Why, Mr. Carpenter. Thank you."

"You are most welcome. The desk was beyond repair, I'm afraid."

"I see." She gathered her courage and took a step closer to him. "May I ask why you came to the school at such an hour?"

He looked away. "I beg your pardon, miss. I succumbed to my weakness and visited the saloon."

Kathleen's eyes widened. "Well, you should be ashamed of yourself. But that doesn't explain your presence here."

He shrugged. "The wind was extremely cold, and it was snowing so hard I could scarcely see where I was going. I knew I couldn't make it home, so I came here."

"Oh, it snowed? I best clear a path for the children."

"Don't bother. No one will be coming today."

"What do you mean? It's Tuesday. Of course they'll be here. It's a school day."

"Look outside."

Crossing to the window, Kathleen peeked through a circle Mr. Carpenter had wiped in the frosted glass. "Oh, my. I'm afraid you're right." Not only was the ground covered but heavy snow still fell from the sky.

"Naturally."

With a sinking—and slightly nauseated—stomach, Kathleen realized one more thing: If the children couldn't come to school, Mr. Carpenter couldn't leave.

By noon, the stench was beginning to waft into Kathleen's own living quarters, and she'd had all she could take. The ham she'd sliced for lunch sizzled in the skillet, the smell turning her stomach.

She tossed aside her book and flung open the door. "Mr. Carpenter, we need to talk."

He sat in *her* chair holding *her* book in his dirt-caked hands.

"Yes, miss?"

Her courage faltered, then revived as she thought ahead to the possibility of days and days with this man. "I haven't

all day, Miss Johnson. I would like to get back to this perfectly delightful book." Kathleen recognized Edgar Allen
Poe's name on the spine and rolled her eyes. She shook herself to get back to the matter at hand.

"Mr. Carpenter, I–I am afraid I must ask you—no,
I must insist that you. . ."

He frowned. "Yes?"

"Sir, I beg of you to fill the tub and take a bath."

His eyes sparked as he jumped to his feet. "What?"

Kathleen shrank back from his anger.

"What right have you to insult me, young lady?" He
glared down at her.

"I–I meant no insult."

He seemed not to have heard. "I was born and bred in
Boston, the son of a wealthy merchant. I attended the finest
schools and served as a schoolmaster in this very town until
the war." He banged his fist on her desk, and Kathleen
jumped, tears filling her eyes. "I am entitled to respect. I
will be treated with decency!"

Fearing the wild fury in his eyes, she turned and fled the
room. Once she was safely inside her quarters, she leaned
against her closed door and willed her racing heart to return
to a normal beat. Fat tears rolled down her cheeks. How
could she have been so insensitive? From their first encounter, she had known that beneath Mr. Carpenter's exterior was a great man. She couldn't begin to fathom why on
earth he would choose to live as he did, but wasn't she called
to love him regardless? Would Christ have insisted he take a
bath without taking the time to have a proper conversation?

*Dear Lord, You brought Mr. Carpenter stumbling into the
schoolroom as a blizzard roared. You knew we'd be trapped*

together, and You know how vile he smells. Please give me Your grace, compassion, and love for the man.

She walked to the stove and removed the slightly burned slices of ham from the skillet. She brewed a pot of strong coffee. When it was finished, she poured two mugs full, piled ham between two slices of bread, and returned to the school.

Mr. Carpenter sat in her chair, reading as before. He didn't look up. "I'd like to apologize, sir."

Still no response. Kathleen set the mug and plate before him on her desk. She took a gulp of her own coffee and nearly choked as it scorched her throat. "B–be careful. The coffee's hot."

He glanced up at her, curiosity in his eyes.

There. At least he was responsive. She began again. "I had no right to speak to you as I did. You are a full-grown man of more intelligence than anyone I know, and you have the right to decide whether or not to bathe."

With a grunt, he eyed the sandwich and mug, then turned his attention back to his book.

Heat flooded Kathleen's face. "Well, I guess I'll. . .I guess you don't want company. I can drink my coffee back in my room." Turning, she swallowed back her humiliation.

"Wait, miss."

She turned back. "Yes, sir?"

"You brought only a cup of coffee for yourself. Are you not eating?"

So heavy was the stench, her stomach revolted against the thought. "Uh, no. I'm not very hungry."

He scrutinized her a moment, nodded, and then returned his attention to the book. Feeling dismissed, Kathleen returned to her quarters and picked up her knitting. Her lonely evenings had afforded her plenty of time to stockpile knitted gifts for her family and friends. Now she was determined to knit a stocking cap for each boy in her class and a scarf for each girl—something for them to remember her by when she went back home.

She had just finished another scarf when a knock at her door nearly sent her through the roof.

Mr. Carpenter handed her the mug and plate. "Thank you kindly for your generosity," he said regally. "Now if I may trouble you once more."

"Of course. What can I do for you?"

"I'd very much appreciate the use of a pot with which to collect snow. And the wash tub. And one more thing. Might I trouble you for a blanket to wrap around myself while my clothes are drying?"

Kathleen collected the items he requested and threw in a chunk of lye soap.

"Thank you." He gave her a stern glance. "You must not enter the schoolroom until I return your items. I'm not entirely sure this is appropriate as it is. But for the sake of your appetite, I see no alternative."

Heat scorched her face and neck. "Of course."

She spent the afternoon listening to the door opening and closing more times than she could count as presumably Mr. Carpenter crammed pot after pot with snow to melt and warm on the stove. Thumps and sloshes were her music while she filled another pot with chunks of meat and canned vegetables—the Trumans' latest contribution to her welfare. She whiled away the afternoon, reading off and on, knitting, checking her pot frequently, and watching the clock. Curiosity nearly overwhelmed her at the thought of what Mr. Carpenter would look like absent the grime, though she was highly dubious as to whether he could successfully remove years of dirt.

The sun had set, and the stew filled the room with a tantalizing and most welcome aroma by the time Mr. Carpenter knocked on the door once more.

Kathleen gasped at the sight of him. He handed her the pot. "I apologize for not returning the rest of your items, Miss. The blanket you so generously supplied is soaking in the tub. And the soap is. . .well, I was forced to use the entire block."

"Oh, Mr. Carpenter. You look wonderful!" And she meant it. His skin, though red where he'd obviously scrubbed and scrubbed, was devoid of dirt. His gray hair hung to his shoulders, thick, with just a touch of wave. His clothes, though ragged and damp, were clean. She couldn't help the tears filling her eyes, and she quickly looked away, so as not to humiliate either of them.

"Won't you come inside and join me for supper, Mr. Carpenter?"

"Now, Miss Johnson. Have you no sense of propriety? Bad enough we must share two rooms. A grown man does not enter a young lady's sleeping quarters."

"Of course. M—may I join you for supper in the school?"

He scowled but gave a jerky nod. "Under the circumstances, I believe that would be acceptable. But only because I am old enough to be your grandfather."

Kathleen beamed at him. "I'll dish up our supper and bring it in there lickety-split."

He turned away and headed away from her door, but

Kathleen heard him mumbling, "Lickety-split. It's no wonder children today have such an appalling vocabulary when their teachers use such common speech."

She grinned as she filled their bowls. Who would have thought two unlikely people stranded together in a blizzard would turn out to be such a blessing?

Chapter 8

The blizzard stranded Mr. Carpenter in the schoolhouse for three days. During that time, Kathleen learned a great deal about the man. The torments of war had caused him to retreat into a shell. By the time he had come to his senses, he'd lost all credibility with the town. He sank into despair. Even before her death, his wife had grown so cold, life was nearly unbearable. Mr. Carpenter bore all the blame himself.

One thing she knew for sure: Mr. Carpenter's love of teaching was nothing less than a holy calling. He adored sharing knowledge. Kathleen had made up her mind to discuss his placement as the town schoolteacher next term. She felt certain if the school board spent time with him they would see him as she did—particularly if he resisted the urge to allow himself to go without bathing and abstained from even an occasional visit to the saloon.

By breakfast time on day four, Kathleen and Mr. Carpenter had pretty much run out of things to talk about, so it was with great relief that Kathleen responded to a knock on her door just as she returned the dishes to her quarters.

Mary and Josh stood outside. At least two feet of snow blanketed the area, with drifts as tall as Flora in some places.

"Mary! Josh! Come in. I'm so glad to see you."

Mary grinned, her face red from the cold. She stomped over to the stove and held out her large, rough hands. "Thought ya might be gettin' powerful lonesome."

Kathleen turned to Josh and smiled. "What are you doing in town?"

He smiled back, but his eyes held a serious look that made Kathleen want to run away, to hide from the temptation of falling in love with Josh Truman. It would be so easy to do just that. His kindness and humor drew her, and she'd never known a man to be so self-assured and yet vulnerable, as when he'd professed to having feelings for her so soon after they met. Josh was a rare man, and she knew someday he was going to make a woman very happy. She was almost jealous of whomever that woman would be.

"I hooked the team up to the cutter."

Mary harrumphed. "Rode those horses too fast, if you ask me. Downright dangerous."

Josh grinned, and Kathleen couldn't help but return it. "Sounds wonderful," she said.

"How would you like to go for a ride? I imagine you're just about crazy being cooped up for three full days all by yourself."

A knock sounded on the door between her quarters and the schoolroom just as she was going to explain about Mr. Carpenter. "Miss Johnson? Is everything quite all right in there? I thought I heard voices."

"Who in the. . . ?" Mary flung the door open. Mr. Carpenter gave a little scream and jumped back, fists up ready to defend himself.

Undaunted, Mary advanced. "Who are you? Whaddarya doin' in the schoolhouse, and what have you done to our little girl?"

Mr. Carpenter gaped. "I beg your pardon? I wouldn't lay one finger on that child, and I highly resent the implication."

Mary squinted and peered closer. "Myles?"

"Most certainly. Who else would I be?"

"Well, I'll be. . ."

Kathleen stepped between the two. "Mr. Carpenter came into the schoolroom to get warm just before the blizzard hit. He graciously accepted my invitation to sleep in the school and has been a godsend. If I had not had his stimulating conversation these three days, I would be stark raving mad."

"Well, I'll be. . ." Mary stared at him. "I sure did forgit you was such a good-lookin' fellow, Myles." She glanced back at Kathleen. "How'd ya ever talk 'im into takin' a bath?"

"Why, Mary!"

"Sorry. But we been stayin' upwind from this fellow for years, and here he is in the middle of a snowstorm, smellin' like a dandy. I never would have believed it."

"For your information, Mr. Carpenter asked me for the loan of all things necessary to accomplish a bath, and I merely handed them over and stayed out of his way. The decision was entirely his."

Josh joined the three of them in the school. "You two stayed together for three days?"

Mr. Carpenter drew himself up with all the dignity

he could muster considering his scarlet face—compliments of Mary's loose tongue. "We most certainly did *not* stay together. Miss Johnson stayed in her quarters behind closed doors, and I, a man old enough to be her grandfather, stayed as far back from her door as possible. However, if you feel she has been compromised, I will do my duty and marry her properly, lest her name and reputation be tarnished."

Kathleen gasped as horror tingled between her shoulder blades. Josh placed an arm about her and pulled her away from Mr. Carpenter. Mary scowled. "For pity's sake. That girl ain't been compromised. Now if it had been young Josh on the other side of that door 'stead of you, old man, we might have something to talk about. 'Sides, when this town gets a load of you in your new clean state, there ain't gonna be no other topic of discussion."

Mr. Carpenter looked as relieved as Kathleen felt at the cancellation of possible nuptials. Still drawn into the circle of his arm, Kathleen turned to Josh. Her face was inches from his, and she could feel his breath warm on her face. She swallowed hard in an attempt to compose herself and stepped out of his embrace. "Would you mind giving Mr. Carpenter a ride home in your cutter? He can't walk in this snow."

"I'd be happy to." Josh smiled—the gentle, intimate sort of smile reserved for a man in love. He stole her breath away, and she felt the heat rush to her cheeks.

"Thank you," she whispered.

"Yes, thank you." Mr. Carpenter's voice held just a touch of amusement. The first hint of humor Kathleen had ever detected in the man.

Josh broke eye contact and shifted his gaze to the former schoolmaster. "I'll wait while you get your coat."

The older gentleman cleared his throat. "I am quite ready when you are."

"You're crazy as a loon," Mary said. "It's at least ten below out there. Where's that army coat you been wearin' since '65?"

"The coat has been properly destroyed, as it should have been years ago."

Kathleen realized now what he'd been doing when he built a bonfire during a letup in the falling snow on the second day of their confinement. She walked to her quarters and hesitated only a moment before she peeled back her quilt. She folded it, then hugged it to her chest. As she walked back to the schoolroom, her mind argued with her nostalgic heart. Could she truly bear to part with her quilt? Perhaps Mr. Carpenter could simply cover with it on the way home and then give it back.

As soon as the thought came, she rejected it. In all likelihood, his blankets at home were as filthy as the coat had been. A new quilt would remind him of the dignity he'd acquired during the past three days and possibly discourage him from going back to his old ways. She had other blankets. But she wanted him to have something special to mark what she hoped was a new beginning.

A sudden image flashed across her mind of the beautiful quilt layered in grime. She shook the troubling thought away as quickly as it had come. She was only responsible to be generous. It wasn't up to her to judge what a person did with her gift. She had only to give it cheerfully as unto the Lord.

Mr. Carpenter's brow furrowed when she handed it to

him and mentioned it was his to keep. "I'd like you to have this as a token of my appreciation for keeping me company during the storms. God knew I needed you here. I would have been petrified alone."

Tears misted in his eyes. Reaching forward, he cupped her cheek in his palm as though caressing a beloved child. "It is I who needed you, dear child. You have aptly spoken, in that God sent me here, but it is I who shall forever be grateful."

Impulsively, Kathleen hugged him. He patted her back awkwardly. Miss Bilge blew her nose loudly. "Well, if that ain't the nicest thing. . .well, I just don't know what is."

Josh grabbed Kathleen's hand and squeezed it. He, too, seemed moved by the scene, and Kathleen could almost feel God's stamp of approval as though He had put a period on a well-constructed sentence.

Mr. Carpenter glanced at Josh. "If you are ready, I must be going, young man. My home needs considerable work, and I'd like to get to it."

"Yes, sir. I'm ready when you are." Josh squeezed her hand again. "I'll be back later to take you home, Miss Bilge. And to take you for that ride," he said, his gaze settling on Kathleen in a way that made her pulse leap.

When the men had left, Mary Bilge stared at Kathleen for a long second. "That offer to save me a seat in church still standin'?"

"Of course, Mary!"

She moved her head in a jerky nod. "I guess iffen the Almighty can change a fellow like Myles, there might just be hope for me after all."

Kathleen's lips curved into a smile, and delight rose

in her chest. *Oh, Lord, Your ways truly are so much greater than mine.*

School remained closed for the rest of the week, and each day Josh arrived by noon to take Kathleen for a sleigh ride. On Saturday she packed a picnic lunch. They sat together under a warm lap blanket in the cutter. The sun's rays shimmered across the frozen lake and danced off the icicles hanging from the barren tree branches.

"I'm sorry we missed the November dance." Josh's voice broke a long silence. Each knew this would be their last sleigh ride for a while as school would be back in session on Monday. The mood between them had been somewhat subdued.

"I don't suppose they'll reschedule since the blizzard caused it to be canceled."

Josh shook his head. "Pa said the recreation committee decided two failed attempts were enough, and God must not want it to go on this year for some reason."

Disappointment crept over Kathleen. "I would have enjoyed dancing a waltz with you before I go home, Josh Truman." She tried to keep her voice light, but even she could hear the false gaiety.

He stretched his arm across the top of the seat and cupped her shoulder, pulling her to him. "I would have enjoyed a waltz, too, Kathleen Johnson."

As his face grew closer, Kathleen fought a battle inside. As much as she craved his embrace, she knew it wasn't fair to either of them. She placed her palm against his chest and pushed slightly. "Josh, please. I've already told you that I have to go home in three weeks. Don't make me take the memory of your kiss with me. If I do, how will I ever fall in love with a man in Rosewood?"

A plethora of emotions seemed to cross his face as though he struggled with his next course of action. Finally, he squeezed her shoulder and released her. Kathleen struggled against the feelings rising in her. All the emotions she'd felt over the past few weeks came to the surface, and tears pricked her eyes.

"Ah, Kat, don't cry."

"Kat?" Only those nearest and dearest to her had ever called her by her pet name.

"You don't like it? Kat suits you so well."

She smiled without elaborating. "I like it." Especially when it came from his lips.

As though reading her thoughts, he raised her gloved hand to his mouth. He kissed each finger, then pressed her palm to his cheek. He closed his eyes. "I want to remember this moment."

"W—we have three weeks. . . ."

"My heart can't take being alone with you and knowing you'll never be mine. Every time I'm with you, I fall deeper in love."

Oh, how she knew what he meant. But it would be so lonely without him for the next three weeks. The last day of school was only one week before Christmas. Then she'd go home and never see Josh again.

That night as she lay in bed listening to the sound of the mice scratching inside the walls, Kathleen remembered her brother's words to her. "Kat, don't make the same mistake I did. You might find that you don't want to stay in Rosewood forever."

Not stay in Rosewood? The thought had never occurred to her. Not in a million years. But now. . .

Was it possible?

Chapter 9

The next weeks moved frighteningly fast but at the same time crept along. Fast because Kathleen was busy with last-of-term grading and Christmas play practice. Slow because her sleeplessness had returned. She tossed and turned at night, her mind racing over and over with scenes from the moments she had shared with Josh. She had seen very little of him since the day at the lake, and she missed him. No longer did she lie awake weeping for her family in Rosewood, though she still longed to see them, as well. Now she wept for Josh. Precious Josh. Josh, who would never belong to her.

The night of the Christmas play arrived with a chill in the air and a dampness that caused the old-timers to predict a blizzard was coming. There hadn't been one flake of snow since the last blizzard, and everyone laughed off the predictions.

The children buzzed with excitement. Kathleen pulled a visibly nervous Andrew Coon aside.

"You're going to be wonderful, Andrew. Thank you for being our Joseph."

The teen had been a model student since the encounter with Mr. Carpenter and had even taken the initiative with the other unruly children. He'd become another gift from God. "My pa came. Said it was about time I did somethin' he could be proud of."

Andrew tried so hard to please the man—to make him proud.

She patted his shoulder. "We're about to start. Are you ready?"

"Yes, ma'am."

Kathleen smiled and moved back to the front of the room.

"Good evening, ladies and gentlemen," she said, smiling at the crowd. A few returning smiles warmed her. Mr. and Mrs. Truman; the pastor and his wife; Mary Bilge, who sat beaming next to Myles. Much to the shock of the town, Myles had done an almost instant about-face and had stayed clean against dire predictions. He hadn't missed a church service, nor had Mary Bilge, and they'd recently taken up courting. Two more unlikely people Kathleen couldn't imagine, but according to Mary, he was teaching her etiquette and proper speech, and she was teaching him to laugh. Perhaps God had sent two lonely souls to one another.

Kathleen's gaze landed on Josh standing in the back of the schoolroom, leaning against the wall. Her pulse quickened at his crooked smile. But there was no time to ponder her feelings; she had a play to oversee. "I would like to introduce our narrator for the evening—a truly brilliant man with a gift for literature—Mr. Myles Carpenter."

He seemed ill at ease as he stood and came to the front. When the idea had occurred to Kathleen that Mr. Carpenter's beautiful deep voice and eloquence of speech would make him the perfect narrator, she'd approached him with caution. She needn't have worried. He agreed to her request without question, and she had grown to love him more each day. At Kathleen's encouragement, he often showed up during afternoon sessions and read portions from Shakespeare, Charles Dickens, Tennyson, and even Edgar Allan Poe. The children adored him, and he rarely had occasion to reprimand.

"Glory to God in the highest, and on earth peace, goodwill toward men." Kathleen came back to the present as Myles's voice accentuated the words. She peeked at the audience to see if they were equally affected. The spellbound looks on their faces convinced her that Myles had a captive audience.

Not a dry eye remained as he finished the story with Simeon and Anna's blessing over the baby Jesus.

Mary and Joseph smiled at each other and held their "baby," which was actually made of straw.

"And that, my friends," Myles said, his voice shaking with awe, "concludes the wonderful story of the birth of our dear Lord."

For a long few seconds, no one moved, then slowly people began to clap, then stand. Barely a dry eye remained. Kathleen had never been so moved by a Christmas play.

The pastor shook her hand afterward. "I'm so pleased by all you've accomplished these past two months, Miss Johnson. Can't we convince you to stay on another term?"

As much as she'd considered staying for Josh, the thought of teaching left her cold. "These children are wonderful, as is Coon's Hollow, Pastor, but I'm afraid teaching isn't the profession for me."

"But you've done so well."

"Pastor, may I be honest?"

He grinned. "I wouldn't have it any other way."

She returned his smile. "Of course you wouldn't. I would like to suggest that you hire Myles to teach."

Alarm shone in his eyes. "Myles?"

"The children are thriving because of his influence in my classroom. Myles comes most afternoons. The students adore him. I don't believe you'd be sorry."

"Well, I certainly never would have thought of him, but perhaps you're right. I will look into it."

"Thank you, sir."

The pastor smiled again and looked over her shoulder. Instinctively, Kathleen turned. Her pulse thumped in her throat. "Hi, Josh."

"Hi, Kat." His gaze perused her face. "Your play was very nice."

"Thank you. I can't take much credit."

They stood at a loss for words. Finally, Josh broke the silence.

"You're leaving tomorrow?"

She nodded, gloom descending. "My train leaves at ten in the morning. Will you come see me off?"

"Won't you change your mind? Say you'll come back after Christmas and marry me."

"Oh, Josh, my mother would be so hurt. My family stays in Rosewood. I just can't go against that."

"Then you're robbing yourself of happiness with the man you love."

He spun around and stomped away, leaving Kathleen's heart shattered on the wooden floor.

With aching heart, Josh watched the train pull away from the station. He expelled a heavy sigh. *Well, Lord. That's that, I guess. I tried. I felt sure she was the one for me.*

The snow was falling with more force, and he turned his collar up to ward off the icy blast of wind. A sliver of unease crept through him as the wind howled. With a frown, he nudged Shasta. Rather than turning and heading home, he found himself in front of the school almost without memory of how he'd gotten there.

His memory played in his head like a picture book. His first sight of Kathleen's blue eyes and sweet dimple. The musical sound of her laughter. Her kindness to Mary and to Mr. Carpenter. There would never be another girl like Kathleen Johnson.

He went home and moped for a good four hours while the snow continued to blanket the area. Alarm seized him when Pa entered the barn near suppertime.

"What's wrong, Pa?"

"I'm not sure, but I'm afraid the train to Rosewood might be in trouble."

Josh's mouth went dry. "What makes you think that?" he choked out.

"A rider came into town. Said it's been snowing that direction for a full day longer than we've had it. Snow's piling up. If it's over the track, the train could be in for some problems. I figured you'd want to know."

Josh had already moved into gear. He grabbed a harness and headed for the horse stalls.

"Josh!" As chaos and panic struck the passengers inside the tipping train, his was the only name Kathleen could remember, and she screamed it over and over as she fell. It all happened so fast that it took awhile for Kathleen to realize the train had derailed and she was falling. Pain hammered her right shoulder. And hip. When the car finally stopped moving and groaning, she tried to stand, but the shape of the train and the benches was too awkward for her to walk on with unsteady legs. So she crawled.

Her head felt light, as though she might faint. Oh, how she'd give anything if Josh were with her right now.

"Is everyone all right?"

The sound came from somewhere outside the train. It couldn't be Josh. He was back in Coon's Hollow. "I'm going to need someone to go to the lever and open the door. I can't get it open from out here." There was no mistaking the sound of that voice.

"Josh? Josh? Is that you?"

"Kathleen? Honey, are you all right?"

"I think so. Just a little bruised."

"Oh, thank God. Can you get to the lever?"

"I'm almost there."

In a moment, she opened the door and felt herself being pulled up. He sat on the side of the train and gathered her in his arms. "My love. Are you sure you're all right?"

"I am now."

"Is everyone all right down there?"

"I don't know. I think so."

He called down, and when no one reported anything

but minor injuries, he promised they would send help back.

Since they were several hours closer to Rosewood than Coon's Hollow, Josh turned his team toward Kathleen's hometown. After they spoke with the mayor about the train, Josh headed toward Kathleen's house, then stopped before they got there.

"Kathleen." He looked into her eyes, and the intensity of his gaze nearly clouded her senses. "I can't let you go."

Tears filled her eyes. "I know. I feel the same way. But my family. That is. . .my mother especially. They expect us to stay in Rosewood."

"Sweetheart, I can't move here, if that's what you're thinking. I have a family, too, and my own squared-off piece of land that I've been clearing this winter."

"I know, Josh."

"I want to ask you something. I can't go all of my life knowing I didn't at least ask."

Kathleen closed her eyes, then opened them again.

Josh took her hand in his and pinned her with his gaze. "Kathleen, I've fallen in love with you. From the moment I saw you, I felt you were the girl for me. I want to ask you to be my wife. Will you marry me?"

"Oh, Josh." The negative response was on her lips, but she realized she couldn't say no. She just couldn't. She didn't even want to. "I will marry you."

His eyes widened. "You will?"

"Yes. I will."

He crushed her to him, taking her breath away. "Are you sure you can leave home?"

"Coon's Hollow is home now. I miss Mary and Myles, Flora and the boys, and even Andrew Coon. I want to go back and be a part of their lives."

"I'm so glad." He lowered his face, and this time Kathleen didn't resist. His mouth pressed against hers, soft and warm and filled with promise. Josh pulled away and looked deeply into her eyes. "I love you."

"I love you, too, Josh."

When his lips descended, Kathleen knew without a doubt that she'd finally come home.

Epilogue

Christmas morning

Abel Coon sneered at the two of them.

"Don't worry about him, Josh," said his wife of three days. "We'll beat him by a mile."

After meeting Kathleen's parents, Josh had asked for her father's permission to marry her. Kathleen had stood strong against her mother's protests, and Josh had returned to Coon's Hollow with Kathleen as his wife.

This beautiful Christmas morning had dawned bright, a perfect day for the Coon's Hollow Christmas sleigh ride— and Josh and Abel's yearly race. Josh hadn't lost one yet, and he'd informed Kathleen he didn't intend to start now.

She nestled in beside him, feeling the muscles in his arms tighten with anticipation.

The gun sounded, and they were off, each cutter sliding through the snow. After a minute, Josh got a margin of a lead and knew the race was all but over. Sandy and Chester weren't going to let Abel Coon win now that they'd had a taste of being ahead. The horses were more competitive than he was.

"Oh, Josh. There's our lake."

Trying to stay focused on the race, Josh didn't comment.

"Our lake. Where you almost kissed me. Where we admitted our feelings for the first time."

With a sigh, Josh slowed the cutter. Abel dashed ahead, a grin splitting his face.

"What on earth are you doing, Josh Truman?"

"I'm letting Abel have the race." He nudged the horses to the right and pulled them to a stop in front of the lake. The frozen crystals shimmered.

"But, Josh, you always beat Abel."

"Some things are just more important. Like a man kissing his wife next to a beautiful frozen lake."

There was no time for her to respond as he pulled her close. He kissed her thoroughly until all thoughts of Abel Coon's first-place finish in the race fled from Kathleen's mind.

"Let's go home," he said.

Kathleen nodded. "Yes, let's go home."

TRACEY V. BATEMAN

Tracey lives with her husband and four children in southwest Missouri. She believes in a strong church family relationship and sings on the worship team. Serving as vice president of American Christian Romance Writers gives Tracey the opportunity to help new writers work toward their writing goals. She believes she is living proof that all things are possible for anyone who believes, and she happily encourages those who will listen to dream big and see where God will take them.

To learn more about Tracey, visit her Web site, www.traceybateman.com. Her e-mail address is tvbateman@aol.com.

A Letter to Our Readers

Dear Readers:

In order that we might better contribute to your reading enjoyment, we would appreciate your taking a few minutes to respond to the following questions. When completed, please return to the following: Fiction Editor, Barbour Publishing, Inc., P.O. Box 719, Uhrichsville, OH 44683.

1. Did you enjoy reading *Christmas on the Prairie*?
   ❏ Very much—I would like to see more books like this.
   ❏ Moderately—I would have enjoyed it more if _____
   _____
   _____

2. What influenced your decision to purchase this book?
   (Check those that apply.)
   ❏ Cover   ❏ Back cover copy   ❏ Title   ❏ Price
   ❏ Friends   ❏ Publicity   ❏ Other

3. Which story was your favorite?
   ❏ *One Wintry Night*   ❏ *The Christmas Necklace*
   ❏ *Colder Than Ice*   ❏ *Take Me Home*

4. Please check your age range:
   ❏ Under 18   ❏ 18–24   ❏ 25–34
   ❏ 35–45   ❏ 46–55   ❏ Over 55

5. How many hours per week do you read? _____

Name _____

Occupation _____

Address _____

City _____ State _____ Zip _____

E-mail _____

If you enjoyed

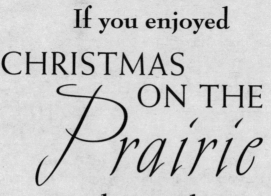

CHRISTMAS ON THE *Prairie*

then read:

An Old Fashioned Christmas

Four Inspirational Love Stories from Christmases Gone By

For the Love of a Child by Sally Laity
Miracle on Kismet Hill by Loree Lough
God Jul by Tracie Peterson
Christmas Flower by Colleen Reece

Available wherever books are sold.
Or order from:
Barbour Publishing, Inc.
P.O. Box 721
Uhrichsville, Ohio 44683
http://www.barbourbooks.com

You may order by mail for $6.97 and add $2.00 to your order for shipping.
Prices subject to change without notice.